CHAPTER 1

A sharp, cold breeze came flowing through the woodlands, hitting every tree and plant that stood in its path as bright, warming rays of sunlight followed. Only the sound of birds in the distance chirping away in their usual tone could be heard, but in the front room of the house it was a different story. A weird house was waking up on an unforgiving morning: one of wiped memories of a twisted game. A loud alarm blared, like a starting gun for a race.

Six people had entered the house and now five of them were in the front room, and not quite with it, having been forced awake by an alarm. They were all lying in strange positions, as if they had all just been thrown about like toys onto the couch and the floor. Dazed and aching, they exchanged looks with one another as they slowly came to: something didn't feel right.

"Ah god, I feel awful! Where are we?" said Steve, staring up in wide-eyed amazement at a beautiful ceiling with detailed coving.

"Jesus, my head! Is everyone ok?" Steph asked. Her ears were still ringing with the shrill sound of the alarm.

"I think so," came a tired, grumpy reply from Fran.

"Yes, all good. I'm ready to start the game! Raring to go." Jason was pacing the room, pumped up.

Steph sat up rubbing her ears and gazed around the room. "Wow, this place is lovely! I wish Jacob would've done something like this at home but no, he was useless."

"Five minutes in and the ex-boyfriends already come up," Steve mumbled to himself.

"Wait...wait, where's Andrew?" David asked, sitting up on the floor. "Andrew! You here?" he called, but there was no response; just the sound of David's voice echoing through the rest of the house.

"What's happened here?" Fran asked, feeling a little freaked out.

"Oh he's around somewhere," said Steph, "he's got to be, hasn't he?" She stood up and stretched out her back, as it felt sore. "God that hurts," she said, wincing. "Did we drink last night? I don't remember anything! Does anyone else?"

Fran was not reassured. In fact, she was starting to panic. "Guys, are we sure this is even the same house we came to? I don't recognise a thing in this room."

David laughed. "Of course it's the same place. I mean, why wouldn't it be?"

Still sitting or lying where they had woken up, the four hey all surveyed the room. It was a big, open-plan living and dining room with a three-seater couch placed in front of a wall-mounted television and at right angles to another, two-seater couch. There was a smart-looking table in the dining area and the floor was covered in a soft, cream-coloured carpet, though it was hard to see it as it was littered with wine and beer bottles.

David reached out to pick up one of the empty bottles. "That's odd," he said, frowning, "there aren't any labels on them." He sniffed at it. "That one was beer, I guess."

Steve was lounging on one of the sofas. "What a weird place! Dave, do us all a favour and open the blinds will you? Let's throw some light on the matter – that'll make things better." He was always quick to dish out the orders.

"Let's not forget they did promise us a nice weekend away so maybe, just maybe, they laid on a nice party thing for us last night and we ended up having a few too many," said Jason who was also studying the bottles. "Hey, maybe it was all home-brewed – let's face it, that would certainly hit you harder," he joked.

"Well I can handle my booze so I don't think I'd get so drunk that I wouldn't remember anything," Steve bragged, even though he was becoming increasingly baffled as to why he had no recollection of actually drinking anything.

Stretching, David padded across the soft carpet, to the window, careful not to stand on the numerous bottles, and opened the blinds. *Zzzzzzp...crash!* The blinds flew up and the fierce morning light blazed through the window.

"Ah Jesus that's bright," David gasped, shielding his eyes with a hand. David looked out of the window at the birds flying around, he almost started to day dream vaguely remembering being in the original house when they signed up for the game and how he enjoying watching the view of the sun setting. Then a thought struck him. "Guys, I don't understand... that window seems to be facing a different way to what I remember... or maybe it's a different window...." He was starting to feel uneasy even as he was attempting to convince himself that everything was fine.

Fran picked up on David's uncertainty straight away: she had the same feeling that something was very wrong. Deciding to check out the window, she stood up too fast. Her head span and, stepping on a bottle, she slipped, hitting the deck hard and landing almost underneath a coffee table in front of the couch.

"Shit! Fran, are you ok?" Steph jumped up to help her, joined by David.

"Damn, that hurt big time. Why are these bottles even here?" Fran exclaimed, annoyed, as she pushed a few out of the way. "Don't worry I think I'm all right." Steph helped Fran slowly to her feet. As she did so, she noticed a key under the coffee table and picked it up. She noticed it had a key tag: there was something written on it.

"Steph, what's that?" Steve asked.

"A key! I think it fell out of Fran's jacket, maybe. It's got something written on it."

"What?" said Steve.

Steph squinted at the tag: "Clue." Puzzled for a moment, she looked up in excitement at the others as she realised that she might have just found the first clue of the game.

Jason piped up: "A key? A clue for what? Does it say what it opens?"

"Well obviously it doesn't, otherwise this game would be pretty short! See, I knew we were still playing the game," beamed Steph reassuringly.

"Yeah, but why is Andrew still missing?" Jason jabbed back.

"Ok, Ok everyone, let's sit at the table and try to work out what's going on and see if we can remember anything, or work out what this key does," Steve said, taking command again.

"Well *duh*, it opens a door," Jason replied, only to get blank looks from the others as they sat at the table. "Jeez, I was only trying to lighten the mood, sorry."

David snapped: "Yeah well, you should be sorry. Andrew is missing and no one else right now is bloody concerned! And there are other things that the key could open."

"C'mon David, Andrew's absence is probably part of the game. Don't stress, and try to be more imaginative," said Steph.

"Imaginative?" David spat, glaring at Steph.

"Guys, guys, just sit!" said Steve. The group gathered at the table. There were five chairs and a gap where one chair was missing, but no one noticed.

"Right, so let's establish the basics," said Steve. "There are six of us, but Andrew is currently not here. So he probably left or it's part of the mystery to find him. We've found a key labelled with the word 'clue', which strengthens the point that we are most definitely playing a game. Yes?"

Steph rolled her eyes. "Yes, thank you Steve."

David spoke next. "According to my watch, we've been in here two days, but none of us can remember a thing, Andrew is missing and the view outside the house seems different. Fran... come on, back me up – you're worried right?"

Fran looked nervously at the others: the mood was getting tetchy. "Yeah, I am worried, but at the same time we do have a clue now so maybe we're judging too quickly, OK maybe I'm judging too quickly. Let's just try and pay more attention to things going forward," she said.

"Right maybe we should just trust that this is the game right now, and try to stay calm and start looking for more clues. What do you think Steph?" Jason said, noting with pleasure that for the first time everyone seemed to agree with him. "Let's start with this room."

CHAPTER 2

The sun had risen high in the sky by the time they began to explore the house. Sunlight slid through every chink and crack in the place, but did little to dispel the creepy atmosphere. Having put their bickering to one side, the group slowly began to expand their exploration of the house, each nursing their own secret fears and theories as to what was really going on.

As they inspected the furniture and fittings of the living room for further clues, David looked out of the window to take stock of their surroundings. The room was stuffy so he decided to open the window for some fresh air. It was a sash window, so he looked for a cord or clamp to open but found none. He began to pull and yank at it, but to no avail.

"Damn, window won't budge," he muttered. Next to the window was an old school-style radiator, which looked out of sorts with the rest of the clean, modern décor of the room. He had a look down the back and felt it to see if it was on then noticed that it wasn't even connected, pulling it away from the wall he wedged it between the wall and his knee so as not to cause a noise.

"Strange, don't you think," he said, but no one was listening. David, being an introvert, wasn't much good at catching attention. As no one paid David much attention let alone an answer he now remembered why he was so inept socially as he never had much confidence to speak up enough for people to be interested in what he was saying.

Finally, Steph looked at him holding onto the radiator. "It's not a real house, is it? It's a set, so of course they won't actually connect the radiators – that'd be a waste of time and money." It was the only reasonable explanation she could think of and

Steph, who saw herself as the most clued-up and smartest of the group, hoped that she sounded convincing. No doubt Steve would give everyone the benefit of his opinion next, she thought.

David let the radiator slide down the wall and onto the floor then continued looking around the window. He focused on a set of shelves hanging, with no visible fixings, on the wall. There was a stack of books on the shelves and he rifled through them, looking at the titles and seeing nothing much of significance. In the middle of the pile, he noticed a book of riddles and picked it up. It didn't mean anything to him right then, but he decided to keep it to himself as he had a feeling it might prove to be important. It just seemed different.

Steph moved over to a tall glass cabinet filled with unlabelled bottles of what she assumed to be alcohol; the same as those lying on the floor. She picked one up and sniffed it: whisky fumes hit her full in the face.

"Damn that's strong: I thought it was going to be fake alcohol. This game spares no expense," she spluttered.

She put the whisky bottle back on the shelf and continued to search the cabinet; moving on to a set of drawers below. In the top drawer she found some spoons along and other cutlery used for making drinks. The bottom drawer was padlocked with a key code lock: she would need the code to open it.

She called out to the rest of the room: "Ooh ohh ooo! Guys! A locked draw!" She ran her fingers over the solid wooden front, feeling it's rough exterior. "It seems we need a four-digit code: has anyone seen any numbers anywhere?"

"No!" came the disappointing reply.

Fran was busy sieving through the bottles and broken debris on the floor, but found nothing of interest. She crawled around, moving rubbish from one side to another, in the hope of finding a clue but discovering only crumbs, bottle caps and corks – the sort of rubbish you find left over from a party. The only unusual find was a few AA batteries, so she picked them up and pocketed them.

Jason floating around being nothing but short of useless almost just aimlessly moving around to make the illusion of actually doing something and half -heartedly checking on top of the previously sat on table and the tv stand. "Anyone found anything, this is hard man."

"Nope nothing yet, just a tv remote in-between the couch seats," Steve replied while looking at Jason's efforts with almost a parental disappointment and turning away to see if he can find anything else within the Couch cushions.

Jason while walking around like a lost child stepped on an extension cable without realising, looking down on it he realised it wasn't plugged in but it had a note on it 'Plug me in' so that's exactly what Jason did, without warning it shot on loud as a gun exploding into life.

'WELCOME NEW MEMBERS'

"Shit that's loud, Steve where's that remote," Jason raised his voice for clarity.

"Here here," Steve shouted panicking and pressing buttons on it "It's not doing anything!" the noise from the Tv still blaring in the room, Steve eventually turning the remote round and realising there's no batteries for it. "No batteries, just try turning it down on the Tv." Steve shouting over the noise, fighting a losing battle while the rest of the crew covers their ears with force hoping to drown out some of the painful blast. Jason desperately slammed buttons on the side of the telly hoping to do anything to turn the noise down but nothing was working.

Fran shouts to Steve "Steve I've got some batteries!! hold on," rushing over to give them to Steve.

Steve eventually puts them in and turns down the Tv to a level that was welcoming, however throughout this time the Tv has carried on with its message and the crew only manage to catch the end of it properly. They all went quiet after a big 'Shh' from Steve so they could all listen to the rest of the message and hope to catch something.

'Let's hope you few have the will power trust in each other and don't end up like the all others falling apart piece by piece. Do not forget if you complete this game a reward of £50,000 will be received'

As them words rang out the gang didn't have a clue what the message meant, only that it must be something to keep in mind although the last part did provoke some kind of memory for Steve. Once the Tv had finished its final part of the message something clicked inside Steve. "Oh snap the 50k! Almost forgot about that, god that'd be nice to win."

"Well maybe, but how else would we throw it above our head and let it rain on us when we win," Jason smirked almost day dreaming of that exact scenario.

Steph looks at Jason while he's daydreaming as she tries to remember the message, repeating it out loud for herself, "Let's hope you have the will power to trust each other and don't end up like all others what on earth could that mean? Of course we trust each other we're friends after all."

"I think I have a good idea what it means" remarks Steve confidently.

"Oh yeah, what then?"

"How can you not get it?"

"Explain then please?"

"Aha, need me to spell it out?" jokes Steve, acting as if he is so much smarter than the rest.

"Guys, guys! If you think about it, it doesn't even make sense really," giggles Jason, but his dumb comments don't go down well with the two alphas of the group.

While the rest of the crew try and figure it out, Fran drifts of into the kitchen to wash her hands after touching the touching all of the grime and dirty on the floor whilst the Tv after sitting on a blank screen for few seconds shuts off.

David still pondering the phrase "Yeah it's certainly something to think about ... trust, the power of trust. It seems like something is going to test us and have us doubting each other."

"Ahhhhhhh!" A scream echoed from the kitchen it sounded like Fran! 'Crassshh' a lot of noise came echoing out of the kitchen, blasting through the rest of the quiet house as the crew rushed in there to see what happened.

Steve led the gang into the kitchen with all of their eyes scanning the room as if they were all part of one huge surveillance system and saw that poor Fran is cowering away while pointing at the sink. The sink was flooded in a dark red liquid and on her panic backing away Fran had knocked a few things off of the side, mainly silverware causing some of the crashing noise they had heard from the other room.

"Is that... is that, Blood?" Fran asks the others as she continues to move backwards away from the sink.

"I mean... no, surely not it must just be something made to look like blood surely..." said less than confidently by David in an attempt to calm nerves without even taking a look as he walks over to Fran to shield her from the gruesomeness "Come here Fran, it's alright don't stress we've got you," David Cuddles Fran as she wipes her teary eyes on David's Jumper, leaving Steve free to act tough walking over to the sink to inspect.

"Right let's see what we have here," Steve was heard muttering under his breath.

"Well, what do you think Steve?" Steph quietly murmurs as she drifts over, a shock to both of them as it certainly looks insanely like blood. Upon closer inspection they start to convince themselves that it couldn't and instead is probably just a prop for the game "Look, the plug chain," Steph said while reaching in and pulling it out without any hesitation.

"Steph!! have a little caution won't you!" Steve wincing a little at the smell as it dissolves down the drain swirling away almost mesmerizing to watch.

"It's fine, I got this."

"I could have got it out if you just waited."

"I don't need a man to do it for me, but thank you."

"Jesus Christ that stinks!" Holding his t-Shirt over his nose Jason remarks.

As the sink is slowly emptying Fran is still being comforted by David, Jason is in the doorway staying out the way while Steve is still with Steph by the sink who both are also covering their noses as the stench still consumes the air around. The gurgling of the plug hole points to the emptied sink with no liquid left in there however there is a Ziplock bag with a piece of paper inside which was previously not visible due to the density of the red liquid inside.

"Guys look!!" Steve and Steph both say out loud almost like a competition to who can say it first and alert everyone of their dominance.

The crew all rush over while still trying to either mask the scent with their T-shirts or plain and simply trying to ignore it, they all glance their eyes over the Ziplock bag they knew they'd found another clue. Excitement ran high for a minute with them all now hitting some crisps high 5s almost as if they were getting closer to solving it. Steve manages to be the one who pulls the Ziplock bag out of the sinks and begins to unzip it almost in some amount of swagger to announce his position of leader, inside the bag he pulls out the piece of paper and unfolds it.

Clue

Your Memories Are Gone.

Or are they...

Write Them Down

Piece This Together.

"Well that's completely useless, that doesn't help anyone? How on earth do we know what will jog our memory?" Jason spits out complaining as per usual, seemingly doing what he's done the whole time so far.

"Wait Jason you're missing the point, they're clearly telling us that they have wiped our memory, no? So... maybe we weren't drinking, they blanked us! God I already hate this, I want to leave." A panicked Fran cuts herself off before frantically leaving the kitchen and heading into the corridor walking towards what she assumes to be the front door.

The front door was beautifully made and some what a feature of the house so far with it being a big Stained wooden door, it looked handmade, with clean Chrome handles on it. Fran grabs the handle and began to turn it "God damn it it's locked! Where's that key maybe it opens this," with everyone still listening and watching, Steph who is still holding the key walks over to Fran to try and calm her down.

"Fran please," Steph moves slowly over to Fran reaching out to give comfort from a hug "Just relax its fine, it's part of the game."

"Give me the bloody key now Steph!!"

"Fran! Relax," Steph already giving up with a softer tone and changing back to her usual grump, groans back.

Fran just stood there at the front door with her hand still in grasp of the door handle becoming more and more irate by the minute with the panic in her eyes becoming more obvious. Fran normally such a calm person really wants to just scream out but before she has a chance Steve pipes up from the other room, "Steph just give her the key, let her out or at least try."

Steph reluctantly passes the keys over sighing as she does it knowing it will cause more problems if she doesn't, without even so much of thank you Fran takes the key off of Steph and pushes it immediately into the Keyhole... A moments silence passes with the only sound being heard is Fran as she rustles with the key and handle "It doesn't work, it's not for here," Fran says in a disappointed tone slowly letting go of the door handle.

Jason deciding to clue everyone up on his movements and hopefully lighten the mood moving it on from the front door argument he informs everyone that he needs the toilet "Guys can we please find the loo, I could really use it aha." the two other men give each other a look of embarrassment and motioning to each other the fact that they are even still friends with him, so the guy's head into head into the hallway together.

The hallway had 2 rooms and a staircase; one room was all the way down the other end of it whilst the other only a matter of steps away. The room at the end of the hallway seemed a mile away, stretching past the side of the stairs and a small unit, but every inch of wall was painted perfectly with the two different colours of wall and ceiling blending into each other with style. The room at the end of the hallway certainly looked like it could be something important, it held that creepy vibe about it, but lucky enough for Jason that wasn't the toilet as he had already opened the first door he reached.

"Well that was easy, maybe the rest will be," Jason said while smirking and smiling as he walked into the toilet closing the door behind him.

"Seriously guys why are we friends with him, why does he even need to tell us that? Was he not getting enough attention or something! Gah he's so annoying and stupid. He is not going to contribute anything to this game," Steph quietly expressing her irk with him.

"Yeah, game," David mumbles.

A Noise from the toilet... Jason comes bursting out the toilet, the noise of a flushing toilet making his burst out almost seem comedic in some sense "Guys I remember something!" The crew gathered to listen with intent.

"Well?" Steph asked with intrigue.

"I had a small vision in the bathroom of me exiting that room over down there," Jason says while then motioning toward the room down the end of the corridor.

"What do you mean?" Fran asks still sightly bemused as to how he'd now suddenly remember something like that.

"So, you're telling us that you remember leaving that room down the corridor," Steve asks pointing to the same room just to confirm with Jason.

"Yes yes, I remember closing the door and locking it," Jason replies "100%, well kind of, I think."

The whole group were all almost excited for a second with a real lead to push on until the words 'I think' came out of Jasons mouth.

"So that sounds super confident doesn't it, well done Jason," Steph sarcastically replies whilst rolling her eyes using any excuse to force Jason down some notches.

"Now now Steph it's the only thing we kind of remember right now, Jason is there anything from the room you can remember?" David questions in a nicer tone.

"Errrm, I remember walking out. As I looked back there was a red couch with gold lining round it, quite fancy now I consider the rest of the house we've seen I mean come on that carpet in there is horrible who has a cream carpet with..."

"Jason?!?"

"Sorry sorry! No that's it, I think it might have been a study or something I guess," Jason answers.

Steve walks down the smart looking corridor which was filled with nice paintings as-well a nice oval mirror just big enough to see waist high upwards until he reached the door Jason was talking about. He looking at the door seeing if there were any clues on or around the it before then trying the handle, it's locked.

"Fran, key," Steve calls out down to a saddened Fran who was still by the front door.

Fran drags her feet over to Steve taking note of some of the nice paintings on the wall as they catch her eye before giving him the key, he takes the rusty looking key off of her and rams it in the lock praying it works.

"Dammit! it's still not the right key," Steve infuriatingly grumbles out "So where is it for I wonder?" Steves next idea is to try and force the door by giving it large nudges in hope it'll budge open a little bit, however to no prevail.

"Steve see if you can see anything through the keyhole," Fran wonders and suggests as an idea.

"Good Idea," Jason says agreeing with her.

Steve gives a somewhat look of disbelief that he's being asked to do that but reluctantly he gets on his knees, closes an eye and has a glance through the keyhole. The room inside was filling up with sunlight as it came flooding through the windows at this point allowing Steve to actually see properly and what he saw is what looks like a red couch with gold as Jason described as well as a solid hardwood desk. Steve slowly pulls away from the door slightly while reopening his other eye in disbelief, annoyance and infuriatingly trying to figure out exactly how Jason knew that considering no one else can remember a thing and yet Jason the less than intelligent human did.

"How! How did you know that was in there! We all cannot remember a thing and yet you suddenly know what's behind this door?! explain yourself now," Steve jumps up and storms over to Jason getting all in his face.

"Woah woah Steve calm down, I'm sure Jason has a good explanation to this. I assume he was correct with his description," David says trying to defuse Steve by trying to get in-between him and Jason.

"Yes, it seems that way from what little I can see. Jason is bang on," with Steves eyes staring deep into Jasons.

"What? No guys you don't understand, I was just in the loo having a whizz and it just came to me; I don't know how, I don't know why. I just know... I swear! Guys," Jason now panicking badly "Steph you believe me, right?"

"I mean you've got to realise, it is suspicious Jason," Steph replies softly but not exactly backing him up.

The conversation appears to be going nowhere so just to break it up and calm things down Fran pipes up "Guys I don't want to be here at all so can we please move this on to try and get out of this house or game or whatever we are doing fast. So, let's just try and clear these rooms as quickly as possible please."

"Good idea," Steph Replied "Fran when you went into the kitchen what was you going in there for? Did you actually search it?"

"I went to wash my hands Steph so, no didn't get a chance because I too busy panicking,"

"Alright, well maybe you and Jason take the kitchen and me David and Steve will head upstairs?"

"Errr Steph, I'd feel more comfortable with David."

"Ok fine," A blunt Steph replied knowing she was stuck with Jason.

Chapter 3

As time was passing the friction in the air seemed to grow with arguments already breaking out, the group decided it was the right idea to split up and look for clues in separate parts of the house to hopefully solve this game quicker with David and Fran heading back to the kitchen, while the rest made their ascent upstairs.

The group going up had a beautiful staircase to tackle, it was so broad while still being fully covered in lovely hardwood once again with a theme seemingly being set, no creaks here this was a nice staircase fitting of the house as they've seen it so far with it. Steve goes first asserting his position as the dominant male; not that anyone was even seemingly that bothered about it, upon reaching the top of the stairs there is a room directly in front of him one to right and two more followed round.

Once Steve had reached the top of the stairs straight away it hit him just how silent it was, with no lights or anything else going on to suggest anyone had been up here previously. Steve could see a couple of rooms up there but no light could be seen coming from inside the rooms either, but unlike the hallway on the ground this floor had no paintings on the wall and on closer inspection no light bulbs were even in the lights.

"Right where first?" Steve asked trying to act like this hasn't bothered him but deep down he was spooked and rightly so.

Steph and Jason both tried to reach over each other's shoulders as they continued up the stairs to get a view however the whole floor slowly came into view, both of them started glancing their eyes over the whole floor taking note of the rooms and noticing that only one appears to be slightly creaked open, so this is where their adventure must begin surely.

"There!" Jason says the quickest as if he's won a game of bingo while pointing to the door.

The three of them all very close to each other almost using one another as shields whilst walking over to what would be the first room on that floor. Steve leans in placing his hand on the door and slowly pushing it open, It gives a small yet screechy creak as it opens 'Eeearrrrrrh' ... Pretending to chivalrous and not at all afraid of what lurks in the dark Steve offers the ever old "Ladies first."

Steph sharply looks at Steve "You wimp," smirks and peaks into the room it's cold, it's dark and it's eerily quiet yet nevertheless clues might be in here so they do need to search it. Steph still taking the lead slowly steps further into the room and in doing so she sees that the King size bed that's in here, it's in an absolute state with the bed sheet thrown half on the floor half on the bed and pillows all over the place yet no sign on the duvet. The others made their way into the room after Steph while she then moved further into what appeared to be the master bedroom, the first thing she done was inspect the bed, she notices a dark stain upon the bed as-well as partially on the sheet hanging off the bed. It's hard to tell what it is but on first assumption it looks like the same liquid from the sink a thick dark blood like stain ... is it blood .. could it be?.

"Guys look, there's a red stain on this bed! I think it looks like the fake blood scene from the sink, don't you think? Maybe them clues are linked." She says smiling away taking no thought to the fact of it possibly being real blood "And, why is it such a mess it! Looks like there was some kind of struggle here ... a fight... an accident who knows."

Steve eventually walks over to the bed properly however merely just glancing at the stained sheet in which Steph was intrigued at, instead opting to go straight over to the big double window taking a second to glance outside at what view it may behold and maybe just maybe it might look like something they recognise. Steve gently moved the soft silk curtain to one side and looks outside, he see's just a singular road out from the house surrounded but what almost looks just like forest and nothing else.

Steve straight away after glancing outside is certain this isn't the same house because he does remember driving in to the previous place and this is not where they originally were... this house is different... but without trying to evoke panic he calmly lets go of the white patterned curtain letting it drop back into position. Steve without changing the manner in which he had moved over there or the expression on his face opts to move away and instead now move over to the wardrobe to the side of the windows.

A very old large robust wardrobe, the doors a bit jammed where over time they have got damaged and moved around on their hinges, but with a little brute strength he pops it open. When opening the doors, he knocks the boxes stored at the top of the wardrobe off the shelf onto the floor ' Baannggg , Dinnnnng' startling both Steph and Jason causing them both to jump. The two of them turned so sharply toward the noise perhaps even moving back and attempting to protect themselves a bit as human instinct would permit you too.

"Jesus Steve, you trying to give us a heart attack or what!" Jason snapped while holding his arms against his chest.

"Calm down Jase it was an accident, didn't purposely do it did I," Steve remarked in a sarcastic tone.

After the boxes had fallen causing the loud bang hearing it echo across the whole floor the room suddenly went quiet again with only the slight whistling of the wind coming through the single glazed window in the room and it was those few moments that reminded them how alone they really were in this big house.

Jason headed over to the fallen boxes whilst Steve searched the rest of the wardrobe seeing if anything else lay about inside. Steve routing through the clothes on the hanging rail noticing certain outfits that looked very familiar, as he stood there holding out a few of the items it slowly came to him. *'What the hell'* Steve thought as he realised the outfits were the same as what some of his friends have worn at some point, noting it in his brain but basically just ended up assuming it was a happy coincidence and assuming he must have been remembering it wrong or differently.

"Hey Jason this ugly shirt rings a bell." As Steve laughs away before letting it swing back on hanger, the shirt was very similar or potentially even the same as part of an outfit Jason wore to his friend Andrews birthday just a few months back, he was mocked some might even say bullied for its ugly patterning and weird fit.

"Yeah yeah! Just because you couldn't pull off a shirt like me Steve, rocking around with ya Dad bod," Jason punching back somewhat serious and somewhat jokingly.

After Jason had finished fighting over his dress sense, he continued browsing through the boxes to see if he could see anything that remotely looked like a clue and continued going through box after box of what turned out to be mainly rubbish. Searching the boxing was boring for Jason as it wasn't exciting enough for his personality and almost on the verge of giving up as Jason does, he struck lucky finding pages worth of 4 Digits codes all different.

Jason pulls the pages out of the box and at first glance is ecstatic that he's found these sheets and somewhat noting his worth in the game to the others as-well as hoping this smart capture will point out his attributes considering how the rest have been putting him down slightly already.

"YO! Yes! Look I found pages of 4 Digit Codes," Jason says throwing his hand with the sheets in the air but there are so many sheets that they're starting to fold over his hand and arm "What a good find by me," a smug Jason calls out "Don't you think guys! Not so useless after all, eh?"

"Ah wicked well-done Jason. Now go see which one works and we'll carry on here," Steph smiling as she says it, knowing full well that it was a good find but now she's got rid of Jason for a bit.

"Wait....What?" Jason's smile and elation immediately replaced by a frown realising he now has to do even more work.

"What you heard her, you done a good job finding them now go and see if they work down stairs... good luck you might be there for a while," Steve also beginning to smile and eventually laugh as he backs up Steph, the two of them were so smug and couldn't be happy to be team players for one moment or let someone else accomplish something.

A disappointed Jason stands up stopping to look at the papers and then at the others *thought we'd all go down and check,* Jason thought as he slowly turns away walking towards the door only once turning back to witness the smirks and sniggers of the others.

Meanwhile downstairs Fran and David headed into the kitchen walking back past the mess in the living room, for the moment just completely ignoring it. Once back into the kitchen the sink once filled with the red liquid, now completely empty was the only notable thing they'd seen so far but there was still a lot to search. The Kitchen itself was a nicely fitted sleek designed kitchen, graphite worktop followed top and bottom by lighter grey cupboards with crisp sharp copper edging complimenting everything, it was beautiful and certainly something someone would have enjoyed cooking in plus it seemed way to plush to be just in a game.

The two of them looking around noticed that everything in the kitchen seemed to be in place, everything from the energy saving light bulbs to the neatly assembled plate stack causing Fran and David to not have much luck hunting down any more clues here however they knew they needed to start looking but not before the teary eyes on Fran were to be addressed.

"So Fran, what's up you seem a bit on edge is everything alright with you?" David sparking up a gentle conversation with ever fragile Fran.

"To be honest with you David I wasn't going to come to this as my mums a bit sick at the moment, but we'd have this booked for so long I didn't want to disappoint the rest of you guys so I decided a few days of fun wouldn't hurt. Plus my sisters in town to help out with my mum." Frans voice cracks a little as she's explaining her situation to David, but just about keeping enough composure by turning her head away pretending to look at things.

"Oh, I'm sorry to hear that Fran! I hope she gets better soon I know how close you two are." David softly answers as he moves over to Fran to give her an embrace before slowly pulling away and looking at her.

"I'm struggling so much David, I'm trying my best to hold everything together but I can't. I want to cry all the time, I just feel like I'm trapped in this life which isn't mine," Fran cries back.

"Oh Fran," David almost unsure of how to reply back in the right way, replies with a continued soft tone "Why?"

"I don't know why, everything is so much. I don't really know how to explain it, I just feel tired all the time and sad but I also know I need to get out and socialise but at the same time that's the last thing I want to do," Fran says "I'm sorry David I shouldn't put any of this on you."

"Fran don't be silly! I'm your friend and I am here for you always," David replies "Maybe once this game is over we can have a proper sit down and talk about it. If you need help maybe I could start helping you out a lot more, friends should stick together."

"That'd be great thank you David, you're so great," Fran smiles and kisses David on the cheek.

"Hey this will be fun it's been a bumpy start but I am sure this will turn out fun in the end and we'll realize we we're all just over reacting," David gently trying to comfort Fran but not really believing the words he is spitting but smiling anyway.

After splitting from the embrace and letting Fran take a moment to wipe her eyes they both give a nod to start the search again and within a few moments David notices that on the worktop there is a rack of knives, strange David thought before mumbling to himself "Hmmm the chef's knife is missing," as he then turns his head away to have a browse across the rest of the kitchen to see if it was left out anywhere. His eyes glazed across the different surfaces with Fran taking notice of him clearly looking for something.

"What is it David? Have you found something?"

The noise of two loud feet jumping down from the last step on the stairs interrupts them before David has a chance to answer Fran, Jason comes bouncing into the kitchen hoping for more adulation than what he received upstairs.

CHAPTER 4

Jason came into the kitchen with a big grin on his face hoping for something more welcoming but instead sees a teary Fran and an almost panicked looking David, confused somewhat his bouncy mood is deflating as quick as an untied balloon.

"Is everything alright?"

David looked at Fran and she gave back a slight smile to indicate she was fine inside was a tough strong woman when needed but she was especially good at keeping herself to herself normally so the fact she has said anything to David is a big deal and David knew it. David's got a lot of love for Fran and always has.

"Alright. So, I found these upstairs." Jason says while holding them up "Pages and pages of 4 Digit codes so I was thinking maybe one of these could unlock the draw surely? I mean I hope so." Jason flicked through all papers quickly before doubting himself a little "Imagine it wasn't and this was a waste of time," A slight nervous giggle came out after he spoke before offering a look to the others.

The two of them take a few papers each and has a browse at a few of them and Jason was right they are all 4 digits and potentially could unlock the code.

"Christ Jason! Couldn't have anymore could ya? There are loads here this is going to take ages where do we even start," David gasped as he watched Jason flicking through the rest of the papers he was holding.

Fran and David handed back the papers to Jason as he was snatched back for them like a kid who'd dropped his dummy, Jason takes seat on the floor in front of the locked draw on the glass cabinet sweeping aside broken bottles and debris making way to lay out his sheets. "Well let's get going?!" a pumped Jason requested.

The draw lay closed in front of Jason with only a code standing between him and whatever is in it, David decides to also get down on the floor to make sure Jason does it properly because trust is not bestowed upon him lightly.

Fran plain and simply looks at the two of them before slowly looks at the sheets, looking away in disbelief wondering how on earth they'll ever find the right combination and who's to say it's even on there, what if this is just a plot to throw you off! Fran is getting anxiety just looking at the sheets with her brain already forcing the feeling of failure onto her, unfortunately she has never been good at controlling her emotions, really struggling with mood swings, dips into depression and being alone has forced her into some dark places.

"I'm going to take a back seat on this one guys and let you two push through."

Team digits as Jason jokingly decided to name them have made a start on attempting to find the correct code with David ticking them off as they go, as a team they're trying to eliminate as many of these digits as quick as possible with button pressing after button pressing, just this process alone is going to be mentally draining, soul crushing with the sound of 'bleep bleep bleep bleep' over and over as time just ticks past.

The air around is filled with silence with only the sound of the slight sighs of disappointment being mixed in is becoming a reoccurring tune that will continue to hammer at the will of the group, with everyone of one them every now and again thinking what is the point in this they're being broken at the very first step. The 3 of them there wasting precious time on codes when really they should still be searching also, who knows how this time waste will affect them later on in the game.

The clock ticks away in the background like a ticking time bomb with Fran slowly feeling like she can feel the tick of the clock inside her brain, with only the soft subtle noise of a pen scratching out each wrong code as they go and Fran has to know "How many have we have done guys I feel like we've been here doing this for ages, I can't take it anymore," Fran Sighed as she looked back towards the clock.

The room stayed quiet as she didn't really get a response from anyone as they were too busy attempting the codes, the guys eventually turned around after a few seconds after hearing the panting of Fran and the fidgeting.

"The clock said 12.47 when I looked earlier, it now says..." Fran turned back round to the guys "Ohh and it still says 12.47, hmm David did you say you had a watch on?"

"Yeah, I do."

"What does your watch say?" Fran asked as she was curious as to what they actual time was.

David once again stops what he is doing to glance down at his watch, he stops and stays silent for a few seconds then slowly lifts his face to look at the clock, then once more at his watch "Dammit, my watch isn't working i'm sure it was working earlier?! Maybe it wasn't but then.. I haven't a clue how long we've been here then because I was sure it was working earlier. God I'm confused I really don't know Fran." David told Fran "If I had to hazard a guess, I'd say we've been doing this for about an hour but I really couldn't tell you for sure."

That wasn't really the reply Fran was hoping for, she didn't enjoy the unknown let alone doing things in a scary house by herself, but there was no way Fran could just sit here waiting any longer for these two to finish what they are doing before they as a group continued searching somewhere else in the house. Fran decides to stand up wanting to stretch her legs a little so plain and simply takes a walk over to see if the clock is working before then slowly moving around the messy room looking at the state it's been left in and pondering why it was left like this.

Continuing her leg stretching she takes a little walk down the corridor stepping on lovely cream coloured carpet on her way down the corridor having a glance at some of the paintings on the wall. There were a few generic paintings on the wall of Daisies and other floral designs as-well a painting of a bridge over the canal of Venice which is a gorgeous sight, she takes a moment to enjoy the simplicity of it. One painting further down is certainly one of a more peculiar nature as it is a picture of group of friends but the corner of the picture is peeling off just enough to suggest that had been planted on top of another.

Fran gently grabs the corner and starts pulling the picture off only to find underneath is another picture, on the picture underneath is one of a confusing nature. It is the view you'd get if you looked directly into the oval mirror in the hallway with nothing different except for a dark shadow on the stairs implicating a human on the stairs. Fran took the picture off of the wall and walked over to the mirror to have a look whether or not it was exactly the same or just similar so she slowly lifted up the picture to get the right angle, as she finally got the right angle she heard a creak on the stairs unusual considering the nature of the stairs.

Fran unaware of where the sound may have come from exactly, shook a little in fright and immediately turned round to look at the stairs, yet nothing had seemed to have changed so, Fran turned back around and placed the picture onto the side underneath the mirror believing it was nothing or maybe she knew it was something but didn't wish to attempt to investigate such a thing by herself.

Instead she decided to have a look around the small unit situated under the mirror as it seemed less spooky and something to cause her less stress, with the only real thing of note there being a shoe rack integrated into the unit. She looked closer at the shoe rack noticing a lovely pair of silver studded heels and deciding to have a closer inspection she picked them up "What a lovely pair of shoes, they look familiar ... Does Steph have a pair of these?"

Back upstairs Steph and Steve were still in the master bedroom stripping it from pillar to post and leaving no stone unturned hoping for any more clues. Each pillow was thrown from the bed and wardrobe ruined, the bedroom was heading towards what would now have to be considered a waste site. Although they had turned it upside down between the two of them they had wrecked it to the point where if there were any more clues in here, they're gone now. While doing so they heard a faint noise causing them both to stop and listen like a meerkat noticing a predator, it certainly was there and they wasn't imagining it but what was making the noise was certainly a mystery.

"Hey Steve you here that?" Steph whispered.

"Yeah yeah I do," Steve replied in an equally low volume.

Steph and Steve look at each other as they take a moment to attempt to hear where this new noise has suddenly come from, so the two of them drop the items they were holding to the floor and headed towards the doorway taking time to slowly move over the items they had thrown around the room.

"Where is it coming from," Steve whispered to Steph.

The two of them reached the entrance of the master bedroom, leaning out into the hallway to listen out for the noise. The door frame was stern and strong, it needed to be with the two of them hanging out of it but it worked a charm as the heard them noise coming from the second floor, so as an obvious next choice they decided to go check it out with Steve leading the charge.

Steve headed up the stairs first but not before he looked at Steph hoping for the possibility she might want to go first, she did not for once so without anymore hesitation Steve continued slowly up the flight of stairs.

"Wow, does not look as nice up hear does it aha," Steve said as he sniggered looking at the poor quality decor.

Steve wasn't exactly wrong the floor was like a whole new house up here, it was like a single soul hadn't used this part of the house in years or at all, which was a confusing site considering how well kept the downstairs was. The two stopped on the stairs with Steph reaching out and grabbing Steve to stop him before he'd got all the way up the stairs.

"Shhhhhh," Steph whispered "Listen."

The alarm was still going off only now it seemed a little louder than previously, it was similar to just your generic wake up alarm and it just kept going and going until it suddenly just stopped before shutting off. A radio appeared to now turn itself on instead with what sounded like classical music playing but this time it was faint almost at a soothing tone, causing Steve to sharply take half a step back and look at Steph. Fear and confusion filled his eyes as to how that changed, was that a person that done that or was it just coincidence.

"Music!? Why is music playing?!?" Steve whispered to Steph.

"I Don't like this Steve; I'm starting to panic," Steph replied with a crack in her confident tone "Why would music start playing?"

Before the two of them even had a chance to continue speaking about the music playing in the background it went silent, the music had shut off almost as if someone had heard them and wanted to listen to the words they were spitting. The silence and the potential of what it could mean caused even more panic, Steve and Steph backed half way down the stairs with no idea of their next move. There is a possibility of someone being up there due to the fact that Andrew is currently still missing from the group or maybe it could it be someone else but right now fear was holding the still in their position.

"It's off.." Steph almost shivered as she said it thinking about the thought of someone else being in the house "The music's gone Steve! Is someone up there do you reckon?"

"Err no idea, I mean it's probably Andrew up there playing tricks on us," Steve still whispering back hoping and praying he was right because even he was starting to get scared now.

"Oh yeah, it could be Andrew. Well I mean I bloody hope it is," Steph hoped saying it back, almost trying to make herself believe taking some of the fear of the unknown away "We should go up, maybe no one's there maybe it's Andrew or maybe it's just a clue."

Steve was watching Steph closely watching her lips move as she uttered the words he didn't particularly want to hear but did agree before then again being hit with a mellow tone of sheer fear. The right thing to do was to go up first so he slowly heads back up to the top of the stairs and keeps peering over the landing. Light was coming from the room they assumed to the noise had come from as it was shining out from underneath the door creating a vibe of mystery and yet welcoming.

The door is damaged and almost rotten but it' still closed properly allowing Steve a few more seconds of peace before looking inside, he looks to heavens above and almost says a little prayer then Steve grips the handle softly and slowly starts pushing it down until it's fully recessed, just before he pushes it open he feels Steph using him as a shield with her hands on his back for cover and gives her a look to suggest whether she is ready or not a gentle nod of the head is given back in response.

CHAPTER 5

The outside world is moving along calmly with the birds tweeting away and wind still blowing with still no sign of any other people or cars, the group are still on their own in the middle of where ever they are but with Steve and Steph on the verge of maybe finding someone else could their fortunes be changing.

Steve once he had the handle recessed he went in guns blazing, pushed the door open fast and stepped through confidently hoping if anyone is in the room then he may have startled them or at least created a moment to see what was going on first, however there is no one in the room. The push of the door incubates a waft of weird smells into the air with no idea where anyone of them had come from just yet, with the first protocol to cover their nose. After a few seconds had passed they notice that one of them weird smells is none other than Andrews shoes which are positioned in the middle of the room, not a lot else was going on just his shoes on the floor. The stench coming from Andrew's shoes is powerful making it even more obvious that they are there but the question is why.

"Look! Andrew's shoes. I told you it was probably him just messing about with us but why isn't he wearing them the weirdo ... Classic Andrew," Steve happily barked once again calming himself.

Steph on the other hand isn't quite convinced at first sight "Steve; I'm sorry but do you not just think that's weird? What are his shoes even doing there."

"Because it's funny I guess, I don't know I don't have all the answers Hun but he always did like a prank." Steve chirped back at what he assumed to be a grumpy Steph.

Steph glared back still not confident in the thought of it being Andrew but also grimacing a little at being called 'Hun', these last 30 minutes have started to cause just a tiny bit of faith in the 'Game' to be lost although still not enough to start all out panic. Steph decided to be brave and move over to the radio to investigate, it was a bog-standard dab radio, a cheap silver boxed monstrosity insulting towards the niche decorating downstairs.

The radio lay upon a bedside table which too was in poor condition with its chipped surfaces and fading colour carrying mug rings stains on it, up here on this floor it is a different kettle of fish as the walls were half plastered with the ceilings almost fully falling down. The room was old with the colour scheme of your nans 1950's bungalow leaving the feeling of time travel as you left the downstairs to be hit by all of this.

"God what is that smell? Or smells should I say," Steph said attempting to hold her breath as much as possible.

"Yeah its horrible, smells worse than death up here! Lets search as quick as possible and move out of here," Steve replied "The clock has to be a clue surely, don't you think?"

"I mean... I'm looking at it but I can't tell that anything is up with it, can you see anything else here that could help? Do you wanna have a look i'm really struggling here," Steph replied in a soft sad tone.

"Sure, I'll have a look," Steve said as he quickly moved over to Steph leaving the door on which he was still holding on too. As Steve lay his eyes over the clock looking for any discrepancies he too could only see it for what it was, but he continued anyway.

Steph continued to search near the clock as Steve fiddled with the clock itself, she was checking in all the draws of the bedside table that it was perched on, there was only two drawers attached to the unit. Opening the top draw was pointless as nothing lay in there except for dust and potentially a lot of bacteria, so she quickly closed that and moved down to the bottom draw pulling that open with same speed; inside lay an old case of what seemed to hold retainers in and to her disgust they were still in there along with a pair of small circle reading glasses.

"Yeah you're right, I can't see anything in this clock. No secret compartment or anything that resembles a clue right now."

The two of them continued their search with Steve only now moving away from the clock and grabbing the duvet from the bed which surprisingly was fitting nicely before thrusting it off the bed without thinking causing the air around it to be thrown about. The room certainly was not giving off a great odor no thanks to Steve and it was starting to become hard to search, just what was that smell.

After a moment's thought and the fact that it smells like regurgitated seafood paired with whatever else may in the air, the pair of them decide to open the window as the smell was starting to get stronger. "I can't take any more I've got to open it Steve," Steph said looking over to Steve for him to agree.

"Yeah. My bad, sorry!" Steve apologetically replied.

Steph stepped carefully over to the window trying not to knock anything else and cause more stench before slowly grabbing the handle to push the window open, the window was a bit tough but after a few nudges it moved slowly and Steph pushed the window open. Outside it was very breezy, a bit cold but apart from that it was greatly helping with the smell so for a brief moment it was lovely.

"See it's fine! A nice breeze to get rid of the smell and alright it's a bit chilly but it's starting to get better already," Steph said being pleasantly happy with herself.

"Ahhh you're right that's so much better I feel like I can actually breath again," Steve said gasping for more fresh air to come his way.

As things began to improve in the atmosphere the two of them became calmer again virtually forgetting about the ghost radio, Steve still standing over at the bed pulling away at pillows and sheets trying not to touch any stains that lay dormant on there. Steph on the other hand was checking behind the radiator and seeing something lodged down the back there so she grabbed a coat hanger from the wardrobe near by and tried to fish it out because for some reason it wasn't particularly covered in dust yet everything else was.

As Steph began fishing for this item she started knocking dust particles into air as she went but that didn't stop her as somehow she knew this was important as it looked somewhat familiar ,once she finally got this item out and blew off any excess dust and realised why it looked familiar..

"This is mine," she could be heard mumbling.

"What's that," Steve asked "You say something?"

"Err, yeah. I found this," Steph replied while turning slowly and showing Steve.

"What is it?"

"It's a hair clip."

"So, why do you look so worried?"

"Because it's mine."

"How do you know?" A concerned Steve asked.

"Because, my nan gave it to me. It has her initials on it," An emotional Steph said back as she threw her hands into her hands and just stood there for a second. Steph continued to hold her hands to her face as she was now flooded with tears, paralyzed in the position she stood only somewhat shaking a little from the crying.

A shocked confused Steve was very unsure how to react to this as it'd all happened so fast "Steph, you alright?"

A few moments passed as he continued to stand there awkwardly waiting to get the go ahead to continue talking or at least comfort her, such were Steph's strong resilient ways people had rarely seen her cry, let alone like this.

"Sorry, this is dumb."

"Hey hey, no. Don't be silly we all need a cry every now and again."

"Yeah but I'm slowing us down, just give me a second."

"Oh don't be silly, I cried at a film about a dog once. Admittedly it was very emotional and I couldn't believe they had to put the dog down. However, it's fine take as long as you need"

Steph took another few minutes to eventually compose herself and stopped crying, wiping the tears from her face before looking back at the clip with a sudden feeling of memory coming back to her as the room went silent for a second. "Ahh Steve, some good news hopefully!"

"What? What's happened?"

"I remember something." As Steph began talking Steve watched her mouth and listened with great attention incase anything was important. "I was in this room! I remember, I was in this room with Andrew." Steph said with somewhat enjoyment so at least there's a possibility she may have dropped this in here. "Well actually more so I remember being in...."

"In where Steph? This might help us?" Steve questioned.

Steph looked like she had just thrown up in her mouth before saying "That bed with Andrew?!"

"What?!" Giggled Steve.

"Don't laugh! You don't think we... do you?" Steph asked but before Steve could answer she replied to herself "Urgh no never, lets move on."

Steve straight away let out a huge laugh and began teasing Steph "Sounds like you were searching for more than clues in that bed hun," Steve said while trying to contain his laughter.

"Eww first of all Steve. My name is Steph not Hun, secondly I would never be bumping uglies with Andrew! Ever, we're friends we wouldn't do that!" Steph grumpily answering back "But what has that got to do with anything and why have I just now remembered that?"

"Maybe it was a joyous memory for you." Continued a childish Steve.

Steve decided to stop searching realising if what Steph has said is true then he's touching stuff he doesn't want to touch it, so he virtually threw it down as fast as possible and jumps backwards. In their search so far nothing they had found has helped at all and it's starting to feel like there was simply nothing in this room.

The two of them stood there hopeless in the room for a few seconds looking around the room wondering where a clue could be, hoping any little open door or moved carpet could show a location of a hidden clue but all they could feel was the force of the wind blasting through the open window as it rattles on its hinges.

All of a sudden a loud crash could be heard upstairs one of seismic proportion "STEPH STEVE, IS EVERYTHING OK UP THERE? WHAT WAS THAT?" David shouted up the stairs!

Steve hollered back down as loud as he could "Yeah we're ok Dave, the wind managed to smash the old window off of its hinges not quite sure how it happened, absolutely crazy."

"You sure?" David calls again.

"Yes, thanks Dave."

Somehow all of sudden a loud noisy gust of wind had come flying into the room sending the window crashing back into its frame causing it to come loose and fall, the window smashing down into the ground outside the noise being heard by everyone in the house but lucky enough the two of them were so busy doing nothing that they were able to move back quick enough when it happened. As David and Steve were having a shouting match up and down the stairs, Steph went back over to the window to see the damages or merely what's left of it.

"Jesus christ, how has this happened?," Questioned a bewildered Steph, must of been one terribly old window she thought.

As her eyes continued to browse over the frame and her hands run along it she couldn't help but then to look out at the same time, outside she saw what appeared to be a shed just slightly to the side of the house. Steve had moved out of the room following the mishap due to the wind continuously now blowing cold air into the room, right now Steve would take the bad smell coming back if it'd just warm up again.

"Come on Steph, it's freezing in here!" Steve said waving his hand for her to leave the room.

Following the destruction of the window and what felt like an ice storm coming through the window, Steve and Steph decided to head back down to the first floor to check the rest of the rooms. Once they were back on the floor they decided to go to the other end of the hallway and work their way back.. Steve walked over to the door first but this time Steph wanted to be the first through the door so Steve obliged, so he backed out of the way allowing her space to get to the door. Her hand gripped the door handle and lucky enough for them it was unlocked so slowly and softly she swung the door open allowing it all to be on show before she entered, a bathroom was on the other side.

The first floor was a nicer floor to be on with the temperature actually reasonable and the decor once again actually nice, this bathroom was no exception giving a feeling of being large however it was actually a bit on the small side. The bathroom was clean, simple and yet beautiful, the big marble floor tiles were complimented by a big shower with a classy rainfall shower head also with the correct lighting coming from the window it let off the illusion of it being sizable.

The bathroom as a while was lined with the slightest bit of condensation, not enough to suggest the showers or hot water been used in the last 5 minutes but certainly at some point somebody had been in here. It didn't take very long foe their eyes to scan the whole of the bathroom and for the most part it seemed plain and empty however, placed inside the shower tray lay something of confusion.

CHAPTER 6

While the others searched upstairs for something to help and coming across nothing but winter through the window the rest were still down stairs hoping themselves to gain something helpful.

The shoes in the hallway were still a strange one to Fran because she knew they looked a spitting imagine of a pair that Steph either owned or ones she definitely spoke about before but Fran couldn't remember exactly but certainly made a mental note of it. While in the hallway she spent some time looking back over at some of the paintings on the wall with them almost being an escape from the stress she was feeling, with the daisies in painting reminding her of the outside and how simple it can be.

As she began to day dream while staring at the paint feelings of guilt came across her, feeling like she should be at home helping her mum instead of having fun with her friends but this so called game they were playing is far away from what she actually thought it'd be.

In this moment Fran was not particularly helping anyone or doing anything but for a moment at least she was out of the way of the others, she assumed they'd be happy they didn't have her standing over for them for a bit. Frans eyes did glaze upon the keyhole of the room at the end of the hallway because some times different eyes see different things, using a different prospective but alas to no prevail she only saw the same as the others.

The two guys in front room were still sat on the floor attempting to crack the code of the drawer and by god they are certainly moving through the codes but so far nothing suddenly they were interrupted by a huge bang from upstairs.

'Craaaaasssssshhh'

The three of them all jumped, not knowing what it was David ran into the corridor to see if Fran was ok or if she knew what it was.

"Fran?! You ok?" David said out of breath as he moved very quickly.

"Yeah Yeah. I'm alright, it came from upstairs somewhere," Fran said attempting to compose herself.

David shouted up to see if everyone was alright "STEPH STEVE, IS EVERYTHING OK UP THERE? WHAT WAS THAT?!"

Steve hollered back down the stairs "Yeah we're ok Dave, the wind managed to smash the old window off of its hinges not quite sure how it happened, absolutely crazy."

"You sure?!"

"Yes, thanks Dave," Steve calls back.

"Well thankfully it seems like they're well! Let's go back in there," Fran points to the front room.

Still trembling from crash and bang of the window Fran ran back into the front room rejoining Jason where he was still in pursuit of the codes for the drawer, David came back in to the front room shortly after Fran. As the two of them sat back down to see how Jason was getting on he was ever so thankful that he had finally got a correct code' 5594'. As he entered the code the draw unlocked itself the crew were giddy with excitement they've been here for ages listening to ' Bleep Bleep Bleep Bleep ' nonstop over and over.

"Guys I've done it... I mean we've done it, it's unlocked!" Jason smiled from ear to ear spitting words, hoping for some kind of applause.

David was left speechless that he actually found the code, he edged closer over to draw before gripping the handle he momentarily had a brief look at the others and breathed a small sigh of relief. David began to pull the drawer open with the drawer dragging on the side as it slowly pulls open but not without some resistance.

Inside the nice solid drawer still looking as fresh as the day it was bought, well from the out anyway, it still left a lot to the imagination. Inside they find another 2 keys with both being different as well as looking quite old with rust starting to form, there was no information with these keys. Something else inside the draw that could actually help is a drawing of the house layout, but it almost looked old enough to be the original layout of what you would have got when you first bought the house as it was stained brown and torn slightly.

"Oooh, we've got more keys and a layout?" Fran expelled with some slight excitement in her voice.

"Yeah, would've been better if it at least showed where these keys worked," Jason Said smiling and hopeful for an easier run at this game.

"Yeah that'd be nice."

"Let's check these keys on that room that Jason said he remembered being in, maybe they fit or worst case it'll narrow it down." David said while taking the keys out of the drawer, closing it and standing up using Jasons shoulder to push himself up off of the floor. Jason and Fran agreed to this idea because as of right now they didn't have many other options, so it was logically to at least try.

As the sun continued to shine through the slightly opened curtain in the front room it almost created a path for them to walk on as well as, keeping downstairs nice and toasty compared to upstairs anyway. However things outside were not going to stay on their side for long as the weather was on the turn with dark clouds moving into view could be seen heading over fast. The three of them walked into the hallway, down the corridor towards the door with Fran glancing in the mirror as she went past and sped up a little to resist catching the same view as before which spooked her, so she managed to reach the study door first.

David looked at the keys and offered them to Fran to see if she wanted to try opening the door but she quickly shock her head in decline so, David moved the keys towards the keyhole and slide one inside, it seemed to fit. David eyes lit up with anticipation slowly turning the key, but it never turned fully it was starting to get jammed inside but he kept trying to force it.

"Careful!! Don't twist it too much, you're gonna snap it," Jason called out grabbing David's arm.

"Fine fine, sorry!" David pulled the key back out but it wasn't plain sailing as it was quite well jammed in there now, but he backed off from the door allowing Jason free roam.

"Here, move," Jason said "Let me try."

Jason actually managed to get the key out before swapping keys with David to give the other one a go, David was more than happy to take a back seat and let Jason take the lead keeping his distance from any confrontation.

"The key worked! It actually worked! This is huge," Jason punched the air overjoyed with his success, giving a slight smug look to David, with David giving back nothing more than a happy smile,. "Maybe I'll even remember something more by going in here."

As the door swung open it was there for all to see a rich red coloured couch studded with gold, it was classy but some what horrid at the same time. Jason's memory was overwhelmingly correct but unfortunately the couch was pretty much as far that went, he walked into the room after David noticing he was correct straight away he scanned the rest of the room hoping something else would jolt his brain into remembering stuff. David however had his eyes immediately fixate onto a big brown desk right in front of him, he felt like it was almost calling him almost like a sign of home sitting at his desk alone where he is most comfortable.

The desk itself was sturdy with a lovely smooth finish to it, it looked expensive as well as having some real class about it.

His eyes took a good look at the desk and it's many draws however; it was littered in papers but all stacked neatly on top and it looked important as if any clues were down here then surely, they would be in there.

Fran was the last one into the room she let the guys go in first, as soon as he walked into the room herself she noticed the guys getting caught up on the different things in the room in which she wasn't all that bothered about and took a seat on the red couch, somewhat surprised by how comfortable it was considering how ugly she it thought it to be.

"So, anything ringing any bells Jason?" Fran calmly asked Jason hoping not to distract him as she parked her butt onto the couch.

Jason dropped himself onto the couch next to Fran causing her to bounce up slightly before letting out a slight sigh "No literally nothing, I barely even remember the couch thing! It's so strange I have no idea what that memory was meant to tell me."

David's hand was running all over the open space on top of the solid hardwood desk feeling for any abnormalities, none seemed present so far instead now moving his attention over to the 3 drawers on the right-hand side of the desk. Each drawer increased in size with the top draw being the smallest and thankfully unlocked so David started with that one, pulling it open he saw inside were blanks pieces of paper stapled together with no indication of why they were like that as well as those, the only other thing inside the drawer was a little pot of liquid with no label.

David had a brief look at both items before closing the draw as he was hoping for something a little more concrete so he moved onto to draw number 2, the middle draw. In the grasp of his hand was the drawer handle so he yanked the draw open to reveal its secrets.

Inside drawer number 2 held inside it a good looking laptop and a calculator so potentially one of them might prove valuable but aside from that there were no more items to be found in there. The last drawer in the set was the bottom drawer, the final draw on the desk which at first glance the desk itself doesn't seem to have been very fruitful so far but nevertheless, search they must. David pulled open the final drawer exposing all of the items that lie within but all that turned out to be was a couple of pens and other stationary items like a hole-punch, stapler etc.

David stood there gutted as he was really putting his eggs in this basket, he assumed the desk would have something for him but so far nothing in it seemed to be concrete proof but the more he looked over it the more his suspicions grew.

"Guys is it me or does this bottom draw seem off?" David asked while signaling his friends over t have a look.

Jason and Fran stood up from the red couch from which they'd made their home, this 'game' is seemingly very slow right now as not a singular search was really going on yet, everyone was just kind of hanging around in the house. The group hadn't really any idea of what avenue they should be chasing, Jason had a slight memory come back to him and the rest upstairs were chasing the music to no avail but the chase was not over yet.

"What are we looking for? looks like a draw to me?" Jason said sarcastically but also seriously.

"No no no but think about it, doesn't it seem like it should be bigger?" David replied as he gestured to the desk pointing at the part he thinks looks bigger.

"Why?"

"What do you mean why?"

"Why should it be bigger?" Jason questions still confused as to why.

"Because it looks way bigger on the front than it does inside," Fran spoke up "I agree David, seems odd but there a slight possibility that it's a design but it would be strange."

Jason still wasn't fully with the idea as to why it should be bigger but instead decided to just go along with it and pretend to understand "Oh yeah! Probably a design to it, think it looks nice."

David knew that he didn't have a clue what was going on but thought he'd just let Jason be Jason "What if there's a secret compartment somewhere?"

"Well let's try and open it up," Fran said, surprisingly destructive from her.

David drags the drawer out and off its runners before slamming it onto the top of the desk somewhat like he enjoyed it, the drawer felt light when he threw it up there so maybe there wasn't anything else in there. The items that he could see in the drawer are thrown out of there in double quick time,

David felt all over the bottom of the drawer tapping on it hoping for a hollow sound.

There were no hollow points just yet as he was heading towards the back of the draw, but wait there appeared to be a tiny bit of string hanging out Davids eye light up in intrigue so he gives it a pull and would you believe it a thin layer of drawer folds back very precisely and perfectly.

"Ingenious," David mutters as his eyes slowly watch the fake drawer layer fold back.

The others were shocked as they watched David take the false bottom out of the draw all with anticipation of something more however there is very little beneath sadly, this false bottom contained a photograph of a big chest with an old frail looking wooden door in the background. Upon picking up the photo David showed it to the others with them all taking a look at the strange but obvious clue, although none of them had seen that chest or any so far.

The drawer was almost empty now except for one final thing while pulling out the photo a note was lurking underneath it was another note with the words written.

No matter what order you find things.

Time is of the essence.

The group must find this chest

All must be present.

"Where do you think this chest could be? That chest must need a key surely," Fran said "I wonder what's in it."

"I have no idea, but I guess we should round up the gang and search for it together, let's go upstairs to find them," Jason suggested.

"Do we need everyone to go, we could just go? The game won't know surely."

"Maybe, you two should get the others," David agreed while distancing himself from going.

"Fine, let's go find the others." Fran agreed but she knew this could slow them down again and they've already wasted enough time, "But wait, why don't you want to come?"

David agreed with both of them to a point before suggesting he would stay and search the rest of the study as they hadn't searched the rest of the study properly and this room must house other things to help solve this game. Fran and Jason agreed to leave him there with them too believing it would be a good idea for him to stay and search the study, David was more than happy to be left alone doing things his own way. The others left the room as Jason lead Fran upstairs to find the others and search for the box as it was clearly something that needed to be investigated, plus by this point the others may have found some clues of their own too.

"Come on then Fran, let's find the others." A delighted Jason said, as he felt a lot of his suggestions were being used and boy did he feel good right now.

"Yeah fine, let's go." Fran said while wondering why they couldn't just look for the chest themselves, but maybe she just felt like she wanted her suggestion to be heard and used so she could feel like she was in control for a minute instead of always being second because even in her mind she was second best.

"You alright Fran?" Jason wondered.

"Yeah I'm fine, let's just get this over and done with."

CHAPTER 7

Back upstairs in the lush bathroom Steve and Steph continued to search in there paying particular notice to the items inside the shower tray.

"What are those and whose are they?" Steve questioned. The shower tray was holding a whole set of clothes containing every item you'd assume to wear day to day, but what on earth they were doing in a shower tray soaking wet is odd to say the least.

Steph picked up a nearby towel covering her hand in it and moved back over to shower tray with Steve watching whilst feeling rather confused right now, as she got back over toward the shower she used the towel to pick up one or two of the pieces of clothing to get a closer look. Upon lifting clothing pieces one by one before letting them drop slightly to the side, Steph got a strange feeling that she had seen these pieces of clothing before but where.

"You alright Steph?" Steve asked still very confused.

"Err... yeah," Steph replied.

"Come on! Spit it out,"

"Is it me or do they look like the clothes Andrew was wearing?"

He took a minute to take a look himself however without picking them up because he was already grossed out a little that she had touched them but he did get closer and closer to them, so Steph jokingly then attempted to throw the dirty underwear from the floor onto Steve. Steve flung himself back but ended up just knocking himself backwards onto his arse still attempting to keep his face covered from Steph as she cried with laughter as he wriggled away.

"Steph! Stop, that's disgusting." Steve said rolling around on the floor.

"I'm only joking," Steph said while laughing away and dropping the underwear back into the shower tray.

"You're so nasty, honestly. Not even funny," Steve said as he slowly got back to his feet still cowering away a little bit. "You're such an idiot, you'd get all emotional if I done that to you!"

"Oh, emotional, would I? Because I'm a girl?"

"No! Because you are emotional about everything, like the other week when I pranked you at Davids and you basically wanted to fight me."

"That was different and not funny at all! I could have really hurt myself, you're just an idiot when you're drunk."

"Oh, grow up."

"Pathetic, now isn't the time so do you have an opinion on the clothes or not?"

"What do you mean?"

"That they look like Andrews?"

"Well right now I am trying to get the taste of underwear out of my mouth, thanks to you!" Steve replied grumpily before slowly glances and having another quick look at the clothes "But yeah, maybe a little bit."

"I'm pretty sure of it!" Steph told Steve.

"Wait so you're telling me he's shoes are upstairs and the rest of his stuff is here? So, what would he be wearing?" Steve said while shivering at the thought of Andrew nude.

"Maybe he's just running around nude somewhere," Steph smirked and giggled.

Steve just stood there looking at Steph weird, she seemed to enjoy that thought even though a minute ago she was almost throwing up in her mouth. The clothes themselves were a mystery because even if someone or Andrew did have a shower, why would the clothes be back inside the shower it just doesn't make sense. While the two of them were in the bathroom pondering, Fran and Jason were coming up the stairs to look for them but that wasn't common knowledge for these two.

"Hey!" Called out Fran as she got to the bathroom door with Jason in suit, causing Steve and Steph to jump out of their skin with Steve almost on his back side again. Those solid stairs really were quiet.

"Jesus FRAN!" Steph took a deep breath while holding her heart and her back against the wall "Do you want us to pass over," Heavy panting and breathing were in full flow "Please give us a bit of warning next time please."

"Oh sorry, I didn't know where you were so I didn't want to start shouting," Fran apologetically replied.

"You certainly did jump," Laughed Jason from the hallway, neither him or Fran had actually gone inside the bathroom yet.

"We just wanted to show you this,"

"What is it?" Both Steve and Steph answered once again both fighting over the chance to be the first one people turn too, the two of them have a history of wanting to be the main person.

"Err, we don't know exactly. It's just a picture of a chest with a note telling us to search for it! Does it ring any bells, like the room or the door?" Jason said as Fran passed over the picture, "Or have you seen a chest?"

Steve was first to take the photo off of Fran and run his authoritative eyes over it trying to notice anything in it but it held no resemblance to Steve from what he'd personally seen so far, instead passing it over to Steph. She did the same and had a long hard look but came up short too, however, she did have an idea of where something that old and badly looked after door could be.

"I have an idea, but you may not like it." Steph said while moving off quickly before stopping and looking back "Well come on," she headed upstairs with the others very confused and worried but also hearing the confidence in her voice they decided to follow. The rest of them followed up the stairs after her with only Steve having a clue where she was going as the others had never even left the ground floor until a few minutes ago.

Steph headed into the bedroom with the dodgy radio and missing window, by this point the weather outside had changed leaving behind the bright sunny day that once was before and bringing with it the clouds leaving the house dark already. The room had become unbearably cold and was painful to stand in with everything cold to the touch, however the view from the room was vital. "In Here guys, this is where I think it could be."

Steve was a bit unsure "Steph, I've been in here too? Where could it be..."

"Ahhh Jesus it's freezing in here," Jason said as he shivered dramatically walking in the room.

The whole crew were struck almost straight away by the frosty wind hitting them violently as it still continued to blow through the room nothing was safe from its ice, as they all walked further into the room they attempted to fight the frosty by hiding behind each other as they headed straight for the window. Steves eyes glanced the floor with even the carpet showing signs of frost and what could be foot step marks in the floor but where it was dark and they had now started walking over them it was hard to tell.

"Steph?!" Steve tried to call out but every spoken word was met with ice flowing into the lungs, cold and unsettling.

"Guys look directly out and to the side of the window, do you see that shed?" Steph said asking all the others while pointing toward the shed. As the others were trailing behind slightly, they took a few more seconds to get over to the window, Steph waited by the freezing cold window as the rest took their sweet time getting over to here.

"Yup." Steve said trying not to stand at the window for too long with Fran and Jason giving a nonverbal reply.

"I think it might be in there," Steph said while gasping at air.

They all moved back from the window nodding and agreeing but mainly because they didn't really have another idea to go with, but how would they even get there as the front door was still locked from before and no one has seen any back door just yet, not that they had been looking for it.

"Seeing as the front door was locked, how on earth are we going to get outside to get there? The windows down stairs were also locked, well the one we checked at least. So what we going to do?" Jason pondered and questioned the others "Climb down that bloody trellis," he then giggled as he went and had another look out the window.

"I tell you what Jason that is your best idea to date," Steph smiled and said back.

"Steph?!" Steve still struggling big time and continuously looking back like a crazy person "The shoes!"

Steph could hardly understand Steve as he sounded like he was struggling with this cold air badly, he was still panting and breathing heavy so she moved closer to him."What? what did you say?"

"The shoes Steph, the SHOES!" Steve said panicking as the shoes had disappeared, maybe they covered them up while looking earlier but it seemed unlike so he frantically looked around the room to see if anything else had changed in the room with his eyes catching the radio also although that remained on the side except now it displaced a time of 11.34.

"Guys I was joking about doing that I don't actually want to climb down that, it was a joke!" Jason reiterating to make everyone was fully aware he was joking because it seemed as though people had taken Steph agreeing with Jason's joke as gospel and that's what they'd do, because no one questioned it.

Steph immediately turned and looked to where they had previously been placed and took a little gasp and a step towards the location, before quickly explaining to the others why her and Steve are so bothered by this. Steph moved ever closer to see if they'd just accidentally kicked them under the bed, covered them or something similar but as she almost reached the bed a noise of a loud creaky door opening could be heard by all and considering most people were in this room, it was a problem.

The noise sounded like it could only be coming from this floor due to how loud it was but this suggested someone was on this floor, however when they had come up here before it seemed as though the other doors were locked but due to the distraction of the radio they didn't check previously.

The noise of the door was unsettling, it was unnerving and had taken everyone by surprise. Not one of them actually knew where the noise had come from, as they all moved backwards and huddled ever closer Jason seemed to believe he had the answer.

"Wow, that was creepy wasn't it," A nervous laugh could be heard from Jason.

"What was that?!" Fran asked.

"It was probably the wind from here, blowing in the hallway,"

"No, no I don't think so," Steve said and for once he had really hoped he wasn't right"All these doors up here are stiff, we struggled to open this one a little."

"And?"

"I do not believe it would just blow open."

As the two of them stood there bickering over whether or not the wind could do such a thing, the two girls stayed close together and you could see that they gently nudged further away from the door of their room. During all the back and forth more noises could be heard with the door moving again, this time sounding like it opened even more than previously, perhaps even fully. The noise was creepy with the rest of house at rest and yet someone is moving a door somewhere with everyone a bit too afraid to actually check to see what or who it was.

"Guys seriously where is David?" Steve asked quickly.

"We left him downstairs searching," Fran mumbled out.

"Could he have come up?" Steph said.

"Possibly I guess, who knows,"

After a moments silence with nothing but the wind flowing through peoples ears a loud crash echoed down the hallway clear as day, the same door that had been creeping open now had been slammed closed with it followed by an unknown voice calling out "I know you are up here." The voice continued with a mild creepy laugh but only very briefly.

"Well, that... is definitely... not David!" Jason said trembling away with nobody being able to tell whether it was from the cold or fear but really and truly, did it matter.

Within a moment of hearing the voice, they had all scampered away from the door with no idea what this was but it was scary, was it the game or something else. They stood there freezing away in the wind with footsteps slow but being heard heading towards them with every step invoking a loud slow creak, the fear sector of the brain took over straight away and it encouraged them to go and fast but where.

"Climb just bloody climb!" Steph shouted as best as she could in the moment with it feeling like the breath taken out of her lungs, she didn't have another plan this was her only plan as she moved fast over to the window.

"What?! You sure Steph?" Jason shocked by what Steph was saying right now, looked at her in disbelief.

"It was your idea and honestly it sounds great right now!" She said as the footsteps continued to move but still ever so slow. They weren't sure how close this person was to them, whether it was Andrew or someone else also none of them seemed too keen to go and find out.

"But… but Steph I can't." Fran said with her head telling her she could never do this.

"Fran I'm sorry but I don't think you're going to have a choice."

Suddenly the footsteps now sounded like they were speeding up and definitely heading toward them only now with intent so Steph took no chances and had a look out before grabbing the trellis and boosted herself onto the window ledge itself while actioning for the rest to follow suit. She gently shifted her weight onto the trellis and began to move down it. Jason urgently followed as-well aiming to be near Steph and he wanted to show everyone he wasn't afraid to climb out even if he was actually joking the first time, plus right now seriously wasn't the time to mess about.

"Fran go. Now!" Steve frantically insisted.

"But..." Fran softly said with a tear in her eye.

"Now Fran!!"

Fran eventually listened and climbed out of the window but not before sitting on the ledge, taking a look out questioning why on earth she was doing this. This was meant to be a game so why was she climbing out of a window, but the noises from the footsteps along with the call of the others from down below caused her to move so she started climbing. Steph had reached the bottom and was gesturing to rest to hurry up while paying no attention to what was going on near her, unsure as to where she was right now with her only concern was to help Fran down with Jason not far behind Steph in reaching the bottom so by this point it was only Steve left in the room.

As Steve watched Fran move down the trellis he too then reached out of the window and grabbed the trellis, just as he did the door smashed open fully causing him to jump almost falling out the window. Within a flash the light turned off so when he had a brief look back all he could see was darkness and a slight outline of a person.

Steve however could not tell whether it was male or female from the figure only assuming it was male from the voice they had heard, so he started his panic climb down without falling and once near enough to the bottom he jumped off. Once everyone was away from the bottom of the trellis, they took look back up but now there was no noise or motion existing by the window with it almost now feeling like no one was ever there.

"What on earth was that or who should I say?" Fran asked as they huddled back together looking back at the window.

"I have no idea but damn this game is realistic isn't it," Jason said while trying to keep it together.

"I don't think it's a game Jase!"

"Oh come on, surely it is,"

"Steve are you alright, you looked like you almost fell?" Steph asked.

"Yeah, the door got booted in and it spooked me, nearly lost my balance."

"Did you manage to have a look back?"

"I tried but when I did the light had gone out, I couldn't see anything but a slight figure but it didn't help." Steve told while moving his hands up and down his arms tried to warm them up feeling the goosebumps all over them.

"Dammit," Steph replied.

Now they stood out in the cold somewhere around the house, the front the back, right now they couldn't tell which was which but at least they were out of that room; however, they all knew they couldn't just stay where they were right now so a plan of action was needed to save the situation. As they stood outside in the cold wondering what their next move was, the figure from the room was now stood in front of the window of someone looking down at them without them even realising.

CHAPTER 8

The sun turned to clouds and warm turned to real cold but David hadn't even noticed, he was spending time down stairs looking through items in the study, he checked the behind the door, under the couch as-well as re-checking under the desk after pulling the nice office chair away.

David was so engulfed in finding some information he had no idea of the commotion upstairs instead had his head buried in the papers that lay upon the desk. The laptop that David found had been opened up and pressed to turn on but it did not start it merely flashed a low battery signal so objective number one was to find the cable, it had to be in here somewhere as it's only logical.

Upon searching for the cable he'd taken out boxes next to the side of desk and with it he came across a load of books in a box all linked to science, more specially Biology and the study of the body. Among those science books were theoretical studies on brain waves and the potential of the brain when put in strenuous situations, some what similar to situations of an escape room.

David wasn't much of an expert on anything scientific but even he found them very intriguing and wanted to had a look through them because it could hold clues on how to control their emotions in this exact situation, possibly but you'd near more time to study it. Even though they didn't have the time to sit and read these books and theories David did manage to notice that near the box of books was in fact a power cable, pulling it up and onto the desk.

The first time today that something had gone their way, as the lead he found did indeed match the laptop, so he unravelled the rest of the lead and moved his chair back so he could plug the other end into the wall.

The laptop powered on after a few moments and as it hit the startup screen obviously a passcode was needed, Shit! David thought to himself so he rechecked all the draws immediately to see if he'd missed anything. The draws were as bare as before which was obvious but still frustrating for David so he put the stuff back in the drawers properly as well as refitting the bottom drawer back in place. David slammed the drawers closed one by one and in doing so heard the pot of liquid tip over.

"Dammit," David said sighing and puffing as he reopened the drawer seeing that some of the liquid spilled over the stapled papers and to his surprise it started turning a funny colour. "That's odd, why is it doing that? " David mumbled to himself before then pulling both the pot and the paper out of the desk and trying to put some more liquid onto the paper.

David saw that it started to change colour revealing some letters as he watched in amazement, as he shunted the locked computer to one side and began putting the liquid over the paper, only a few little drops at a time. The liquid dripped slowly with the paper began to change colour completely and information was slowly revealing itself.

Once the paper had fully changed colour it showed itself to be exactly what the guys needed earlier as it listed the passcode to the draw safe and the laptop code which happened to be the same, insinuating the same persons stuff and this person might be a creature of habit so if anything else was coded then it's possibly the same code.

David started monologuing curiously "Oh I see, it's invisible ink. Now that certainly is very clever indeed and yet so obvious why did we not notice this the first time or even think of it. So, if this first paper housed the codes to get into things I wonder what the other pieces of paper are holding secret from me, I must know. The others are going to be so excited to see my break through."

David folded back the first paper and went through the same process to ink the following two papers with more information coming to light, one of which was a map of the house hinting at where certain things may be hidden in the house and the second piece of paper was almost blank, it did have something written on it but with it mostly scribbled out it was impossible to tell what it was.

Something just didn't quite add up for David, as he sat there looking at the information he had gathered from these pieces of paper it dawned on him "Wait, wait, how on earth could we have possibly found this paper beforehand, it shows us where to find the drawer and other places of interest and yet we wouldn't have got into this room without finding and getting into the draw first because the key to this room was in the draw? That doesn't make a shred of sense..."

David was very confused and wasn't sure to what to think and decided to just open up the laptop hoping to find something else, "Let's get into this laptop and see if this has any more information" Davids mind was doing circles because he just did not understand.

David typed in the passcode on the laptop 5594 and the laptop unlocked itself, coming up with the previously loaded screen or what David assumed to be the clue screen but what loaded up was photo album of groups of people. All the groups in the photos appeared to be previous contenders in this game or house at least, all of the pictures had two copies and both copies showed a group of 6 with one being a normal picture and the second copy being the exact same photo except with one person in the photo being a blacked out over and every other person having a green tick over or red cross.

Every group photo had the same background the same location and photo after photo with the exact same marks what could it mean, the person blanked out is in a different position every time so maybe that person was the winner. David remembers their group photo was also taken in the same place, it looked similar to the previous house where the game was meant to be held so a possibility was that there was a problem with the other house that is why it got changed to here or maybe that was always the plan.

David continued flicking through the pictures before opening up anything else that would work on the laptop but so far it doesn't appear to be holding any clues as such, David wasn't sure why the laptop was here then so instead picked back up the sheets of paper he had. The paper which he picked up first was the one that held a map of the house on it, on the map it was confirmation of where clues would be roughly found and it even had the shed outside on it although unaware that's where the others were attempting to head.

What was extremely odd for him was that it strangely said there was a basement on it and yet no one has seen a door to it or any idea of a basement, even on the map it simply listed the basement but not a location of entrance on it. All the map told was that there was a basement however logic dictates that it would be located somewhere in the hallway and the entrance would be under the actual set of the stairs.

As David was looking at this map by himself a message popped up on the laptop leaving David in a little fright.

'Is the house safe.. Is the room safe.. I hope no one has a heart attack.'

David was very confused he didn't know where it came from or how it played but subconsciously he replied to the message mumbling his response out loud "I'm not alone my friends are upstairs." Before pausing for a second as he saw his reflection in the mirror before speaking again "Look at me replying to a laptop must losing my mind." He said while laughing to himself before hearing another message popped up.

'Oh but are they, because as far as we're concerned, you're alone.'

David jumped back in his seat throwing his hand over his mouth not knowing what to say next, breathing heavy through his nose before slamming the laptop closed and looking all around the room for indication of who or what is watching him. David is 100% sure that there was no way of the laptop pre predicting his responses because that's just impossible, isn't it?

Silence filled the room as David continued to sit speechless in his chair without a thought running through his mind he just sat, eventually after a while he slowly removed his hand and opened the laptop back up hoping somehow he had imagined it but as soon as the laptop was opened up properly, a message straight away popped up and it turned out to be his 3rd and final message.

'We are watching.

You will not see where or how.

Alone is never a good way to be

Good Luck'

David felt instant panic inside of him with the heavy breathing continuing and with him now aware that he was no longer in control, he hadn't the foggiest idea of what to do next instead just aimlessly slamming the laptop closed jumping back onto the couch attempting to get a breather. The empty room filled with Davids breath as he started breathing deeper and heavier than ever before, it took a while before David had managed to calm himself down a little and reopened the laptop one last time, however it no longer started up it merely displayed a time 11.00.

A new plan was now in place and that plan was to find the others stay as a group, then go looking for the basement but the only problem with the plan is that he wasn't exactly sure where the others were, were they upstairs or was he alone like the voice said. David quietly left the study leaving as if nothing was wrong and crept to the bottom of the stairs before lending his ear up the staircase carefully listening out for anything, it was suspiciously quiet for what should be at least 4 people upstairs.

After staying there for a few seconds listening David did eventually hear a noise but it seemed to just be the wind slamming a door closed upstairs somewhere with nothing of note going on, which seemed rather strange to him. Instead he decided there and then he would move on to the next part of his plan without the help of the others as he didn't want to wait anymore because admit it or not, he was a little scared.

David moved his head away from the bottom of the stairs pulled himself together, stood up straight and faced back down the corridor towards the study door to start his search for where he thought the entrance would be for the basement or even if anything looked out of place. David started his search from the bottom step heading toward the stuff, feeling over every surface the only thing that even remotely looked out of place appeared to be a picture frame that had been left on the shoe rack so he made his way over to it.

"That's strange someone's touched them shoes also? Fran was out here earlier maybe she liked the look of them." David giggled to himself trying to ease his fears and anxiety, he picked up the photo and straight away noticed it was a replica of a view of the hallway/staircase in the mirror. Unsure of why it was like this he looked it over a few times, spinning it over and checking the back of the frame too but nothing else was there as a clue and it was only due to the fact he was in-front of the mirror he himself too tried to match up the view in the mirror but mainly because he wanted to see if he could actually do it.

"Almost got it," He could be heard mumbling to himself almost as if this was a little game, using this to calm his nerves "There! Got it!" And in doing so he too heard a creak come from the brand new stair case behind him which confused him more than scared him. David turned away to look behind him to see for what could of made that noise and in doing so he moved the photo out of frame, putting it down and moving over to the staircase.

David's hands felt all over the side of staircase as well as each step individually to feel for anything out of place or some kind of a button or hatch, alas nothing.

"What was that noise, if it's not the actual stairs then what is it." David was getting agitated from not finding anything yet and was attempting to think of all possibilities no matter how outside the box they were. Although it happened at the same time he wasn't actually sure whether it was just a coincidence or it actually had something to do with the photo so his next idea was to try again to be sure. David grabbed the photo frame and attempted to match it up again in the mirror once again because that is when he heard the noise before.

The photo frame all old and busted was in his grasp as he tried his best to realign it to how he had it before, to add to his suspicions and he stairs made the exact same noise as before.

"So, every time I match this view up something creaks but what. It can't actually be the stairs so it has to be a door or something attached to the stairs!" His eyes in the mirror looked all over the beautiful looking stairs questioning every bit of moulding or mark." Where is it! It's here somewhere it cannot keep being a coincidence," David said questioning everything "God i feel so crazy right now, if only someone could see me now."

He decides to have a closer look in the photo to look for anything different compared to what he sees in real life, it appears that in his photo to the left hand side of the towards the study door there appears to be a slight lip in the panels underneath the stairs. Once again he matches up the view in the mirror while looking for the lip in real life on that specific part of the stairs and once again there's a creak once the photo matches up however this time he sees that part of the panels move just ever so slightly and it matches the creak noise.

"Got ya," David says with a grin on his face, he doesn't know what he's got but he's found something.

David puts down the picture and moves towards the staircase panelling where he knows the opening is but for some reason as soon as he does the panel closes and it's almost impossible to see it anymore. "What?!" David says mildly annoyed "So how does this work, how am I going to get that panel open?"

David could barely remember where the panel was when it closed and considering he was literally just looking at it, that made him feel extra crazy, something is behind that panel and David knows it. The panelling was built to perfection there was no way that is was just suddenly going to be forced open, David knew that it is going to be incredibly hard to get open, if only he had someone else to help him because then it was for sure an easier task but where were the others.

A noise, a faint noise from upstairs, footsteps but a not on the immediate floor, they seemed like they were above that. David stopped moving and listened to these footsteps but they for sure sounded like singular steps indicating one person and they weren't getting closer or louder they were getting quieter so, David ignored them and continued his mission.

David had to find a way to get to in too the room on his own but how?

CHAPTER 9

Back outside with the majority of the group, all of them were finally starting to calm themselves a little and could actually start focusing on what they were meant to be doing again. Steve stood there while still rubbing his arms with his hands in any attempt to warm up slightly, as did a few of them and all they knew right no was that they were just standing outside in the cold.

The world around them was beginning to get really dark with the wind blowing hard on the backs of their necks and down their spine, it was starting to really get horrid for them as none of them were dressed for the occasion, well realistically how could they possibly be as they believed they would be doing this game somewhere else.

"Right is everyone ok, does anyone have any ailments?" Steve asked attempting to put himself back on top of the authoritative ladder after Steph's emergence on it.

"Err yeah," Fran said as she shivered away "Where are we? Like what side of the house are we?"

Everyone was thinking the same thing, nobody had the foggiest where they were because of all the excitement and fear from climbing out of a second-floor window they had lost all sense of direction. Once again no figure could be seen in the window, it was empty so maybe that person or thing could have been part of the game because nobody actually saw anybody or anything but another possibility was that person could be on their way down to them right now.

Everyone seemed to be in fine nick with no complaints and nothing to attend too, so they all span around to remember which direction the shed was in as that was the only place and direction they could remember right now, after a brief stint of staring into space they saw it. The shed actually seemed further away than at first inspection from the window, it was at least 50 metres away but nonetheless it was the next stop on this strange ride so far.

"Hey look!" Jason called out "Is that the shed?"

"Maybe," Steve said as he looked back at the house before looking back toward the shed "Seems like it would be in that direction, so yes let's go for it."

"So, we've got to go there...right?" Fran asked to the group.

"Guess so, that seems like the next stop. We don't have much else right now, plus we're already outside," Jason replied looking into the distance.

Not for the first time during this day so far Jason was right again, it was virtually all they had to go on for now so exploring this lead was worth it, the four of them began walking in the direction of the shed. Surprisingly as they walked toward the shed and started entering a small plot of trees it was slighter warmer than it was before hand with the wind not being able to hit them so brutally and so often, but this still was not a very comfortable journey but every single step the did edge closer and closer to the ever more visible shed.

The only new issue they had now come across was with every-step they got closer to the shed, it was a step further away from the house and more into what could now be described as a patch of woodlands so the imagination ran wild with fear as well as their ever-changing sense of direction with every section of the trees staring to look the same.

"What's that?!" Jason said panicking as he heard a crack in the trees.

"Nothing Jason, there's nothing there," Steve said in a strange amount of confidence "It's just your brain playing tricks on you."

"Are you sure? Ahhh!" Jason jumped as he thought something had touched him when it was just Steph stroking him with a stick ever so slightly trying to make light of a serious situation so they stayed strong and light on their feet. "Why?! Why would you do that?!"

"Woah, watch your mouth! I was only joking." Steph said giggling and threw the stick on the floor.

Fran bless her was also trying her hardest not to freak out as-well attempting to not seem even more scared than she already was, so forcing her fear and troubles inside, she decided to join the light jokes on Jason "Come on Jason don't be such a girl, it's only a stick."

Walking in a woodland cold as hell they all needed a good laugh and in the end even Jason let out a little giggle, admitting that maybe it was slightly funny and for a few minutes they were all genuinely having a little amount of fun, until something did actually make a noise in the woods. A branch cracked and leaves rustled as something came moving over them, leaving the group all startled realising that noise was genuine, they all had a minor heart attack and as they turned it was right there behind them.

"Ahhhh!" Screamed Fran with similar screams coming from everyone, even Steve could be heard making a weird high pitch scream.

The screams slowly finished and they opened their eyes properly before realising that it was just a singular deer and now it seemed as though the deer was laughing at all of their expense as it gently made its way over a little patch of leaves and sticks again before leaving. The group all let out a sigh of relief realising how easily you can be spooked in these kinds of situations, after the sigh a slight giggle could once again be heard as they moved forward again away from where the deer once was.

"See! It's spooky out here isn't it," Jason said backing up his need to be worried "Did you scream like a girl there Steve?"

"Shut up, no I didn't. I was merely mocking you guys," Steve said straight away with his chest, secretly afraid to be shown as anything less than the manliest of men.

A few eyes thrust upon Steve not believing him at all as they all heard him scream like a girl but it was fine, they weren't judging him at all it was just funny to hear and very unexpected but, Steve rolled his eyes pretending not to be bothered instead choosing to go to the front and start leading the group in its hunt for the shed.

They finally reached the Shed and by this point when they turned around the house seemed a real long distance away and it was getting dark quick also they did not fancy being out here at all, especially not for much longer. When Fran looked back at the house and more specifically back towards where they had climbed down from she felt some amount of pride for overcoming her fear quickly albeit thanks to a huge amount of adrenaline but a feat nonetheless, and it was a huge moment for her knowing she is strong enough inside to be in control.

Although when Steph looked back at the house, she felt like she could see what looked like a figure in an adjacent window to the one they'd climbed out of and it gave her the creeps because it seemed to vanish just as quickly as it appeared.

"Let's go and get this over with." Steph said gulping with a degree of fear as she moved towards the Shed door and went to give it a push open, surprisingly it was very easy to open however it was extremely dark inside with them barely being able to see. The shed seemed very empty with nothing but the chest, thankfully with it being the only thing in the room it was quite obvious that this was the chest they were looking for.

They all shuffled into the shed and Fran almost by accident slammed the door behind them. 'Boooom' once again leaving everyone on the verge of a heart attack and also leaving the room in complete darkness now, she threw her hands up in apology not that anyone could see before then reopening the door to allow some light at least.

After everyone doing a shuffle in the dark trying to feel what may be in the room and eventually working out where the chest lay exactly, the time had come for them to open the chest and see what they had been searching for. Each of them gathered around the chest on the floor with strangely just enough light to be able to see a note on top of the chest, almost perfectly actually.

The note had an instruction to follow which requested everyone be there at the same time and open it together, except David was missing and he was nowhere to be seen, neither was Andrew so they had a decision to make.

"Right we need a Key?" Steph said.

"Yeah, do we have one?" Jason asked.

"I've still got the key we had from earlier when we tried to open the study," Steve replied.

"Oh yeah," Jason remembered "Did that note saying anything else Steph?"

"Yeah hold on." Steph continued to just about read the note "It says..We all have.. to reach in .. the .. Chest at ... the same time." The darkness was forcing Steph to almost keeping turning and twisting the note into the one bit of light forcing its way through the old slats on the shed. "But we can't do that because we're not all here."

"But, does it mean everyone or does it mean everyone who is in this shed right now?"

"No idea, that's all that it says to be honest."

It was getting cold in the shed, especially as they were not moving around anymore so they couldn't just sit and wait here forever, a decision had to be made. The chest didn't hold any more information of the top of it, there was no indication of what was inside it or why they all need to be there but except for David and the missing Andrew they were all there.

"Let's just do it." Steve told the rest "There's no way the game knows if we were all here or not so let's just do it."

"But.." Steph mumbled to the group.

"Yeah, alright" Fran actually agreed and was at the forefront of the decision making, she felt alive right now.

"Ok, let's do it then." Jason too agreed with the decision.

"I have the key ready" Steve said as he pulled the key from his pocket moving closer to the chest and made sure everyone gathered around " Right are we ready?"

"Let's do it, what's the worst that can happen." Fran said to the others while making sure she was close enough to the chest to be involved.

The whole gang gathering closer in-front of the chest, they all seemed to take it a large quantity of air at the same time in preparation of the unexpected however, upon opening the pushing the key in and unlocking chest another note fell out as the lid was lifted slightly. The note although extremely hard to see in the darkness, Steph managed to just about use the light again to just about work out what it said.

Inside this chest consists on 5 Items.

Each of you pull out what which your hand grabs.

No exceptions.

The note was bare and yet informative at the same time, everyone was well aware of what was to come with them actually understanding of what the note required or so they thought. Steve watched as everyone nodded agreeing they were ready to reach in and take an item, so as a group they grabbed the lid at the same time pushing it up with one hand and moved their other hand into the chest.

It was extremely dark inside the chest as it was expected to be, reaching into a void of darkness feeling what seemed to be a slightly wet and damp substance they began swirling their hands around attempting each to grab an item from the chest, it was exhilarating yet scary at the same time.

One by one they all brought their hands out of the chest pulling out an item with them before moving back to give the remaining people more space, as time passed and they all were out of the chest the time had come to identify what they had but with the very little light around it was going to be virtually impossible right now to be 100% accurate.

"Right I cannot see what on earth I'm holding so let's move over to the light unless you can see what you're holding, as it could be a vital clue," Steve asked of the gang as he ran his hands over his item attempting to find out what it was.

No-one was particularly able to see what they were holding so they all wanted to move into more light but that was hard to come by, by this point the sun was gone and there were no lights or candles in this old school shed so they needed to move out and use whatever moon light was available.

Steve led the group back out of the shed leaving behind the chest and its remains desperate to capture whatever amount of light outside they could. Jason himself actually felt pretty confident that he was already aware of what he was holding way before he had even left the shed so, he came out slower than the others but still holding his item more in pure shock and intrigue than anything.

"Why? this can't be a clue surely," Jasons soft confused tone was straight away obvious and it alerted the others.

All of the others turned around to see what Jason was holding before actually looking at what they were holding, Jason was standing there holding a chef's knife with what looked like blood on it dripping onto his clothing and hands, the rest of the gang were shocked!

After seeing what Jason was holding they were all curious as to what they were all holding, prompting them into quickly working out what they had. The moon was graciously helping them with some bright rays from above allowing them the perfect angle and amount of time to visualize what is in there hands, it didn't take long for the rest of them to work out what they were holding.

Jason had pulled A Chef's Knife out.

Steph had pulled A Broken Bottle.

Steve had pulled An Old Classic walking Cane.

Fran had pulled A Bottle of Ultra Strong Bleach.

"What on earth are the items?" Fran wondered as she spoke out loud to the group very confused as to why they had these items..

"I don't know but I really don't like it, something seems off. Very off," Steph said as she looked over at Fran "Plus my hands wet," Continued a grossed out Steph, upon catching her hand and forearm in the fading light she could see a small amount of red fluid had dripped onto her, it seemed like the sink liquid all over again.

As everyone else seemed to notice liquid had dripped over them too. they all dropped the items they were holding except Fran, she didn't have any liquid on her nor was her item dripping liquid over her. As Fran took another look at the item she was holding she noticed that her fingers are getting slightly stuck to the bottle, like an it had adhesive coat on it which was strange.

"Did it say how many items were there? Surely there's 5 or 6 then if it wanted us all there. So there's another item in there at least?" Steve wondered almost hinting that someone should head back to check and possibly get it.

"Yeah it did, should I get it?" Jason jumped at the chance to go back in to confirm the information feeling like he was taking charge.

"Err yes and no? I don't know if you should, but I guess we also need to know what it is," Steph said for once not being contradicting and harsh back to Jason.

"So, what do we reckon? What should I do, grab it or not?" Jason again queried "I'll just grab it," Jason headed back into the dark shed towards the open chest with even less light than before however before he got to the chest he started to second guessed himself in his mind stopping in his tracks, trying to work out if he should grab it or not.

Jason eventually gave up thinking about it and just went for it, he bent down to reach into the chest and began routing around for the final 'clue' in there but for all his reaching around he couldn't find anything in there so, was the note a lie or was something missing.

Jason walked back outside to join the others, who were all standing there nervously scanning the surrounding area for any movement because thanks to these strange items theirs mind were already going crazy a little bit. There have been many studies based on the possibility of your brain causing visual hallucinations based on memories or possible fears being seen by people.

The possibility of something being out there in the woods isn't zero, it's the woods there are animals in there or worst case maybe someone, however the mind will make you see things anyway as it is the most powerful tool a human has.

"So, there isn't anything else in there...There were only 4 items in the chest, I searched it fully," Jason told everyone leaving them all very confused.

"Wait are you sure?" Steve asked quite confused.

"Yes 100%, I searched it properly I swear."

"Right I don't like this and as much as I don't want to touch any of those items again, lets grab these and head back inside it's starting to get spooky out here and I don't like it," Steph requested as she bent down and grabbed the item she had dropped.

Everyone there was conservative to only pick up what they previously held just in case anything else was unjust about the situation. Upon picking up their items they headed back towards the house following the path they took before or at least hoping to anyway, it seemed awfully weird that they'd trekked to the shed for these items and yet more strange to be carrying them back to the house along a dark almost woodland path and yet they were. Realistically what would these' Clues' do to help solve the 'Game' they were in if it was still what they were doing.

As the crew continued along the pathway they had forged on the way here and were getting closer to the house they were beginning to remember that the front door and ground floor windows were all locked before, with the only way they knew how to get back into the house was the way they came out of the house which involved going back up the trellis into the broken window, possibly towards the person or thing. In a situation like this what is the best option do you climb back up , try to break in downstairs or find if there is another option. Once back close enough to the house they knew had to search the outside of the house fully there had to be something or possible another window to climb to on the floor below.

"We have to find a way in," Steve remembered!

"How? The front door was locked remember?" Fran reminded the others.

"True, what about the windows?" Jason asked hoping for a good answer.

"Nope they were locked too, there surely has to be another way in?" Steph wondered and came up with an idea. " I think we split up around the house, 2 and 2, meet round the other side and see who saw the best option to get in?"

"Hmm seems dangerous," Fran mumbled with her not liking that idea.

"Yeah it does, however it will be the quickest way to find a way in. We can search the outside twice as fast," Steve said backing up Steph's suggestion.

"Don't forget that's how people die in the movies." Mumbled a worried Fran.

The group eventually decided to split up and meet up back around the other side to decide the best way to get back in, that way they wouldn't get split up when they went back into the house. Jason and Fran headed one way with Steve and Steph heading around the other, the plan was to get in any way possible with the extreme last resort being climbing back in the window they had climbed out of.

CHAPTER 10

As day time was ticking to a close, clues were in short supply and with the group starting to split ever more with them now in three groups instead of one, things certainly were not looking up right now. The house was getting darker ever more with the game a foot, but were they going to be good enough to solve it or will it best them.

We continue with Jason and Fran as they split from the other two to search one side of the house, realistically the house itself was not huge so they could have stuck together and searched but mutually it was decided that this would be much quicker.

"Do you think we're going to be alright?"

"Yes Fran, of course." Jason stopped walking for a second and turned to look at Fran "Look, we may have split up and things may not be going our way but we always get through these sorts of scenarios. Just think back to all the times when we have got ourselves into sticky situations and we're still here!"

"What times?" Laughed Fran as she had no idea what sort of times he was talking about.

"Alright, so maybe there isn't as many times as I thought but you catch my drift, we will get through this." Jason looked at Fran and smiled, she smiled back at Jason appreciating him and what he is attempting to do.

They continued walking again moving their feet across the cold grass which felt like it was wet from the frost flicking little droplets of water with every step. Jason and Fran walked past the window they had originally climbed out of and completely ignored it, instead going straight around to the side of the building, immediately seeing a window on the first floor that looked like it could be opened.

The climb up to the window on the first floor seemed an unfeasible climb for Fran up the drain pipe, maybe it was doable for Jason but not possible for Fran so maybe they needed a new plan. Frans's problem wasn't necessarily through size or weakness but more weakness of the mind, she never wanted to climb out the other window but had too due to previous concerns.

"Jason you could make that couldn't you? " Fran wondered as she looked up it.

"Err yeah I guess so; I mean of course I could. Probably pretty easily," Jason replied trying not to sound to smug or proud of himself for being able to climb.

"Well, that's an option then I guess."

"Well no? Because how would you get up Fran?"

"I Wouldn't be able to climb but I could wait for you to open the front door or maybe a window down stairs," Fran suggested.

"Yeah but Fran how would we open the door we don't have a Key? And if the windows don't open I can only try and smash them. That wouldn't be the safest thing to climb into, let's keep looking" Jason insisted and slightly started moving more down the side of the building only stopping slightly to stop, look back and indicate for Fran to come on. Fran was reluctant as she believed her option to be a good choice but eventually agreed starting to walk with Jason to check for anymore possible entrances into the house.

Over on the other side of the building and making their way round the opposite side was Steve and Steph they too were checking to see if there was a plain and simple way of getting in the building from their side.

"There must be a way in to the house surely and we're going to find it," Steph said to Steve with intent in her voice.

"Yeah, we will," Steve said back in the same confidence.

The two of them started covering ground at a fast pace attempting to one up each other and being the person to lead causing all types of problems, they almost both fell over trying to out run each other. The woodlands around were bringing forward some awfully strange noises to their ears, bucks fighting in the forest clashing heads creating a wave of vicious grunting causing Steve to stop and look with Steph not one to be alone also stopping to have a look.

"What's that noise Steve?" Steph questioned to the unknown noise.

"Not sure, but it's got to the animals surely?" Steve responded "Let's just move."

They continued moving around the building and in doing so they missed the back door attached to the kitchen as the light was off and with the buck in the forest got them riled up as-well as unfocused.

"Can't really see one, I mean there are windows up there but none that are easily accessible plus who's to say that any are even open," Steve said as he led the way.

"Can't believe we haven't found any way in yet? This is crazy," Steph said impatiently as she turned back to have a look but it was dark leaving it hard to distinguish actually opening, she was so desperate to be the one to find the right way.

They turned round the corner to reach the front of the house within view of the front door just as they had agreed to do, upon waiting there for a few seconds for the others they started to hear some commotion going on inside the house. Their ears turned towards the house to what sounded like some crashing and banging around coming from the kitchen almost as if someone was looking for something but what and who.

"What was that? Did you hear that?" Steph panicked and turned around moving to the corner of the house looking back towards where the kitchen was, after passing it blindly without realising.

"Yeah! But where was it from?"

"I'm guessing the kitchen, as it sounded like plates and cutlery crashing about," Steph says after already making her move, she was so confident she knew and didn't stop to think, she just acted.

"Wait!" Steve said as Steph the stopped in her tracks "What about the others?"

"We won't be long and when we get back, I'm sure they'll be waiting here," Steph explained.

Steve trusted her instincts and just decided to follow behind as the both of them moved quickly crouching down alongside the house trying to keep in cover to sneak up to the kitchen. The window of the kitchen was positioned toward the back of the house, once they had reached the window, they both stayed below the window before a synchronized head nod then they raised their heads just enough to see into the window. In the window a soft white curtain was hanging down making it harder to see in, as they peaked into the window to get the first glance at there was nothing going on and nobody to see.

Their reflections could be seen in the window looking back, staring at their reflections feeling so alone as they sat there crouching outside a house in the middle of nowhere looking into a random kitchen window. The two of them slowly moved back down away from the window taking a moment to breath and calm themselves before going back up for a second look as it seemed like nothing was going on, their breath could be seen on the window and after a few seconds a figure ran into the kitchen but that was as best as it got, a figure.

The lighting in the kitchen was poor which really wasn't helping them, the figure that came into the kitchen was frantically looking around the kitchen throwing open drawers and slamming them closed again with the stuff in the drawers spilling out bouncing off of the tiled floor.

Whoever this person was they were looking for something specific as they were checking every single draw with no luck so far, it was manic in there and it was all happening so fast as they watched from the window with their breath still pressing against the glass, when all of a sudden the figure turned around while looking around in the kitchen. The figure seemed like it had looked directly at them and it spooked the two of them like crazy so, they ducked back down with both of their hearts pounding like crazy not knowing who that was, was it David or the person they had upstairs with them.

Jason and Fran finished moving around their side of the house and have now reached the front of the house with unfortunately no more available options to get back into the house, the only option they have right now is to climb in the window they had noticed. The only way they could get into that window was to use the drain pipe and potentially leave Fran outside, while Jason climbs the Drainpipe or they smash and go in another window. The two of them waited at the front of the house like the plan was, so decided to go through their options while they waited for the other two to arrive.

"Fran, I reckon you're going to have to try and climb the drainpipe," Jason recommended to Fran.

"I can try but I really don't think I'm able to I don't have that kind of upper body strength Jason."

"Well, that's the only way up or in it,"

"From what we have seen, maybe the other two have found a good way in," A slightly annoyed Fran told to Jason, rather upset by his insistence.

"Hmm, maybe you're right. I guess we'll see when they turn up, where are they anyway?" Wondered Jason as he stood there looking in other direction to see if he could see them.

They were in a predicament now as they need to get back inside there because there is no way they can stay out here in the dark, in the cold absent night with distant strange noises echoing in the background or potentially in their head no one knows for sure. Their eyes were covering every inch of the building stressing and panicking as they continued to look for way in but nothing is poking its head out to scream come in.

"Jason plain and simply you have to go climb into that window.".

"But how will you get in?"

"You'll find a way to let me in," Fran said while standing there with goosebumps covering her skin.

"You cannot just wait outside in the cold Fran! Moreover, I don't even know how I'd get you in."

"You'll find a way Jason!"

"No no no, let's find something to smash a window on the ground floor and we'll just have to be careful when climbing in," Jason said as he refused to just leave Fran out in the cold.

"Ok fine!" Fran said with frustrated tone but found it nice of Jason "First of all let's go around the other side and check on the other two maybe they've found a way in."

"That's a good idea, I feel like they definitely should have been here by now anyway." Jason was right, they should have been there by now so what was keeping them "If they're not there for some reason strange reason then we should just break back in a window."

"Why wouldn't they be there?" Fran questioned.

"No idea, but it seems odd that they're not here yet."

Neither one of the two actually knew what the right thing to do was right now, they just knew they had to stick together if they were to get back into the house so finding the others could only help them in their efforts. Between them they decided to head around to find the others, keeping close together Fran and Jason moved across the frosty grass with Fran holding onto Jason's arm to feel safer.

Steph and Steve were still ducking and panicking by the window knowing they too need to find a way to get in but they can't go in on this level because this doesn't feel safe now, the could hear footsteps in the kitchen of the figure heading toward the window.

"Oh god! He's coming?!" Steph panics grabbing Steves arm tight even hurting him a little bit.

"Ouch! Steph!" Steve called out, with her slowly letting go and apologizing "How do you know it's a dude?"

"Is that really the thing right now?!" A stressed Steph looked at Steve with a dumb look.

"Yep, yep you're right!" Steve replied to Steph breathing heavy and attempting to apologize before slowly lifting himself to try and get a glance into the window again, only to get deterred by two hands seemingly like they slammed against the window. "GO GO!" Steve called out in a panic and ran around the back of the building, just aimlessly moving away from where they were.

"What happened?" Steph called out after Steve as she followed him in moving quickly away from the window.

"The person or guy or whatever it is, slammed it hands on the window! I think it knew we were there!" Steve said as he continued moving fast around the back reaching the corner of the house, where the others started their search. "Let's face it, it's a he or a she. It can't be a thing can it."

"Damn. I don't like this Steve, let's find the others. They must be around here, let's face it they won't be as quick or efficient as us," Steph said with some arrogance.

Steve looked at her believing she was potentially right but didn't say anything back but decided to go with it, they were hoping to catch the others up and they praying that they had a way into the building. Although it was hard to see in this dark it was almost obvious that no-one else was round this side of the building with them so the only logical explanation was that they were waiting around the front for them.

"I guess they're at the front."

"Must be yeah," Steph agreed as she moved towards the front of the building at a faster pace now just hoping to find the others, but she didn't actually want to admit it was a bad idea as she stopped before the corner "Wait, but what are we going to do if they're not?"

"Well..." Steve said but with no real answer because he didn't know, what was the next plan or option. "Well I saw a window that could be opened just back there," He said pointing back to where the window was "We'd just need to climb up but at least we haven't got to go into the ground floor."

"Maybe they went up?"

"Surely they wouldn't go up without us?"

"Yeah you're right, let's just round this corner and I bet they're standing there laughing at us for being so stupid," Steph said as she walked away from Steve and looked around the corner. "Well, not exactly...." Steph said as she had got around the corner before Steve had.

"Mad! So where are they?"

"It's getting cold out here, I can barely feel my hands anymore. Should we just go up and in that window?" Steph asked Steve, she could barely take it anymore and she was sure with how cold Steve was that he would definitely agree.

"Yeah, let's do it. I'm bloody freezing too; we'll find them inside." Steve headed back around the corner moving over to the drainpipe and motioning to Steph that they would climb this to get in, the both were well aware that it wouldn't be easy in the dark but yet they were confident that they would be able to get up as neither one wanted to show any weakness.

The woodlands was such a prominent feature of where they were with it surrounding them almost creating a new world that only involved them, the wind blew around them with noises getting picked up and getting pushed from one section to another giving no indication of where it came from. Jason and Fran were pushing around the other side with them walking that way to find Steph and Steve hoping to get back together, shockingly as they got around that side they found that the others were not actually around there and instead only getting greeted by the emptiness of the dark staring back at them.

"God. Where are they? I'm worried now Jason."

"Yeah, alright. You're correct, this is very odd," Jason too was a bit confused as to where they would be, but wanted to keep strong for Fran knowing for sure that she wasn't feeling great.

"So.. What now?"

Slowly taking footsteps around the building with their feet getting ever wetter from the grass and their hands becoming more numb by the minute, they just went with the irrational. "This window! It's the kitchen and we can get back in near to where David is so, let's get back in here we'll smash it," Jason said.

"Really?" Questioned Fran as she didn't wish to start breaking stuff.

"Fran?! What choice do we have, it's freezing!" by this point he was right, the wind as darkness has caught up with them and the temperature was very low.

"Fine.Fine. Let's see if we can find a rock or something."

The two of them straight away just started feeling around in the dark for something, anything they could use to smash the window with but for some reason the grass behind the house is unmistakably empty looking.

The night sky was getting darker and it seemed colder too as theirs hand became more and more engulfed by the grass somewhat making them wet from the frost, after a while they eventually found a small rock. The rock was passed over to Jason, he took it and moved back closer to the window before looking at Fran before doing so and without a second thought smashed the rock through the window, a loud smash echoed the silent surroundings carrying it for what felt like miles.

They were now able to get in, but they themselves questioned their desperate actions and whether it was worth it."I mean we can get in but surely the game didn't want us to break anything? Like surely this can't be how it's done, so what are we doing," Fran worrying said.

"You're right Fran, I don't really understand it either but there is no way we could've stayed outside." Jason replied with an honest answer before slowly tapping out the rest of the glass panel every time with some regret on his face, upon doing that they both now had a way to get in the house.

As the rock had gone flying through the kitchen window, so did the sound 'Smaaassshh' echoed throughout the area scaring the animals in the woods with a flock of dark looking birds departing the trees in a horde, as-well as blowing the sound in the house.

"What on earth was that?!" Steve jumped out of his skin as he stood staring at Steph.

"I Don't know but it sounded like it came from the kitchen, maybe that person spotted us and is trying to get out" Steph also very startled somewhat still spooked from before and just began acting irrationally " I'm going up! Come or stay your choice" Steph immediately grabbed the drainpipe and positioned herself to start ascending.

"I told you they saw us!" Steve said in an desperate voice.Steve was in no hurry to stand around to see what that noise was as he too decided to grasp the pipe and begin his journey upwards.

Panic stricken the two of them climbing fast and with purpose, Steph was obviously first to reach the first-floor window pushing the slightly stiff sash window up with one hand and desperately clinging on with her other limbs. The window took a few seconds before it budged properly and started to lift squeaking like crazy as it did but right now causing more noise was not an issue for these startled humans. Steph grabbed hold of the side of the window frame making sure she had a tight enough grip before relinquishing any grip she had on the drain pipe.

Steph made it in the window with no grace what so ever but she was in there and that is all that mattered. It was Steves turn now, he was on his way up to the window without the urge to ever look back down with heading up and moving fast seemingly being the motto they were living by right now. Steve was holding onto the rusty drain pipe using all the limbs to get up at the same time and effectively, with Steph in the window motioning for Steve to hurry up she lent out and offered some help.

"Steve grab my hand," Steph said while giving herself a proper support system inside the window making sure she didn't lean over too far or lose her footing.

Steve reached out and slapped hands with Steph gripping their sweaty palms as tight as they could, as Steve was pushing off the drainpipe Steph was pulling him in, pushing herself back using her foot at the same time.

Steve eventually was flung over the window ledge coming in head first but little did he care right now because whether or not someone was chasing them was of no concern to them anymore as they felt safe but just for good measure Steph popped her head out the window to search the dark for something, anything.

CHAPTER 11

Inside the house feeling alone and getting desperate David knew somehow he had to get into this basement but how, how would it be possible without a second pair of hands. He had a to find a plan, maybe he could find something to hold the picture up or somehow push something it the way to jam the door open while holding the picture up, both ways would be extremely tricky. David eventually settled on an idea, he put the picture frame down back onto the shoe rack and moved into the dining room, a chair, David's plan needed a chair so he grabbed one of the chairs positioned at the big table and carried it back into the hallway placing it in front of the mirror.

The next part of the plan was to find some boxes to stack up on the chair which was going to be hard to come by considering he hadn't really seen anything that resembled a box yet. David was stumped and was frantically grabbing the books he remembers were on the shelf next to the window before bringing them back to the chair but of course they were never going to be high enough alone, so he needed something else as-well.

"The bin?! There was a bin in the kitchen," David remembered, so he headed into to the kitchen and grabbed the bin bumped it into the wall as he turned quickly knocking it over, it didn't spill out because it was empty because who'd fill up the bin for a game, right?.

David picked the bin back up and headed back into the hallway trying to be careful to balance the bin on the chair properly, the bin alone wasn't high enough but combined with the books he brought in earlier it might just do it. David really needed his vertical jigsaw puzzle to work so he could continue his journey and realised he'd need some tape or something to hold the actual picture up if he removed it from the frame, so that is exactly what David Did.

David removed the picture out of the frame leaving the rest on the floor and began eyeing it up in the mirror against the bin and books, he had to turn the bin slightly to make it work but lucky enough for him he realised that it would work and all he needed was tape. David was looking at his invention reeling with some amount of excitement from making this so-called mechanism, he was on the verge of working out the mystery of the door.

Tape this there and bingo David thought as he held the picture up exactly where he would tape it and what would you know 'Creeeak' the door does open so David knew this works so tape, tape is definitely all he needs. As David puts the photo on top of the propped up bin so he can go and find some tape from somewhere, taking a walk to the front room entrance his eyes glanced around the room wondering where tape would be kept in here if there is any, with his eyes catching the window located in the corner of the open plan living room.

 David stopping in his tracks, were his eyes deceiving him because he feels like he's just seem some flashes of figures go past the window in the dark, David is so unsure of whether he's actually seen something or not, but he is not willing to take any risks at all so he runs into the kitchen believing there must be a draw with at least some generic cello-tape in one of the draws as that's where he keeps his at least.

David enters the kitchen at a fast pace and immediately starts opening draws as if this is some kind of Olympic sport with stuff from inside each draw flying out hitting the floor causing more chaos. Right now he hasn't a clue where the others are or what the noise was upstairs or who's watching him or who's outside right now if anyone even is. David feels alone, so very alone his heart is racing like mad, he's even hearing things now believing he has heard voices coming from outside.

David instantly spins 360 degrees on the spot with his panicked eyes hitting the window, its dark way too dark he can't see anything especially with that soft white patterned curtain in the way but with him believing he can here voices he moves over to the window to have a look before continuing his search.

"Jesus something weird is going on." David finally finding the cello-tape and with that his exit from the kitchen is as quick as it was to enter, racing back through the living room and to his chair sculpture or modern art as some people might describe it.

"Where on earth are the rest of the gang?! Maybe I should look for them before doing this." David manages to slowly spit out in-between big deep breaths recovering from his fast-paced action moment, before David finishes off his modern art he does try to take a few seconds to calm down incase his heart flies out his chest and does a runner. "They must be upstairs surely, where else could they be?"

David doesn't decide to go looking for his friends and instead goes to finish what he started. He begins positioning the picture up onto the bin and in view according to the mirror, the tape is lifted to his mouth to tear of a part to use, he manages to get a big enough amount off of the roll and lets the rest hit the deck as it's services are no longer required.

The tape is placed on the picture and wrapped onto the bin at the same time before one final twist and turn off the bin. Time felt like it was now standing still for David as he stood waiting to see if his experiment had been a success, once he'd let go of everything and it sat in position for a minute he heard the ever weird creak come from the stairs, with that noise there the icing on his cake.

"YES! Thank god that was stressful." David mumbles to himself while placing his hands on his knees to just take a moment to breath even unzipping the hoodie that he was wearing as he was hot as hell right now, sweating like a pig. The structure was solid at the moment but only just and just before he goes into the room he thinks of his friends and checks one last time, he takes a few soft steps towards the bottom of the stairs to again check for noises or motion.

Upon hearing no noise from the edge of the stairs David was slightly worried about having no company going into the possibly, and highly likely scary basement alone is not a great choice. Potentially it's wise to wait for backup but after hearing weird noises earlier coming from upstairs and outside, as-well as the spooky messages David is already on edge and doesn't really have time wait.

'Smaaasshh' A loud crashing sound comes rattling through the house, it sounds like it came from the kitchen, someones trying to break in David thought as he began panicking, no chances are being taken here. David now has zero interest in waiting for his friends to make some kind of vocal call from upstairs instead deciding to boot leg it into the basement, he ran away from the bottom of the stairs and starting throwing the basement door open but in the process of panic David manages to nudge his work of art.

The sculpture that he built up began to wobble as David was busy squeezing himself inside the door under the stairs, his modern art slowly began to cascade downward, lucky enough it didn't matter now with David now inside "Good news, I'm safe from whoever was breaking in. Bad news, I might be trapped." David said to himself as he watched the door close itself, closing him in safe from whoever was outside.

As the sound of smashing rattled around the house with the rock bouncing along with floor, with glass not long behind it, they two outside watched as shards fell all over the floor and all over the worktop, so they would have to be extremely careful when climbing in. Jason offered Fran to go in first to get her out of the cold, which for once she accepted to go first and began putting her foot onto Jasons hands as he pushed them together to push her up with. Her arms reached through the window trying not to catch them on the glass that was still in the frame, taking her time to get through managing to get her leg through and pretty much standing up on top of the kitchen worktop.

"It's an absolute state in here?" A shocked Fran gasped as she looked around the room, the lovely sleek kitchen was no more instead cupboards were left open, knives and forks were on the floor scattered around, somewhat like a bomb had gone off in there.

"What?" Jason asked, with the wind blowing hard for a moment that he struggled to hear her, with him also not really listening because he wasn't expecting her to wait around and chat before moving so he could get in.

"It's a mess!" she said once again but this time a little louder and more direct to Jason.

"Ok Fran! I need to get in, please move!" Jason said very emotionally tapping her legs.

"Alright! Sorry, damn!" A disgruntled Fran moved away from the window and climbed down off of the worktop.

Jason then climbed into the window pushing the soft curtain aside as he did, with glass everywhere he done his best to get down off of the worktop without slipping or putting his hand on any of it. Now that Jason and Fran were both inside the kitchen they started looking around wondering who or what has made this mess. Taking a guess it looks like whoever or whatever it was, they may have found what they were looking for, although the glass on the floor was the two of them.

The items the two of them picked up in the chest were still being carried every step of the way with Jason still holding chef's knife in his hand while Fran was holding a bottle of bleach.

"This game is really weird don't you think Fran?"

"Yeah it's odd and honestly I don't even know what we're doing any more, like are we still looking for stuff? We could just jump back outside and leave but at the same time I don't even know where we are so maybe that's what we should figure out?" Fran said to Jason, while giving Jason a look of optimism.

"That is actually a really good idea! We'll keep an eye out for clues but maybe we should make that our priority and we'll try to figure out our location, to double check to see if we are in the same place as before."

"Really Jason? We are not in the same place as before, like how can we be?"

"Fran, I was joking obviously!" Said a less than confident Jason as he looked at Fran hoping she'd believe him.

"There's no noise from anything in the surroundings except hungry animals where are the cars the surrounding street noise?"

"Well for starters Deer will not eat humans so we don't need to worry about the hungry animals, and secondly do you really think they'd let area noise and cars get into the game. It' be a distraction," Jason said with some degree of sarcasm.

Fran was not impressed with Jasons sense of humour right now as she glared back at Jason with a confused look suggesting she was very concerned as to how his brain works, questioning how he's ever even made it this far. "Sure Jason. You're correct," Replying to Jason in the same sarcasm he gave her and yet he didn't pick up the tone, so she smirked to herself more in fear of being stuck with him incase anything bad happens, she's screwed. "Let's find David again."

The two of them had a look around the kitchen even opening a few of the drawers around the mess wondering if they could work out what had been taken out from any of them. The only issue with this is that they never searched the kitchen properly in the first place, so it would be really difficult to actually work out what was missing.

After a few good wasted minutes just looking around a kitchen staring at utensils they decided to move out of there, through the still messy living room straight away browsing the room as they went looking for anything new. The room looked pretty much the same with them not realising that one chair was missing and a few books were too, but they were going to see them pretty soon.

"What the... why...what," Jasons mind was blown, he ended up speechless with his words not even coming out properly. On the floor in front of Jason a chair, a bin and a bunch of books.

Fran just stood there and didn't reply hoping to piece anything together in her mind, but this was such a random mixture of items that it was almost too much to comprehend what had actually happened and really the truth wouldn't be must easier to comprehend. Frans first idea was to not touch anything and move into the Study as David must have some idea of what this was, he probably done it or at least knew about it surely.

"Right Jason do not touch anything do not move or anything just gently step over everything and let's go into the study and see if David's in there."

"Yeah, I agree!" Jason agreed and was very careful to step around or over anything laying in his path, as he went passed he still had a look at everything trying to piece things together. Upon opening the study door it was immediately clear that David was not in there, leaving behind only the laptop which he had out because all the other items like the map David had taken with him in case it helped him with his basement situation, neither Fran or Jason knew this map existed.

"David we're coming in I hope you've got clues for us. Oh, he's not in here," Jason commentating on his movement hoping to keep himself calm.

"Where is he, he's had the laptop out or did we leave it out?" Fran double backing and trying to remember.

Fran goes closer to the laptop to check it out and pressed the space bar hoping it would turn on considering it was still plugged in, but nothing happened so she clicked the mouse pad but this time the laptop flashed leaving the number 9.57 but disappointment for Fran as that was all that happened the laptop would not turn on or show anything else.

Fran and Jason decided to re-check this room properly as they had only briefly checked for clues last time so for starters they headed over to the bookcase and started searching, plus this might give them a clue to where David may have actually disappeared to.

CHAPTER 12

As the ever present wind followed them into the window Steph and Steve both lay there on there floor by the window, taking a few minutes to just stay there as Steve threw a hand up to push the window back down closing it to keep the wind out hoping to warm back up. The room appeared to be some kind of child's bedroom it looked very elaborate in here, with a lot of eye catching colours and features.

"God what was that smash," Steve just about managed to say with his heart still pounding a bit.

"I don't know but it can't be good surely, Jesus Christ this game is immersive and scary I love it."

Steve just looked at Steph and wondered what was wrong with her, why was she loving this 'game' so much, seeing as it's been a complete and utter mess so far with seriously terrifying events condemning them. Steve didn't even respond to Steph instead opting to reply with a confused scared look in his eyes as he saw some excitement as she had her hand on her chest feeling her heart beat racing.

Steve had now got his breath back after laying dormant for while, he decided now was the time to get up to actually see where they were because they have not checked that yet. He rolled off his back like an old turtle and slowly made his way to his feet but in stages it must be said, using whatever it close to him as support.

"You're getting old Steve," Steph laughing to herself watching Steve struggle to get back to his feet "You alright? Something wrong," Again Steph continued laughing "I should get David Attenborough to come and have a look at you, you're like an endangered species of old man"

"Ha...Ha funny, I'm fine just in a bit of pain," Steve replied trying not to feel sorry for himself at all, as he got to his feet smirking at Steph but in the most sarcastic and unwelcoming way.

"We only ran a little and climbed a few things you can't be in that much pain." Steve was getting grilled by Steph, she had seen an opportunity and took it.

Steve was reluctant to talk about it anymore and instead tries to just move the conversation along "Where do you think we are, a kid's room?"

The room is most certainly a kid's room or at least was when there were children in it but right now it's a complete mess with toys and stains all over the carpet, it possessed a smaller bed not exactly a child's bed but certainly not an adult one. That wasn't the only clues to point this towards it being a kids room, it was also dressed in a young hearted red with a white feature wall littered with pictures of this young child's favourite footballers and so-called celebrities.

The only thing currently lighting the room is one lamp on the bedside table, shaped as an ironman mask, prospectively giving a weird shape to the lighting and shadowing giving off a real strange vibe. Steve looked around being somewhat spooked by all toys being scattered but he knew he had to start searching soon so he walked over closer to a set of drawers which was supporting a rather large vibrant looking fish tank.

It was a lovely big tank littered with lovely plants and algae giving off a full ocean vibe it was memorizing to look at, there was no way on earth you'd be able to miss it but unfortunately it was anything but lively in there. Steve noticed all the fish were swimming upside down except for one or two fish in there one being a Plecostomus which seemed happy consuming the bodies of the rest and a potentially dangerous but soft swimming Lion fish.

Steph seemed to be a few minutes behind Steve as she finally got off of the floor while wiping very small tears of laughter from her eyes, as she then perched her bottom onto the bed with her noticing the size of the bed before then deciding to scowl the rest of the room with her eyes.

"This room is giving me the creeps it's so dark, I need that light on now." Steph for the first time today really starting to feel uncomfortable and just had to stand up from the bed to head over and switch on the main light. The flick of the light switch was meant to bring more light to the room but it did nothing, it didn't even attempt to turn on it was just completely dead so all they were left with was the Ironman lamp. The situation was not ideal at all for them, they were in a scary child's room with no lighting and no idea what direction they were meant to be going in.

Steve on the other hand was still by standing by the fish tank intoxicated by its aura, his eyes fixated onto the tank while the small light inside the tank glowed back at him ever so slightly, one fish was really catching his attention because it was actually still alive in there consuming raw meat off of its compatriots' while questioning Steph " So, what do you think we're looking for ..."

"Honestly, not a clue Steve! Normally I'm not bad at escape rooms as i've done a few in the past" Smiling to herself in acknowledge of her greatness "But this time I am fully stumped, like what is the purpose of anything we are doing?"

"Finding Andrew, I guess?" Steve shrugging his shoulders with little passion for what him and Steph are actually talking about, he just didn't want it to go silent in the room.

"But like... is that it? We find him and then they suddenly go well done, you can go," Steph replied "There must be a second find to this game, it must be to find Andrew and then something because I reckon Andrew is holding a clue himself or something surely otherwise why would we have to find him."

"Yeah you're right!" Steve nods and agrees that a clue or clues are exactly what they need right now because all they have to help them is a broken bottle and an old school cane both of which were what they've brought into the room with them. Steve finally took his eyes off of the fish for a few minutes to start checking in the drawers that were supporting the fish tank, opening each slowly with his eyes fixated on what's in there and to his surprise it was neatly folded clothes exactly what you'd expect to find in there so it shouldn't be much of a surprise but considering the room, it is.

Steve goes through every single drawer being very meticulous with his search but nothing in any of them drawers shouted clue, instead standing back up to have a look across the room to see what else to search.

Steve's eyes scanned over whole the room once very quickly with it dark yet colourful, large yet they felt almost claustrophobic, as his eyes done a full circle of the room they hit the fish tank again, only this time he notices something new in there, a Phone. The phone looks suspiciously like Steve's but he couldn't tell at first glance he needed a closer look, Steve leant over the top of the fish tank to have another look in but as he looked in he saw closer up all the dying or dead fish laying about with little bits of flesh hanging off of them.

Steve felt slightly reluctant to reach in there without touching dead fish or starting a territorial war with the potentially vicious fish living in there, but the phone may hold clues because otherwise why would it be here now with them.

"Steph it looks like my phone is in this fish tank..."

"What? Don't be stupid, how could it be your phone?" Steph questioned as she looked at Steve.

"I'm not sure, but come take a look. I mean it's definitely a phone for sure," Steve motioned for Steph to come take a look at the phone.

Steph walked over to Steve and ducked down slightly to glance into to the tank, as her eyes got closer to the tank the fish launched itself against the tank at the same point warding off Steph causing her to let out just a little scream, this fish was intent on keeping its dead fish for itself. The fishes that were alive were beautiful, they were magnificent but the tank had some scary looked fish left and unfortunately the two of them didn't realise how deadly they were, Steph instantly covered her mouth as if she wasn't scared and that scream was an accident or joke before turning her attention to goading Steve into just being a man.

"Yeah you're right that might be your phone just lean in and grab it," Steph said as she backed away from the tank without it being too obvious to Steve.

"You saw how that just reacted it! It's a very angry little fish," Steve said as he looked at her as if she was crazy.

"Just do it Steve! Or do you want me to do it and prove I'm more of a man that you are?" Instantly poking at the bear,

Steph knew what she was doing because she was frightened too but knew this would prompt Steve.

"Fine Fine, I'll do it ... I am a man," Steve continued to mutter that phrase over and over again to himself as he pulled up his sleeve to lean in preparation to grab his phone, even though he really didn't want to.

Steve took a real deep breath over and over as he went to slowly lower his hand into the tank, as he began he just with one finger slowly pushed the dead fish aside, it was a horrid process with Steve straight away trying to blank it out and ignore it as his hand dived further into the tank. The water inside was actually rather warm as he felt the presence of the fish moving around, as he getting closer to his phone and going slowly hoping not to disturb the waters too much, he was just beginning to get some small nibbles off of the Plecostomus.

Each bite forced a reaction from Steve as well as each bite getting harder and harder until Steve pushed back eventually with just a slight little nudge, it worked in his favour for a minute as the fish backed off allowing Steve to lay a hand on the phone at the bottom.

"I've got it," Steve was filled with glee with himself for reaching into a fish tank and retrieving the phone but on his way back out of the tank the fish once again took a nibble out of Steve causing him to flinch away and virtually impaling his hand with the other fishes' spikes and within seconds, he immediately felt searing pain.

"Don't worry you done it now you've got the phone, I wonder whether it still works or not," Steph said taking no notice at first of Steves injury, if anything finding reason to ignore it "Try turning it on."

The phone itself seemed to be undamaged by anything so far although it isn't turning on but thankfully for them, it is saying it just needs a charge so that will be a positive as long as they can find a charger. Steve however is in a worse way than the phone as he was still reeling from that spike he took off the other fish with his hand throbbing away like mad and within minutes the pain became excruciating, he could feel his hand going numb. The only positive is that lucky enough he managed to get the phone out of the water first but that was the it because little did he know what he was in for now with things about to get a lot worse and a lot more painful for him.

CHAPTER 13

David wanted to take no chances so he forced the little under stairs door to close behind him, the door clicked to lock itself and bring on pretty much pitch-black light, except for a few glares from what seem to be a door in the near but pitch-black distance. David went to maneuver towards the door to inspect hoping for a positive ID on the current situation however after a small amount of movement in this area 51 of darkness and secrecy, he felt steps but not before they felt him.

There were rigid hard wooden steps that the darkness did not tell David about causing a full-on tumble down the stairs falling into everything the stairs had to offer, it was painful it was fast it was a nightmare, finishing its self-off with a crash into the door he was actually looking for so, silver lining I guess but surely someone would hear his tumble considering the eerily quiet nature of the house in this present time.

"Ahh F**k Jesus that hurt ..." David was all folded up like origami at the bottom of these steps pushed up against the door pressing force against its hinges, this door was still solid though David himself surprised it hadn't forced its way open.

"God... Why not have a bloody light on them stairs or something, it's like they're trying to hurt people on purpose!" David angry at somebody anybody but even he doesn't know who anymore, after taking a few minutes to compose himself and continuously rubbed all areas of his body that was in throbbing pain. Shortly his attention turned to actually getting through this door and his mind was running wild at what could possibly be behind it. Was this it? Game won? More Twists? Andrew? Maybe even a way back to the previous house, if that was even feasible.

None of the above particularly applied as David began getting to his feet running his hands all along the wall and door until he found the handle, he began to turn the old rusty knob handle which to his surprise the door was not locked, that was bloody lucky David thought to himself because he did not have a plan B. What David did find strange though was that there wasn't really any creaking on the door it seemed fresh almost as if it had never been used or it at least had scarcely been used.

The door now opened into another dark room it was so hard for David's eyes to try and adjust to what was even in here the only thing David could see what the glare off of a phone propped up on something which seemed to be facing the door with the brightness up fully, it also seemed to have a lead plugged into charging it however, it was still suspect considering phones automatically turn themselves off after a while and it didn't appear to have any messages just come through, so how long had it been here.

"A phone! But whose?" David was full of questions but for now no answers were arising from it, it just sat there displaying a time and a note just in front of it so David closed the door behind him and moved over to attempt to read the note using the phones light to read it.

'Pick me up, you'll need me for reference'

David slowly read the note and read it a few times but it meant nothing, reference to what he thought but willingly he obliged picking up the phone also attempting to unlock the phone or use it in anyway but what flashed up was that a passcode was needed so, in good knowledge he tried the passcode from the laptop but it was not correct it just left the phone vibrating in failure. This left David confused, unaware of why he would need the phone so instead, he attempted to flick on the torch of the phone and bingo he managed to get that on at least. The torch now being on he used it to help him search for a possible light switch or something as he clearly knew the power was working down here.

David's first thought was to follow where the lead led too so he followed it across the floor to a singular plug switch but that was all the was apparent over there, due to the fact that as he was lifting slowly up the wall it seemed extremely bare with no other switches near this one. He slowly followed the wall back toward the door with David still using the phone light to inspect the walls for anything but preferably a light switch of some sort and to his delight there was a light switch, with a slow flick of the switch it brought on some really bright shining lights behind him.

Without knowing what to expect David took a moment to take a breath and prepare himself before he turned around and see what lay in this room, so as the phone was no longer necessary he flicked the phone torch off and placed the phone into his pocket along with the map and passcodes for the previous laptop, with the phone now safely stored in his pocket he made a slow turn of the head followed by the rest of his body to see what he was to discover.

"What the?" Confusion arose as David looked at the interesting objects.

In the room was a small desk littered with papers and a computer with a few screens attached with a small logo bouncing around them all displaying a different time to what was on the phone he saw which wasn't first picked up upon by David. The bright shining light was beaming down revealing what the rest of the room had in it, on one side a surgical bed with fresh sheets on it with no equipment currently near it nor were there any in sight. Over in the corner there lay many containers and boxes up but none of them labelled but all of them different colours, also pushed onto the wall attached to a rail on the ceiling was a plastic curtain the kind you'd find in a meat factory.

"What on bloody earth is this place and why is it here? Did someone know I was coming?" David decided to move over towards the monitors attached to the computer to see what they would display, as he walked over to the screens he noticed how unbelievably clean the floor was. Upon reaching the screens he placed his hand on the mouse and gave it a quick click to see what would turn on and only one screen came on with it being the left-hand screen, within seconds it displayed the visual for the hallway having a camera mainly capturing the hallway.

A look of thought come across his face "Ohh, maybe that's how someone knew I was coming!" David glanced at the monitor and saw his chair sculpture was on the floor assuming that was where it had hit the deck after his dash into the staircase, none of the other screens flashed on but after a few seconds a bleep could be heard on the computer with it matching the cameras changing views with the previous camera no longer on the screen as it was now displaying a different part of the house, he assumed it to be the first floor.

David was worried after noticing the hallway camera realising that maybe someone has been watching them this whole time, but his intuition was getting the better of him and he needed to have a look around the rest of the room while he was alone in this room. Where the boxes were situated in the corner close to the boxes there was an almost medical looking set of cupboards so he decided to check it out and try and work out some more about this room.

A shiny clean white melamine cupboard fitted with large draws and a mini fridge down the bottom, instantly that was first port of call to find out what is inside the fridge because who keeps a fridge in their basement. David slowly bent his legs and his back to get to the handle of the fridge with a push and a click the fridge opened, inside was not what was expected because it was very normal inside as it was just a can of coke and left-over food almost as if someone's lunch was placed in there.

David was so engulfed by the fridge and units that he got really startled to what sounded like a noises coming from the other room beyond the plastic meat curtain dropped from the ceiling creating the illusion of a wall and door. Something somewhere on the other side of this sheet had dropped with that being followed by a strange vague voice "Ah! For god sake, so clumsy" David was immediately silent as a mouse and didn't know what to do but his decision was made for him as in a flash when he heard footsteps coming closer and potentially into the room, he span on the spot, his eyesight seemed to grow larger covering the room double quick time.

"Shit who's that! I need to hide but where?!" He stood there panting like mad with no idea what his options were and the best he ended up coming up with was under the chair in the room. The chair was laid out flat and the fresh sheets that covered it flowed down the floor so he decided under the chair will do for now. David as quietly as he could he ran over to the chair almost sliding fully under it SAS style however, the slide was short so he was budging and budging slowly underneath it just as the plastic sheet sounding like it would open, the footsteps turned away after a bleeping noise faint in the background, no one had come through yet.

David was still taking no chances as he kept all of limbs underneath the table trying not to touch the sheet as it hung off the bed, even though the footsteps had moved away slightly he still kept his hand over his mouth trying to breath as softly as possible. While doing this David realises he had turned on the light "Shit the light! It wasn't on before, David is caught in uncertainty does he try and make it over to the light to turn it off or does he just wait, however neither seem a particularly a good idea right now.

CHAPTER 14

The study wasn't massive in size so it shouldn't take too long to search, however it did harbor many books and papers to sieve through and that was exactly what Fran and Jason were doing with Fran taking apart the bookcase shelf by shelf and doing it in the messiest fashion.

"You found anything Jason?"

"No not really, I mean David was already in here so surely if he found something, he's already acted on it I guess?"

"But what? He's gone without a trace and we have no idea where he is."

Upon searching the bookcase Fran comes across a photo frame which seemed as if it had been shoved down the back to be hidden, it seemed to be a photo of a family but all the people in the photograph had been scratched out but on the first appearance it seemed to be a dad, mum and two children one a fair amount older than the other.

"Hey Jason, look at this photo don't you think it's weird? They're all scratched out and it was thrown down the back? Is this a clue or missed item the company seemed who organized the 'Game' missed when getting the house" Fran glaring at the Photo but nothing in the photo was ringing a bell, not the people not the background in it, nothing at all but as-well as that it also wasn't in an actual frame either it was just a folded old picture.

Jason turned to Fran to also have a look at the photo but all he end up doing was backing up Frans claims, he too didn't have a clue about the people in the photo the only thing he did find mildly amusing was that the man in the picture had the same pair of not so fashionable shoes Andrew seemed to wear "Hey look it seems as though Andrew isn't the only one who likes them ugly shoes!" Jason burst out in a little laugh while pointing out the shoes in the picture.

"Hmm yeah," Fran staring at it and hoping it means something but in the end gives up trying to solve it and begins laughing too "Yeah they're not the greatest are they, I knew there were other people out there with them!!"

They had a right giggle between the two of them as previous to this his shoes were a certain point of friendly bullying so to see someone else own them brings a little bit of happiness and joy into the situation but at the same time it reminded them that they still had to find Andrew, not that they'd forgot. Apart from finding a few moments of joy in someone else's fashion sense the two of them don't seem to be making any progress what so ever right now and were beginning to get really stumped as to what to do next.

"So enough laughing! What are our options right now, we're here and there isn't much going on here or so we can see so what should we do?" Fran asked Jason as she whimpered ever so slightly feeling a little defeated by the whole thing.

A gentle "Mmmhm," from Jason as he wasn't fully paying attention to what she was saying.

"David is missing, Steve and Steph were outside but weren't when we looked. We have no new clues and the last time we were upstairs someone chased us out of a window? And all we have on us is two weird items we have found in a chest in basically the woods!" Fran getting more and more wound up as she spoke getting to boiling point of severe frustration but at what, she isn't sure. Everything that's going on right now is a complete mismatch and there is no light at the end of tunnel right now "JASON?!"

"Fran Fran calm down it's going to be ok," Jason certainly began to pay attention moves over to console Fran and gentle puts his hands round her, she falls into his shoulder and lets out a small number of tears while still trying to stay strong and hold it together so Jason doesn't ask any more questions.

"That's it, get it all out Fran. I get it's all a bit stressful right now but it will be ok, it'll all be ok i'm sure of it," Jason tries to reassure Fran as best as he can.

After a few moments Fran and Jason's embrace ends and she backs away wiping tears away from her face attempting to sort herself out and compose herself, Jason simply smiles at her to remind her that is most certainly there for her they may think he has a small mind but he wants them to know that he does have a big heart. Jason is fully aware of their current situation but is hoping acting light hearted about things will help ease the tension and make things easier for them overall.

"Hey I've an idea seeing as this room seems a bit bleak why don't we check out the stuff in the hallway, maybe we can find out why all that stuff is out there?"

"Good idea Jason, forgot about that!" Fran was more than happy move on, "Let's try and refocus on something else, start fresh and maybe something will come to us."

The two of them left the room with Jason shutting the door behind them with their first idea being to try and look with a prospective view of what could have genuinely happened here, on the floor lay the aforementioned chair, a bin and some books each separately don't really hold much value but together they acted very importantly for David.

After standing at the door for a while and both had glanced over all the items, Fran decides to move closer to the dismantled sculpture and upon standing over the top she noticed the frame on top of the shoe rack was empty, the picture she'd noticed and messed around with before was missing.

"Jason! There was a picture in there," Fran staring and pointing at the frame trying to get Jasons attention.

Jason looked at Fran as she shows him the photo frame, he was mystified and thought she'd lost her marbles as she was pointing at photo frame claiming that it had a photo in it "Well yes that's a possibility Fran, seeing as it's a photo frame."

"No Jason no." Fran slapped her head into her hands before once picking up the frame and frantically pointing to the frame again but closer in Jasons face "You don't understand there was a picture in here! I saw it"

Jason's mind is still left bewildered and just gives back a blank stare back at Fran watching as she started to get stressed rubbing her eyes with her free hand, indicating she's is struggling with Jason right now. Although Jason wasn't the brightest she had to admit that maybe this time she hasn't been all that clear so she tried to explain it a little bit clearer this time.

"Right, in this frame Jason, was a photo of this exact hallway. When I picked it up and attempted to match it up in the mirror just as a joke , like completely match up the photo in the mirror, I suddenly heard a creak from the stairs. It was so weird, so spooky and I don't know what or who it was," Fran explained to Jason.

Fran span the frame around for closer inspection and on the back was a tiny little bit of electric, like a really tiny circuit board but so minuscule, between the two of them they hadn't a clue what this could mean or do but it certainly was something. Jason decided he should have a closer look and took the photo frame off of Fran, he had a look beginning to immediately pretend to have some understanding of what this could comprehend but even Fran knew he didn't and could see through his waffling.

Jason after playing Sherlock Holmes for a few minutes he moved some of the items from the floor intending to put them back in their original place, but as soon as he picked the chair up he decided he need a few seconds so he parked his bottom the chair and started picking up the books instead. One by one he picked up books off the floor with none of them a reference to anything just random books, the only one that caught his eye was a riddle book which was a little unusual because it had a bit of tape on it like it was being held together some what.

"Ohh look a riddle book, I love riddle books," Jason said from his comfortable position on his bum doing virtually nothing again.

Jason was starting to get so comfortable on his chair he started forgetting what he was doing and where he was, casually browsing through it reading out some of them and saying random answers that he'd sneakily find in the back, pretending he was uber smart. Inside however, this book seemed to have a few pages missing and seemingly pretty much ripped out but why who rips out riddles. Jason put down the riddle book to one side to suggest he was now bored of it, he then persisted to pick up the remaining books carrying on the search.

"Anything there Jason that will give us a clue?"

"Not that I can see so far, just a bunch of science stuff."

"God sake! So this is all just a pile of sh*t then," Fran blew her load, she was getting so sick to death of this house and this game, just everything in general.

Fran and Jason again were running out of clues and ideas fast, nothing was helping and nothing was pointing in the right direction, what to do... they were stumped. The two of them pretty much had no choice but to go upstairs and try searching up there, they had no other choice because down here was bone dry for clues and even all of the previous clues they had been given were completely useless but before they ascended up the stairs they backtracked on the previous items they found to see if they could put anything together.

"So the clue in the sink, the Photograph of the chest which we opened with the key we found, some strange things we pulled out and that seems to be about it no?" Fran asked Jason.

"I think so, well that's all we've been told or found ourselves and that note from earlier what did it say again?" Jason replied as he tried to remember the statement from earlier.

"Err something like 'Your Memories Are Gone Or are they... Write them down, piece this together' or some rubbish like that, but that doesn't help because only you had a memory and even that was pointless, none of this game makes sense we don't even know the objective because if it was to leave that's easy, we could just go out the window?" Fran concluded as she lay all of the cards on the table with no clue how to win at the casino.

Fran and Jason were fed up and right now didn't want to go upstairs so they walked slowly back into the front room and slowly slumbered onto the couch to relax themselves just taking a moment. Jason realized he had sat on the tv remote and made a joke about them watching Tv while the others finished the game so he pressed the on button and to his shock it did actually come on.

A little announcement was made on the Tv, it seemed as if it was almost just a continuation from the earlier announcement but considering that they didn't hear it properly earlier they couldn't be sure.

As you see you have awoken with little memory and little idea of what to do.

The main clue is that only one person may be a winner.

Only one person walks away...

So help each other and maybe they'll share the prize money.

Clues go up with the floors

but the best investigations involve solo work'

Just before the Tv switches itself off it leaves a riddle on the screen.

'Round and round I go

never stopping in a continuous flow.

I hang out with numbers each and every day and nothing ever gets in my way'

Fran actually slightly pleased with that scenario seeing as she's stuck with Jason who proclaims to be good at Riddles so she straight away turns to him in hope and expectation, when her eyes hit Jason's you could see the fear build up in them. Jason was merely making it up and is only good at riddles because he normally just looks up the answers in an attempt to try and show off, but no matter however silly it was that they have a riddle to solve, it's nice that they do now have something to work out.

CHAPTER 15

Steve was in serious pain now with his hand throbbing like mad up until the point of it turning numb, he doesn't know what to do or how to make it stop all he could do is grunt from the ever increasing pain but Steph was covering his mouth hoping to keep the noise down as not to attract any unwanted attention from anyone around. Medicine, Steve needs medicine, they need to head downstairs and hope there is a medicine cupboard in the kitchen but Steve cannot move right now so Steph moving her hand away from his mouth offers to run downstairs for Steve and check.

"Steph please get me something!" Steve stressed as he started to panic.

"What? Like what?" Steph said trying to help but unsure on what was even wrong.

"I don't know, anything to take the pain away! It's getting worse," He said as looked at his hand, feeling like his eyes were getting blurry "I don't even know what happened, I just hit that fish by accident."

"Ok, ok. I'll try and find something," Steph said agreeing to find something for Steve, she didn't even know if there was anything around but she had to try at least.

Steph moved over to the door and tries the handle but as she gave it a tug it falls off in her hand, the handle is no longer attached as it fell out of her hand slowly falling onto the floor, fear set in and quick. Steph ran back over to the window where they got in but without realising due to the pandemonium of Steves hand she didn't notice that where they forced it shut earlier they had somehow locked it, because she couldn't force it open at all.

"What?! What? How is this even possible! We're locked in Steve," Steph was in a real panic now and collapsed to her knees after trying hard to open the window, she almost sheds the smallest tear but seemingly sucks it back up before Steve notices it.

Steve only just starting to realise what Steph has said almost allows his body to stop fighting the pain and just accept it or give up whatever's easier, within seconds he fainted with his body just going limp as hit the deck, hard. Steph jumps up straight away and moves very fast back over to Steve pushing on his cheeks trying to get something out of him anything, any noise or words but nothing, Steve is out cold Steph can faintly just feel the breath of Steve knowing he is alive but it is extremely faint.

"Ahhh Steve! What, what happened?!..." Steph is speechless and doesn't know what to do, she feels hopeless, lost, she just let her emotions go with her eyes tearing up as slowly one by one they dropped from her eyes and before you knew it she was crying her eyes out.

Steph just sat wallowing on the floor as she cried for a while just allowing herself to be emotional for a bit, she was at breaking point she constantly tried to stay strong and not let anyone know how emotional she could be behind closed doors, not that it was bad thing at all as we can all be full of emotions sometimes but for some reason she felt like she had to hide all of them.

As time had passed and she began to compose herself she still had the issue of being stuck in a child's room knowing full well she needed to find a way out and fast because if she wasn't fully afraid of this room before, now that Steve had fainted it's all gone catastrophically wrong fast. Steph decided to retraces the steps they had taken in the room but it was very short and obvious as they'd basically only searched the fish tank before Steve collapsed from going near the fish tank, so apart from that horrific moment the rest of the room is a mystery as even the room itself seemed to be unused, a mess but almost unused.

The question on Steph's mind, was this room actually someone's room or was it just created for the game because if it was created then the fish tank was slightly unnecessary but if it was someone's room then A) What sort of kid owns these fish? And B) How is the room basically untouched but yet the fish still there.

Steph just has to start searching this room around Steves lifeless body otherwise they'll never getting out of there so she decides to start with the bed, first stripping it taking off the duvet along with the pillows leaving just a sheet, as she stripped to the sheet a thin layer of dust was left on the sheet indicating no one had changed anything in here for quite a while, let alone slept in here.

Next to the bed sat a little bedside unit with an ironman helmet lamp light sitting aloft with it still shining bright spraying its light across the room but it was rather dim with only small patches of light actually illuminating around the room. Steph picked it up looking at it but it seemed to be an ordinary light or so it looked anyway.

There was one draw attached to the bedside table it was unlocked so Steph pulled it open and inside lay comic books showing off more favourite characters of the 'Childs' if that Child was real. All the comics had the same theme as they all involved super smart people creating things or over inventing, trying to create better version of themselves or humanity except for the occasional few which involved Heroes/Antiheroes being able to heal themselves, all of these meant nothing to Steph to her these were Childish and stupid nothing for a grown up to enjoy.

Apart from the set of draws that Steve already looked in earlier and the bed that Steph had only just checked, the only other thing in the room was a wardrobe facing the bed with one door ajar slightly, it looked very normal exactly how you'd expect it to look for a child's wardrobe. Steph moved over to the wardrobe stepping around Steve as he lay on the floor as-well as the toys that laid dormant getting closer to the cheap wooden wardrobe.

As she moved over to the wardrobe Steph tried to see if she could work out how old this child could be but she didn't have a clue due to the strange items in it, but upon reaching the doors Steph decided to open the door that was already slightly open and work with that first, it opened easily showing its dark interior and not giving anything away before the opening of the other door.

Steph grabbed and pulled open the other door revealing what lay inside it was actually boring and very predictable this didn't seem to have anything at all to help the situation, within the wardrobe was loads of kids clothes and they all insinuated a different kind of dress sense with stuff not many people would bother trying to wear without fear of being bullied.

She began routing through the clothes one hanger at a time looking at the item of clothing before slamming the hanger to the other side, eventually Steph got to the end of the rail with just one singular metal hanger left to go and she got an idea straight away, the hanger now firmly in Steph's hand snatched from the rail.

She moved over to the door as fast as she could clutching onto the hanger, she picked up the door handle hoping it may go back on somehow as she pushed it against the door and fiddled with it but to no prevail, so she went with the idea she just had. Steph got onto her knees before peeking through the keyhole and she thankfully saw no key pushed through the over side meaning she could see light coming through from the other side, so the plan was simple turn this metal hanger into the right size put it into the keyhole and hope it forms to the right pattern and unlock the door.

The plan was a solid one and actually was quite a good plan as being a child's door the lock isn't going to be fort Knox so she started bending and twisting, squeezing it down till it fitted and pushed it into the hole hoping it would be correct, while it is in the hole she is attempting to turn it almost molding it into the correct form. Twist after twist, pulling it out, reshaping it again and again just praying it'll work. The makeshift key wasn't working so far so as she pushed it in again to give it another go slowly running out of steam, she's getting fed up but this time it seems to have got jammed in the keyhole but does that mean good things or bad.

"Oooh!" Steph said as her eyes lit up with excitement feeling as if she just got a second wind she started yanking and twisting at the hanger but nothing budged as of yet, with it finally coming loose causing Steph to fall back onto her bottom bouncing off the floor slightly "Arrgh" Steph called out as she thought she was getting closer and yet back to square one.

She got back onto her knees deciding to have another look into the keyhole however this time it's dark, it's pitch black she couldn't see anything at all so she moves back away to take moment to question why it could have gone dark with nothing changing on her side what so ever, so she puts her eye back to the hole and to her absolute shock an eye is already in the keyhole staring back at her.

CHAPTER 16

David is in luck as he hears a door close in the distance and by the sounds of it the other person may have gone, so this is as good a time as any to move and move fast away from where he's trapped. David scrambles back out from underneath the chair throwing the sheet out of his way almost throwing it off of the chair completely as he done so, he moves over to the light switch and switches it off slowly trying to even reduce the noise of the 'click' of the switch. Now the light is off he moves over to the plastic sheeting and as soft as he can, spreading the strands of plastic hung from the ceiling poking his head through ever so slightly, David uses his beady eyes to take in as much information as humanly possible.

The other room didn't really consist of anything with Davids inquisitive eyes looking over everything in the new room with it baring more fridges but on a larger scale, these were more like freezers on closer inspection. David was curious as to what they actually were so he went to find out and pulling on the handle what followed was a hard press release noise confirming the cold temperatures, inside these new found freezers were more of the boxes previously found in the other room seemingly stacked neatly in colour coded piles.

"What on earth are these boxes, they kind of seem like they're colour coded. Which would assume they contain different things, I guess." David mumbling and essentially answering his own questions as he continued to look inside the freezer, before trying to check inside a box to see what it could hold.

The boxes were all locked with the same generic padlock, every single one so David closed the freezer again and turned around to inspect what else was in the room but it was bare, it contained merely just a trolley that lay in the background he guessed. A tunnel entrance of sorts was the only other thing that was in there too and it seemed that could potentially be the only way out, so he decided to head down that tunnel to find a way out and as he headed down the tunnel the lights flicking on censored by his walk setting the tone.

The end of tunnel had a small sloping ramp up to two big flat grey metal doors that opened upwards insinuating we were slightly further underground now somehow but whereabouts it led up to was harder to grasp and David wasn't even a hundred percent sure which direction he was facing anymore, the only way to find out was to go up.

David was anxious as he walked down the hallway not knowing what to expect as he didn't know if there were any other rooms down there or other exits but his thinking was that he needed to find the others to try and solve this quickly because something didn't feel right, the room had creeped him out profusely. The metal doors were heavy nor were they easy to open, it took quite a bit of might to push them up plus once they were fully up the seemed to click in place holding themselves open, David only opened one of the two doors with the door leading to outside with the icy cold wind straight away hitting him as he poked his head out of the door.

"Where is this, where has this gone?" Poking his head up out of the door all David could see at the present was a car as it sat near by, quite a big one basically a 4x4 even that wasn't easy to spot being a dark coloured car in this moment. This whole idea underground tunnel was shrouded in mystery.

David stepped further out of the almost makeshift bunker with nothing else to notice as he looked into the bleak night time, his eyes slowly turning following his body round in a gentle 360 spin hoping to see where on earth he was. One thing he did notice was that in the opposite direction of the car was a fence, covering a small amount of metres blocking the view from the other way, so he had to walk towards the car to go around it, but from the other side of the fence you couldn't see the car.

When he looked back at the doors the one door he had opened was now slowly closing itself with a click to initiate locking, while doing so the grass was attached to the door to leave them fully covered in grass and dirt when closed, they were a real secret set of doors when the car isn't here they are completely invisible.

His next move was to get around the fence which weirdly was coloured in a camouflage paint causing it to blend in with the surrounding area, once he had reached the fence it became clear how odd the positioning of this bunker opening was. David could see the house which he could only assume it was the one he had just came from, but it seemed far away considering he had only gone into the basement. However, right now his only choice was to reach that house and find the others.

"I have to get to the house and tell the others about the room! I know how to unlock the door again using the picture or we could come back to here and try to open the doors." David felt confident they could finally be getting somewhere, so as he could see the house, he decided to head back there but was also trying to count his steps back to the house to roughly remember where the bunker basically was.

Every step David took he pushed through the cold air attempting to find his friends, his feet getting wetter through the grass causing his body to get even colder. The journey although not that far seemed a million miles away on his own but eventually he reached the house, he seemed to reach the side of the house where the downstairs toilet lay. This is the first time David was outside the house so he had no idea how to get back inside, but he knew he had too.

As he hadn't seen his friends for a while he had no idea that the others had been out of the house so this was all new to him. Davids first thought was to try the front door even know it was locked from inside, you never know they might had figured it so he ran around to the front of house, well the way he assumed it might be anyway and lucky enough he was correct reached the front of the house.

"The door! Aha that was lucky," He spotted the front door, David continued running to it and caught his breath at the door before quickly spinning his head behind him to check to see if anyone was out there or close to him, it was pointless it was too dark to see anything but he could hear the whistling wind. There David was, standing in-front of the door taking a few deep breaths as he prayed that the front door would open for him as he placed it hand on the door and began to press down on the handle to open it and to his shock it actually opened.

"But but, we tried this earlier. Maybe the others did get it open then," David said walking in the door having it close behind him, confused and interested he tried the door from the inside but it was locked again so he was back inside but accidentally locked himself inside again. David let go of the door handle after standing there for a few seconds working out how it is open from the outside but not from the inside, he span around and pushed his back against the door glancing at what lay in-front of him.

David saw that somebody had touched the sculpture he made, so he had a look around quickly before taking a few moments to walk over to the stuff to work out what had been touched and what hadn't. At first glance it seemed like only the chair had been picked up with a book placed on the seat of it so he picked up the book taking a quick glance at it before throwing it back down and take a few steps back toward the front room to have a brief look in also.

CHAPTER 17

As time slowly ticked past with his brain in full flow almost looking like it might start steaming as he strained away, Fran continued to look at Jason hoping for something from him or anything from him as he just blankly stared back at her. Jason had nothing to reply, in-fact he just didn't reply at all, he didn't give any type of answer so after a while Fran started to realise it was futile so she decided to make a decision.

"Right while you think about that riddle let's go up to the first floor and start searching for stuff upstairs because this is hopeless down here, you can either come with or sit on your arse pretending to think about that riddle the whole time," Fran expressed firmly knowing full well Jason had zero idea about the riddle.

"Woah woah, I can think and search," Jason defended himself standing up quicker than Fran to show he is ready to rock and roll "First floor, yeah? Are we sure it's safe?"

"No." A firm blunt answer from Fran but nevertheless she then stood up as-well moving away from the couch and headed towards the stairs, they had no idea where anyone was and if only somehow they knew where David was because he would be here in a few minutes but unless they were psychic there was no way of knowing.

Jason moved quickly over to stairs almost racing Fran and getting there first still trying to indicate he was ready but for some reason still looking like a maniac by brandishing the Chef's knife in his hand slightly spooking Fran and making her feel uncomfortable. Fran however left her bleach bottle in the kitchen where they first came in and she no longer saw the need to carry it around as it seemed to have zero relevance right now plus, she knows where she left it anyway.

"Jason would you please put that bloody knife back! It's not funny or nice to carry that around plus it's making me feel really uncomfortable," Fran insisted.

"But we might need it."

"For what?! You going to attack someone or find an onion upstairs that needs chopping?!"

"But.."

"Just please Jason put it back for me, I don't feel comfortable with it being with us," Fran begged Jason as he eventually agreed.

"Fine, I'll put it back." Jason finally agreed racing back to the kitchen and placing it on the side near the chopping block but not actually in it, before racing back to Fran at the stairs.

"I'll go up first," Jason insisted and took a deep breath before moving onto the first step. Each step he took was slow with a huge amount of caution keeping his eyes peeled on the top of the stairs, hoping and praying that nobody was up there because he had no idea how he'd defend the two of them but it was quiet up there, strangely quiet.

Fran followed slowly behind Jason keeping nice and close to him feeling a little bit safer with him in-front, upon reaching the top of the stairs Fran was still hiding behind Jason ever so slightly, asking the question on their mind right now "Where on earth is everyone? This house isn't that big and yet right now we haven't the foggiest where anyone is or heard any one in ages."

The two of them moved onto the hallway taking a quick look around before trying the first few rooms but the first was the room they found Steve and Steph had been in before so Jason had told Fran, so they assumed it'd been searched. Another room being some kind of bathroom again which the other two had been in before, Fran saw another room before the bathroom at the end of the hallway and suggested they try that room. Jason agreed and went over to the door first, he tried pulling down the door handle while Fran came behind him and lucky for them the door become pushed open easily, turning back to Fran, Jason applauded Fran for her guess work.

"Nice one Fran, it's open and it seems big. Surely this has to have something in here," Jason smiled as he looked at Fran.

"I'm smart what can I say," Joked Fran as she smiled back.

Fran and Jason move into the room flicking the light switch straight away and on came some pretty decent bright lights, this room was big and well prepped but seemingly forgotten now, just seemed like a bit of storage room. As the two of them stood just inside the room they both had a look around to see if anything stood out straight away, what they saw were loads of metal shelving units on the walls holding piles of yarns of string and materials for knitting or sowing, it was weird it could have possibly been a little work station before but hadn't been used in years.

"Oh look a lovely top for you Fran." Jason joking pointing at some incredible stitch work on some items that were hung in the background with some of them finished and some unfinished but whoever had done these before were really good at what they did.

"Ha ha. Hilarious Jason," She said as she started to slowly move over to have a look as she was genuinely intrigued because they did look quite nice, but before Fran could have a better look at what was going on, she heard the front door go downstairs and heard a voice 'Hello, guys!' It sounded like David; Fran was ecstatic. "Huh! David, Jason it sounds like David. I'm going to go and check."

So she moved out of the room fast but silently before Jason even had a chance to discuss if it was a good idea, she was gone with Jason being to slow to turn as he was so engulfed as to what was in the room so he decided to stay in the room and search as she went to find David. The room certainly was big as well as being more vibrant than they realised as Jason moved around the room touching everything, the different styles of clothes were becoming more obvious as he looked around.

Jason had always been useless when it came to needles, not only could he not used them or even put the string through the eye he was always afraid of getting needle injections so getting close to a sewing machine was almost like overcoming a fear for him. He was slowly moving over to the machine then proceeded to feel his hand over the machine wondering how it worked and accidentally turned it on, the noise of the machine going off seemed so loud in this quiet house, he panicked like crazy before turning it off.

The loud noise and slamming of the needle from the machine made him jump but he also laughed to himself reeling at the fact that maybe it wasn't as scary as he first thought but he did decide that he didn't fancy going near it again.

Eventually Jason heard a door close from elsewhere and heard footsteps coming into his room and towards him, they were so light, undetectable almost. Jason had moved over to inspect the clothes that were hung on the rail as-well and being folded on the metal shelving units, he was genuinely intrigued by everything. The soft footsteps were just about noticeable to him, but he only just became fully aware of them once they had come into the room he was in.

"Back so soon Fran, was it David? Also come check out these, aren't these well done and nice looking," Jason being distracted as per usual "They are so well made, I imagine all hand stitched."

The footsteps came closer to Jason almost breathing down his neck and a voice replied to him "Yes delightful aren't they, she was fantastic at it."

"She?" Jason replied about to spark up a conversation taking a second before realizing that is not a voice he recognizes and turns round too, starting low due to him bending over to look at the clothing items, starting with shoes upwards Jason did not recognize anything. Jason scanned the whole strange figure and before he had a chance to say or do anything he received a cloth over his mouth which contained chloroform and so he began to pass out. While struggling to get out Jason's eyes almost burst out of his skull staring directly at this person.

Jason slowly collapsed.

Meanwhile Downstairs....

'Hello, guys" David says standing near the front door after taking a look around for anyone downstairs having a look at his dismantled sculpture in the hallway as-well as the mess in the front room but nobody seemed to be around so he called upstairs before attempting to make his way up he heard someone call back, it was Frans soft voice.

"David, is that you?"

"Fran! Thank god."

Fran jumps down the last few steps as she sees that it is actually David and she is delighted so she grabs hold of him immediately just cuddling him for a few minutes so tight that he didn't even have time to get his hands up so it's a one-way hug at the moment. Eventually as she lets go they both go to speak as they both have questions they need to ask but they decide here is not the place deciding instead to move over to the couch and talk through what they have been through with Fran just completely speaking over David at the minute.

"David where have you been? We've been worried! We left you in the study and you weren't there but also we all went outside to a shed and found weird items in a chest which the key unlocked and we thought we saw someone upstairs and and we climbed out the window, came back but lost Steve and Steph now I've found you," Fran just simply could not get her words out fast enough.

David tried to calm Fran, immediately putting his hand on her leg "Fran Fran, Shh it's ok just calm down. Let's try this slowly."

Fran tries to calm down and compose herself but it's hard for her because she doesn't like panicking or stress in-fact she really struggles with it, so after all of that for her to just sit down and reprocess all that has happened is weird. David is well aware of how Fran reacts to situations so is patient with her trying to slow it all down, and begins to ask her one question at a time.

"Right Fran, where was the chest you said you found?"

"Outside, in some kind of shed."

"Hmm ok, was there anything else in the shed?"

"Not that we could see, it was dark."

"Who's we?"

"It was all of us except you."

"Ok, Ok. Wait how did you get out of the house?"

"Well, a window broke upstairs so we climbed out of it."

"What?! how did it break?"

"I don't know. But we thought we heard someone and panicked so we just jumped out climbing down some trellis."

"Someone? Did you see anything?"

"I Didn't but I think Steve said he saw a figure."

"Hmm ok, I see. Wait so what was in the chest?"

"Just random items really but they were all covered in a weird liquid like the sink was, I didn't get any on me though."

"Right, weird. So did you come back through the Front door and where is everyone else now?"

"Oh god Jason, I left him in a room upstairs! Steve and Steph I don't know they disappeared when we split up on the way back from the shed."

All of this information hasn't really given much insight to David as he is still no closer to having any idea what is going all he knows is that there is a secret bunker which appeared to have someone in but at first thought he did not share this information with Fran as he was slightly suspicious of why she was alone. However, Fran was interested into where David had actually been and decided to ask him some questions in return but yet for some reason, he seemed to be being vague.

"So... where have you been?" Fran asked David.

"I was following up a lead I found... What's that?" David pointed out the Tv which was still sitting there with the riddle plastered on it.

"Oh, that just popped up when me and Jason were in here, it's just a riddle any ideas?"

David leant forward a bit and read the riddle in his mind, he read it a few times before Fran changed his attention back to the fact she'd left Jason upstairs alone and suggested they go find him so they can start to stick together again, the more the merrier as you would.

"Oh Jason I keep forgetting let's go find Jason, he was in an almost workshop type room upstairs," Fran suggested while standing up "There were some nice looking clothes upstairs."

A workshop room was exactly the sort of thing David was interested in seeing this room maybe more so than seeing Jason again, it could potentially help give a better idea of what the basement room was for so he obliged and stood up along with Fran. The Tv still flashed with the riddle with the rest of the Tv blank and dark having the reflection show David and Fran walking away from it clearly no closer to solving its question, but David did keep it in the back of his mind.

"So, where is this room?" David asked.

"First floor, we just need to follow the hallway round, next to the bathroom and thankfully it was open."

"Was this the only room open?" David questioned.

"Well I think that the first room is open but I think the others said they'd already checked that and the other room is a bathroom and that is where they were when we found them earlier," Fran told David as the moved toward the stairs getting prepped to go upstairs.

"So, they're all open except one? So why this room Fran?"

Fran simply turns to shrug to David shrugs her shoulders and carry on because she simply just picked a room and they rocked with it.

So, not as straight forward as David thought because another room is open but Fran didn't want to re-check it out because apparently it had been done, David is getting more suspicious. Everyone seemed to disappear and now he thinks Fran is telling little white lies, is he over reacting. It's Fran surely, she isn't in on anything, she's too innocent but realistically David has no reason to be suspicious over Fran his brain is just using that as a logical reason to be afraid right now as he has zilch else to go on.

They headed up the stairs one by one with Fran leading as David had no idea which was they room it was, as he followed her around the hallway and walked past the other rooms David felt the handle of the doors he had passed in which one did open onto the bedroom which Fran said had already been checked by Steve and Steph. However, the 3rd and other room along was locked and there was no way in there, it seemed to be locked good not even a sign of a budge to the door it just seemed solid. "This is it," Fran said upon reaching the open doorway "Jason it was David, at least we're starting to get people back together," she said turning and smiling back to David.

David merely gave a faint smile back turning around checking his six making sure nobody was else was about before slowly following Fran into this new room as he moved into the room after Fran. The first thing he saw in the room as he was a few seconds behind was the sight of Fran standing there silenced looking around lost, Jason was nowhere to be seen and this didn't spell good news for David who was getting more paranoid as it went on.

"Fran..." David said slowly and subtly to Fran "Where is Jason?"

"I don't know? He was right here when I left him."

"Are you sure?" An undermining tone was used from David as he didn't know what to think right now.

"Yes!! David!" A quick hard response from Fran before a softer "I don't know where he has gone, why does everyone keep disappearing. I just want everyone back and to go home, we started at 6 and now it's just us."

David straight away became more sympathetic from Frans sad and soft tone almost implementing she had nothing to do with anything, she was just a confused lost woman who was scared just wanting to feel whole again with things going back to normal as she can't lose anyone else. They embrace for a cuddle with David still keeping his wits about him to any possibility, any potential outcome with the embrace not lasting too long before it stopped as they pulled away from each other David was keen to get straight back to work moving over to some of the shelving units.

 Fran Followed over to also have a look hoping this would give them some idea of where he went, the shelving held some of the different styles of string and cloth that were so vibrant so unique.

"So, this was the last place you saw Jason?" David wondered.

"Yeah we'd just came in here as I heard you, so I came to check you."

"Why didn't Jason?"

"I don't know, he wanted to stay and look at all the stuff I guess?"

"Strange. So very strange," David finished with.

The two of them knew searching this room might be vital to what happened to Jason, if he did actually stay in this room after Fran left that is, the lights in the room flickered on and off for a few seconds almost as if thunder was about to strike that room exactly until one of the high-quality bulbs seems to just burst and shatter flinging glass everywhere.

"Ahhhh," Fran screamed causing David to jump.

"God why did it explode like that?" David now cowered back watching the last few pieces of bulb hit the deck.

After the bulb finished its descent to the floor the lights came back on properly with only that light out and no more commotion although this room was filled with a lot of different type of things, they were all related to what seemed to be a business room dealing with clothes, sowing or something along those lines. The trail for clues or ideas were cold with this room being no help at all as they searched all over and only found the same sort of things everywhere, if Jason was apparently in here then there is certainly no sign of him now.

"Fran this is useless there's nothing in here except clothes unless Jason is passing himself of as one of these headless child mannequins then we should go elsewhere," David was fed up and started acting slightly weird as he seemed in a rush to search elsewhere "Let's go and check that first room you said they had checked or maybe even go upstairs where you said you had heard someone before because we need to retrace some steps."

Fran didn't particularly like the idea of going upstairs but knew it still had to be done no matter how horrid it may be, so she agreed to go up but they decided they would search the other room first seeing as it was on the same floor. They left the room and heading toward the other door they had a few seconds to stop and listen, first wondering whether they would hear any noise from anywhere, but it was completely silent and considering there was meant to be 6 people in this house that was extremely suspect.

"Right so we agree, we'll check this other room then head upstairs," A firm comment from David as no noise came from anywhere else.

"Yes yes ok, the room here and then upstairs." Fran said while gulping and running her hands through her hair to put it into a pony tail knowing business is the most important thing right now, they need to focus hard and get down to business.

"What about that bathroom?" More questions came Frans's way.

"Err, we didn't check that either just went straight to that room."

"Right. I see." Blunt from David as he was confused to why they started their search in the workshop room.

Fran followed David as he headed back to the bathroom instead as he was concerned that they weren't checking things properly, so as Fran was starting to get curious as to where he was going David made a suggestion. "Let's just quickly check this too Fran as the doors open anyway."

Fran didn't argue and moved into the room after David, Frans eyes fixated into the shower with all seeming clean and clear with just the bottles of shampoo sitting in a suction cupped holder on the tiles. Beyond the shower was a sparkling clean sink and toilet, nothing particularly seemed to be out of place, even having a tooth brush still sitting in a glass cup on the sink.

"This place is spotless, no wonder they didn't seem find anything in here." David still checking the small cupboard underneath the sink but all that held was spare toilet roll and toothpaste.

They continued looking in the shower which was new with a lovely rainfall shower head, very sleek and nice as she spent a few seconds admiring its architecture she continued looking around turning away from the shower having a mirror face her. For the first time today she saw what she looked like and she certainly felt as tired as she looked.

 Fran closed to the door a bit to check behind it to see what was there but behind the actually door was just as bare as the rest it merely had a small plant laying there next to a pile of towels, hanging on the door was a few robes and a shower cap nothing out of the ordinary.

There was nothing happening in the bathroom so their decision was to leave the bathroom and re-check the first room which apparently had also already been checked but they had no other choices really but to go over everything that had already been done. They were at a loss for clues right now so unfortunately it had to be done.. Fran led David away from the bathroom and into the hallway as they kept looking around for anything however it was still so quiet with the only noise going on being them.

"Right so I believe this is just a bedroom?" Fran said upon getting to the door.

David followed into her the bedroom which was so dark in there now, they pressed the light to come on in which it did but not very bright at all still leaving a dimmed setting but it did allow them to have some visuals in the room and what they saw was virtually a bomb site.

"What on earth happened in here?" David staring into the mess and disaster of the room, if it can still be called that.

"I don't know. God it is crazy messy in here isn't it" Fran also shocked at its state "Jesus what did happen in here though, was it already like this?"

"I don't know but let's be careful when stepping around here and checking," David reminded Fran.

The duvet was positioned on the floor revealing a stain on the bed which was a weird colour to say the least, a stained dark dirty red patch laid on the sheet, they both moved closer to the bed stepping over everything on the floor in the way careful not to move anything out of place, if it was even in a place to start with.

"What do you think it is? Blood or like wine?" Fran wondered to David as she moved in for a closer look.

David didn't have an answer right now he didn't have a clue what it was he merely shrugged to Fran and replied "No idea."

David moved around to the other side of the bed to Fran closer to the window accidentally kicking the boxes the had fallen out of the closet earlier what Steve was searching, David's attention firmly fixated on to the box after seeing some papers fall out of it. Bending down slowly looking at the box, it seemed at first like a whole bunch of useless old papers but it wasn't till looking at them further David realised that some of these papers were a bit more useful than that and that they weren't all just a ruse.

The papers inside were hiding around a folder inside the box which held information that the other room was used as a workshop with the business being called 'Handstiched' it appeared to be a clothes distributer specializing in hand stitched craft clothing.

As David searched through more of the boxes as they were a few smaller boxes inside the boxes like Russian dolls with more papers seeming to unravel themselves giving more information about old shipping orders. Not only that but the papers held information like tax returns and it seemed like a lot of the shipping ended up going to the same place, an address in the city.

All of this information intrigued David so he moved over closer to the cupboard to see if anything else lived on the shelf. "Fran it seems that, this house was used for a business. When?

I'm not sure, but some of these shipping notes are less than 2 years old.".

"So, this hasn't always been a game house? This was someone's property and actual house."

"Well more than that, it was their whole life by the looks of it. So, what happened to the business then? Because I don't recall a shop down town called 'Handstitched' do you?"

"Not off the top of my head but maybe it was a smaller business?" Fran followed up "So if this is someone's house there should be more information like that about no?"

"Yes. Well you'd imagine so, let's turn this room upside down even more than it already is!!," David suggested to Fran.

The two of them started searching even more precise straight away with David flicking through the clothing inside the wardrobe searching all the pockets he could find, on the rail were suits, trousers and tops hung down with only the suits seemingly what you'd class as average or normal clothes if you will, the rest were a bit more abstract and fluent in colours. David continued down the rail not finding anything inside any of the pockets but he did come across a shirt he'd swore he'd seen before "Fran isn't this Jasons?"

Fran looking over at it "Err well I think he did have something similar at the least, I mean how would it be his?"

"Well he not long moved back into the city a few years back, roughly a similar time this business seemed to suddenly stop, his top is here? How much do we even know about him, we've known him the least amount of time."

"David, surely you're not suggesting Jason is involved in this? And how were you so quick to put all them things together?" Questioned Fran as she looked at David being taken back by what he said.

"Well not fully but I mean, where is he now? And don't forget he is the only person who has said they'd remembered something, which would be easier to remember what is in the house if you owned it."

Fran hoping David wasn't serious about Jason, she herself wasn't his biggest fan but surely this house doesn't belong to him. However though, as she thought about the hilarity of the suggestion things began to start making just a little bit of sense as they had known Jason the least amount of time and he hasn't seemed to take any of their situation serious so far, and now he went missing in a room of a business he could own.

The two of the continued searching with the idea of Jason having anything to do with it buzzing through their minds, why wasn't he taking this serious, did he actually know something they didn't and but they don't even know what is going on so to accuse Jason of it is harsh...isn't it.

CHAPTER 18

The two of them had to put their accusations of Jason to one side at the moment to continue searching and they were flipping the room upside down along with the mattress, that got lifted off of the bed frame by the two of the room leaving nothing underneath. After they dropped the mattress they had a quick check under the bed and what lay there was an old bottle of red wine no glasses present just an open bottle which could potentially explain the stain on the mattress.

"David look maybe this is what the stain on the bed is, red wine?" Fran showing her discovery.

"Hmm potentially, is there anything left in it?"

"Yeah there is still some in there why?" Fran giving David a confused look wondering what he wants it for.

"Pass it over please."

Fran looked at him still quite confused by obliged none the less and handed the bottle of red to David with him taking it off of her and grasping it firmly as he had a look at the bottle before doing anything else, even giving off a smirk to how fancy the brand was. He then slowly poured it onto the bed to attempt a colour match, Frans face lit up realizing she was being rather stupid with that now being quite an obvious thing to do and that he wasn't going to do something weird like drink it.

"Yeah I think you're right Fran, it seems to roughly be the same colour," Once poured David sees the colour matching being pretty legit so he concluded that it probably was the same.

"Who makes that much of a mess drinking wine in bed," Fran giggled "You wouldn't catch me spilling a drop, I'd catch it all in my mouth before it hit the sheets" Fran having a good old laugh to herself.

David looking at Fran smirking and letting out a little giggle but not sure if Fran realizes what she has unintentionally sounded like she's said, but nevertheless it's still pretty funny so he just moves on and forgets about it but does continue to snigger to himself. They move back onto searching the room however there appears to be little left in the room, they have turned over everything there was to turn over in here as well as the bathroom so there wasn't any more clues for them to find up on this level.

The two of them realise this now means they have to go search upstairs seeing as they cannot get into the other room just yet, it's still locked without a trace of why or what's in there so without breaking the door down they just need to ignore it for now. David and Fran leave the bedroom before looking around the hallway which of course is in the same state they saw it in a little while ago but thankfully thats all they can ask for right now.

The next flight of stairs is certainly looking more rough and ready than the previous as would be the destination of the next part of the search, they moved over to the stairs they start to slowly make their way up it noticing slight creaks and a harsh cold breeze coming from somewhere.

"Fran what is that cold! Jesus was it this cold before?" David starting to get cold already almost as if a ghost has just walked through him, it just hit him quickly and will not leave.

"Well that window I said we climbed out of, which I said was broke... By broke I meant it was no longer there," Fran explained as she too started to shiver as she looked at David.

"Ohh yeah sorry! I've just realized that's what Steve was shouting about earlier when I called up... Sorry feels like forever ago" David realising he already knew as he had been told earlier.

Fran too realizing how cold it is grabbing her arms while folded and rubbing the goosebumps like mad hoping to warm up a little, the cold was becoming almost unbearable already so how on earth would they deal with this for the whole search. David too shivering as he walked up the stairs one small step at a time as the last he had heard from Fran was that someone was up here, so caution was well advised.

The stairs really did seem to lead to a whole another house, this part was worse than anywhere else they'd seen so far like it had been almost forgotten about or purposely ignored, upon getting to the top of the stairs the hallway showed a few different rooms with one door seemingly open with that being the room the frost was originating from as it had the broken window.

They came up with a plan and their plan of action was to try and close or block up the window slightly with anything to try and hold some heat inside otherwise it's going to become a real problem seeing as neither him or Fran have anything significantly warm on.

"Fran lets go in that room," David told Fran as stared back at him with a shocked look at his face.

"But that's the extra cold room?" Fran told back extremely worried as to what he was thinking.

"Yes... So let's try and block the window with something to restrict the cold coming in."

"Oooh Good idea David! Knew you were useful for something." She laughed at him as she tried to move a little quicker to warm herself.

"Oh Cheers," David replied sarcastically feeling his paranoia towards Fran depleting and feeling a lot more comfortable around her again even questioning himself as to why he would even assume sweet innocent Fran of any wrong doing.

As they both agreed that would be a good idea they moved into the room with a fast pace with no time to dwell before it starts getting really cold, looking around the room for something to use they realize that there isn't actually much in there to use.

"Fran! The Mattress it's the only choice, not a great choice but something is better than nothing," Suggested David.

After frantically looking around the room and attempting to move wardrobes that are fixed to the wall the next best as well as particularly the only realistic option they have to is to pick up the mattress and lean it against with some weight to hold it there. Fran quickly moves over to the mattress attempting to grab one end to help out but David grabs the top end of the it and throws it up without any warning causing the mattress to flip on its side hitting Fran square in the face. The hit from the mattress wasn't painful but the fall to ground wasn't delightful to say the least, attempting to throw her arms out to stop herself hitting the ground hard seemed to do the trick.

"Oh god Fran sorry!!" David threw the mattress back down and ran to help Fran, trying to help her back up to her feet being very apologetic.

"It's fine honestly don't worry, my fault." Fran calmly said while grunting in a little amount of pain as she was pulling her self up using Davids help" Ahhhhhhh," Fran screamed.

As Fran was sorting herself out lifting herself off of the canvas her eyes unintentionally caught the underneath of the bed in doing so noticing a little scared mouse running out towards her, causing her to scream and panic. She jumped as high as she could from a ground position which was very impressive to say the least, while the little white mouse ran out from underneath the bed and out of the room however still being spooked from it Fran still moved further away from the door not looking back for a good few seconds.

"Is it gone?" Fran cowering and looking over to David.

"Yes it has appeared to leave the room," David laughing out loud at Fran trying not to make her feel as silly as possible but she did look a little silly.

"Hey! stop laughing you arse! That was terrifying," Fran sharply replied which seemed to calm David's laugh almost to a halt, as he turned away no longer laughing.

"Ok, ok sorry Aha ... Just come and help me with the mattress then."

During the last few moments of laughter and pain it didn't seem to be as cold however they still saw it as necessary to cover the window so the two of them picked up and turned the mattress length ways to cover the window and moved it over to the window and Fran lent on it to hold it in place while David went to find something heavy to lean against it.

"Fran stay there I'm going to lift the bed frame against it to hold it," David believing he was going to show an amount of strength and guile which quickly turned into a struggle for him and it somewhat became painful to watch as well.

When David finally lifted the wooden bed frame onto its side, he slowly walked it corner by corner over to the window taking a bit more might than originally accounted for, tempted to stop for a break but David didn't want to damage his manliness anymore without realising Fran would not care anyway. Finally making it over to the window Fran moved out of the way while David pushed the frame watching it fall into the mattress wedging it against the open window with the cold breeze stopping almost straight away, although this wouldn't make this place any warmer it would certainly stop it getting much colder.

"There we go... Think that will work at least a little bit," David said while puffing his cheek, he certainty wasn't warm but at least he wasn't getting any colder.

"Yeah I hope so, can't make it worse can it," Fran gave hope to David's plan "So now what?"

"Well let's see if we see why they were even in this room in the first place, because Steve and Steph were in here when the window broke, I'm only guessing that because Steve was quick to shout down what it was," David explained his thought process.

Where the bed frame was and had been for a very long time the carpet underneath was a fresher colour than the rest of the floor which implied it hadn't been moved let alone cleaned in ages and yet the rest of the carpet around the bed had dirt stains lay upon the floor but not stains like blood or wine more so just generic wear and tears stains.

The bedside table was bare only holding onto old glasses and a set of retainers left behind by life or preservation at its finest, a radio sat aloft slightly more modern but still not new by any stretch of the imagination. Around where the bed frame had sat were wardrobes which would have surrounded it but once again, they lay bare and bleak holding in them nothing but dust along with a few very old dresses in fashion at some point in history but way before their time.

The house itself held a weird old and new vibe at the same time attempting to preserve the old yet incorporate the new, a weird blended attitude towards house architecture, almost one family blending their timeline together in one long memorial with most things in the house seeming to hold memories or some kind of importance to one set of people's lives.

The room had run its course in terms of information as nothing in here was any more help or seemingly at any point, even the window itself appeared to break plain and simply due to woodworm or rust and damage to the windows integrity nothing more or less.

"It doesn't seem like anything is in here Fran, just a bit of dirt and mould. The window isn't a clue nor are the dusty old-time machines called wardrobes in here," David disappointingly spat out.

ng to take ages to search? Where do we even
dered as too stood there locking at this
room.

, David almost gob smacked at the amount of stuff
crammed into one room, it was filled to the brim as he
breathed out a big sigh of almost regret.

All the boxes in the room seemed to be blank with no proper
indication as to what was in them, they were marked but it
seemed to be in another language but what they didn't know
language it could be. David and Fran moved further into the
room both standing there looking around not willing to touch
anything before knowing where to start but they reckoned they
would just have to pick a box and go for it.

"What language is that, you got any idea?" Fran asked as she
assumed David was as smart as he looked.

"No idea honestly, maybe like eastern European?" David gave
back an answer of his best guess.

Both of them looked hard at the writing on the box hoping to
get a glimpse of what it may be however it didn't seem to be
giving away any clues of what it was or even potential words
to help give any clue as to what may be inside the boxes before
opening all of the boxes. All of the boxes were made of
cardboard taped closed, the question is do they start searching
and hope for the best or move on and try somewhere else.

No matter what the two of them chose they knew at some point
they would have to come back to this room and look at some
point because no other room so far had given them any hope of

getting out of here, everything had just led to more questions so what would be the harm in searching.

"What do you think should we do, try and search this room or should we try a different room?" Fran asked as she passed her eyes over the boxes.

"Well to be honest Fran we're running out of rooms... There is literally nothing left for us to find, all of these rooms just seem to be normal rooms with normal stuff inside there isn't any special game going on here or it doesn't seem as so. What on earth are we doing here and why? We need to know whose house this is and more importantly why on earth we are here!" David very irritated by all of this as he replied coming to the conclusion that something else was a foot and that this wasn't actually a game.

Fran was left speechless at the way David had just come across so irritated so stressed and yet Fran agreed, she realised the situation they were in was a crazy one but right now there wasn't much they could do about it apart from working extra hard to find a way to win or leave or anything just anything.

The house they were in was strange, unusual and no matter how hard they tried they had no idea how they got here or where here was, so any idea of how they would solve this is so far and few between right now, so do they just keep running about the house hoping for something or leave the house in an attempt try to find something that symbolizes normality and hope to find help.

The bad side to the plan is that it is only these two, their friends are gone or missing at least, they need something to give them hope or just something to push them in the right direction or just something to push them in the right direction. What they need is to work out some idea of where their friends are, they need to get back together but right now this room is staring them in the face and the two of them still had no idea how to move forward to gain knowledge, the only option they had was to search this room.

Without any hesitation David fell to his knees and put his head in his hands, he was lost and the more he looked at these boxes the more he just couldn't be bothered to keep this dumb charade going. David always seemed to always have a sense of what to do and what to follow by using his wit as well as following his gut, but right now he was at a loss and Fran saw this, shocked she moved over to David and put her hand on his shoulder, it was her time to comfort him.

"Sorry Fran, I just...I just don't know what to do or how to go about it," David quivered.

"David it will be ok, we will get through this. There must be a way to work it all out." Fran said while consoling David thinking back at all the things she has found or discovered so far in this house, which actually seemed to be very little but she didn't want to tell David that.

Fran decided to get cracking and moved the few closest boxes away to see if anything was hiding underneath or beside them, box after box seemed to be extremely similar in size and weight although the writing on them were very different. Fran moved back over to one side where a screwdriver had been laying and brought it over to the few boxes she moved, because seeing as they were all so similar there was definitive started point so any box was a good start.

Fran decided to open them to see if there were anything similar inside or if it could be coincidence as to the weight and size, a swift drag of the screwdriver across the few boxes slowly cutting the tape across the top and sides rendering them open. Inside the boxes lay different books on ways to stitch like old techniques and different patterns, more leftover items to coincide with the industry. The last and most intriguing thing inside the box lay old documents for the company that had been set up and that there was in fact a shop connected with the business.

"Hey David, there are a load of documents here regarding the business that was apparently set up downstairs, maybe there is something her to help indicate who owned it?"

"That is a great idea Fran!" David slightly more enthused and energized thanks to Frans almost immediate discovery knowing full well moping around wasn't going to solve anything, "Let's do it!"

CHAPTER 19

They spent a while searching through the papers trying to understand what sort of operation was being run down stairs and at first it seemed to be a legitimate business with good and true purposes however, the more they uncovered and discovered things turned into a confusing mess.

The business that they were discovering and learning about was headed by a woman and by the judgement of when the business started as-well as the ages wrote down on the startup form the poor lady would have to be into her late 70s' now, yet the business is apparently still operational. At first it seemed strange to them as no lady would want to be working into her late 70s surely however the more they processed that information it became less weird or strange and actually was a real possibility.

"On the startup form the main head of the business was a woman called Ms. Lamia, it says nothing on a husband or partner. Just her with a sole heir to her business, her Child should she bare one" David read out the piece of information out loud offering up the information he had "Have you seen anything about a first name or even child Fran?"

"No nothing like that at all, there are a few shipping invoices here but none of these are up to date, the newest one being from 3 years ago," Fran replied to David giving back her information.

"So, maybe this hasn't been active for a few years and this isn't that persons house now because it seems abandoned," After David said this, they both looked around the room to almost solidify that statement that maybe this hadn't been used in a few years.

Although this would raise more questions as to what they're doing here now, or more so why they are, maybe they had a closer connection to this woman than they realised or was this literally a game house with an amazing set up because neither one of them seemed to recognize the women's name or this company nothing. Everything that they had found in the house or had seen lying around, nothing seemed to correlate with anything else, it was almost like everything in the house was just generic stuff and not clues.

"So, do you think we've ever had contact with this woman or maybe know her?" Fran questioned.

David unsure of why it would even matter if they had or hadn't, what does it have to do with them. "Actually I just remembered on the laptop that was down stairs I saw a picture file that had pictures of groups that have entered, there were at least another 20 groups that have been in this house, since what year or date I couldn't tell you but I don't think any of this is personal," David explained to Fran calming her down from thinking it's personal.

"Did anything seem out of the ordinary to you?"

"Err, not as far as I could tell but one person was blacked out in the photos as-well as others being coloured in green or red. I never saw a picture of us but I do remember one being taken before we entered the game properly," David trying to remember back " Ohh, and none of the pictures were in this house, or they didn't seem to be. Plus I think we'd remember if we had been in this house." David is remembering a little bit more from the laptop adding more information to the fire that is burning inside them to work out everything but Fran having more questions than ever that needed answering but not knowing who can answer them right now.

"Why would someone be blacked out or coloured green?" Fran said confused more so than ever before in this house.

"Well I don't know Fran, I mean this really doesn't feel like a game anymore." David not quite having enough information to explain stuff to Fran as well as keeping back information of the basement room he found.

The two of them continued to search as they had warmed up slightly compared to how they were before as his window barricade was working which for a bonus for this first time today. The more boxes they went through the more information about the business unravelled itself but all of it dated back a few years, so there is nothing recent about this business at all, does it even still run.

"Look, David... There is a notice here about the previous owner purchasing this house 10 years ago with her being listed as the only tenant but I mean this house seems pretty big for an older lady and in the middle of what looks like nowhere at the moment," Fran tells David feeling like that could be important.

He looks back at her with gracious eyes taking in that information with little to add to that without them going round and round in circles, plus David knows that certainly can't be true considering the room he has seen there is no way that an old lady lived here alone. "Hmm, just by herself. I don't know if I believe that, that seems odd there must have been someone else here surely."

"Why, why do you think that?" Just merely asking for David's opinion but she gets shut down quick with no real response.

"I Just do. I mean look at this place."

Fran somewhat agrees, considering the size of the house along with all of the different heirlooms that appear to lay around the house, granted there isn't many but there is still enough to question who was here. The house appeared to be getting nicer as the downstairs had been changed, made to be fresher so potentially someone was getting the house done up.

"Have you come across anything that says if this lady is alive or dead? Anything to suggest either," David is trying hard to piece something together.

Fran moving around the pieces of papers she has been routing through double checking if she had indeed come across anything that would help answer that "No the only thing I have in a rough guess on her ages but that wouldn't really help would it."

"Well just for reference what is that."

"Seems as though she would be roughly 72 considering what year this house was purchased and that's if the information is correct," Fran tells David what she knows.

David stands up away from the boxes he's got all this random information but how does it all add up and piece together, there has to be a constant because something must be holding this all aloft, what is the glue. Thinking back again at the things he knows looking around the room there are just boxes upon boxes which could take ages to go through, it would take so much of their time as he stands there in silence with him only being able to hear noise of the ticking clock.

"Time!!" David just says out of nowhere.

"I don't know David, I don't have anything on me to tell you," Fran stares blankly at David waiting for more reference.

"No... No... Well more specifically clock hands but time."

Again, Fran is lost she needs more she needs something to work with, David panics and pulls out the phone he's had in his pocket the whole time and looks at it, with it displaying the time 6.30. "It's not the actually time" David says muttering to himself as he stared at the phone, as Fran stared at him waiting for more "It's a countdown, but for what."

"Errm where did you get a phone from?" Fran curious and a bit furious "Does it work? Can't we call for help?!"

"No, it doesn't it only says the time. Well not the time, a time. It's a countdown Fran."

"For?"

"Well that I'm not sure.What did you say you found in the chest?"

"Knife, Broken Bottle, Cane and bleach why?"

"Potential weapons?" David said as he thought about all the things that she said they'd found.

Fran gob smacked and throws her hands over her mouth holding in her voice from spitting out any scream or noise, before taking a look at her hands and arms wondering if she got anything on her from the bottle as now she was extremely worried as to what the liquid was. Thankfully for Fran the bleach bottle she held didn't have anything on it except for some kind of sticky substance.

"I don't know but they are suspicious items don't you think," David then said as he noticed Frans shock as she realised David could be right, but he didn't wanna cause too much panic.

Fran doesn't like the sound of that feeling a little bit sick inside and the more she thinks about it the more she hates the thought of it especially after touching the bleach, even though there wasn't any liquidated substance on them she decides she needs to wash herself and without warning stands up and runs out of the room.

"Fran where are you going?" David shouts after Fran.

David too moves out of the room chasing Fran who is heading down the creaky stairs making a huge amount of noise that would wake the house, running as if her life depended on it. Fran is making all kinds of little moaning noises as she goes, David hasn't a clue where she is going but she leaves the stairs case after one flight and heads into the spotless bathroom.

Step after step he chases her down the stairs and onto the hallway before David too enters the bathroom after Fran, slowly catching his breath as he isn't the most athletic of people. David watched as he saw Fran move over to the shower grabbing the shower head to wash herself down almost and flicking on the mechanism only to have no water come out of there, the water appears to be off or not connected for some reason.

"It's not on David!." Fran says acting weird.

"Quick put your hands under here," David tells Fran as he turns the tap to one side assuming it would come on but to no avail "Oh that's not working either, how weird." The bathroom appears to have no water running through its pipes, it's bone dry which is very odd. "Why would the water be off?" David questions as he scratches his head curiously.

Fran breaks down and crouches onto her knees, head in her folded arms letting out a small cry perched near the entrance of the shower the thought of anything harmful to have happened in this house is too much for Fran, she knew this was no longer fun but to have anything violent in it is just starting to take it all to a whole new level and she hates it.

"Fran it's ok, we will get through this and out this awful house," Attempting to calm her down but even he didn't know what to say or do because even he was getting disillusioned as to what is honestly going on.

"I knew I shouldn't have come to play this stupid game! I should've stayed with my mum. Who was I to think I deserved a slight break to have fun! So selfish and look what happened." Fran letting her emotions be her guide right now, speaking exactly how she feels and although it wasn't helpful she felt like she needed to do it.

David has no idea how to reply or what to do next so he just takes a minute and sits by himself on the toilet, staying quiet letting Fran be for a moment as it seems the right thing to do.

Silence fills the room with the exception of the occasional cry and moan coming from Fran, as the two of them take some time in the bathroom for a little break.

Eventually Fran slowly composes herself before David realises that a hell of a lot of time has passed since he first headed back from the basement room and not a lot have been accomplished. A lot of noise had been made from the running down the staircase having the creaks and the thumps of footsteps hitting the deck is enough to wake the sleepiest of creatures and that it has done.

CHAPTER 20

Waking up in the locked room spread out on that floor was Steve awoken by the noise of the staircase but more so he was just coming back too and that only helped speed it up. Steve was opening his eyes facing a white ceiling unaware for a few seconds of where he was, before he could even attempt to work it out his pain gave him a huge reminder. Steve went to push himself off of the floor but he could only use one arm as although his other arm was still attached to his body it was completely numb, he could not feel anything from the elbow down and even going up the arm was fifty percent numb.

Steve using his other arm managing to throw himself up to his bum instead of his back, viewing the room as it was but the room still looked exactly the same, nothing seemed different than what he could remember except for the fact that Steph wasn't there not at all and no mention of where she may have gone. Pain was now present in Steves head assuming from when he hit the deck hard passing out or something because he doesn't remember much of why he was down here, a thumping headache as well as a numb arm, things can't be worse for him surely.

The feeling of the numbness in his arm was less like pins and needles, and more like complete absence except for physical viewing as he tries so hard to move it but all they could do was swing it with no control that was it. Attempting to get to his feet using just one arm and with his legs also feeling slightly like jelly was proving slightly harder than he could have ever imagined, it was certainly entertaining to watch if anyone could have seen him.

Mumbling under his breath as he moaned and groaned before repeating slightly louder "Ahhh," holding his head at the same time "Steph, you here? What happened?" Hoping for a response from somewhere anywhere as he didn't want to be here by himself and hoped she would just be outside the room. Steve did remember what happened eventually as he looked over to the fish tank to see the fishes still there feasting.

"Fucking fish. As if I'm gonna die to a bloody fish," Steve says mocking the fish and making rude gestures towards the fish as if any of that is ever going to effect the fish or make him feel better.

"The phone..." Grabbing his left pocket before realising it was in his right pocket and attempting to reach his into his right pocket before again being compromised by a numb arm he had to re-adjust his attempts and doing so with his left hand, he felt the phone in there "A charger, I need a charger to turn it on."

The phone in Steves pocket is actually his phone as he could tell by the unusual colour of it, he purposely got it in this colour but what an earth Steves phone was doing in a fish tank was much more confusing. Considering Steve never felt like he had stepped foot in this house let alone this room he doesn't know how it got in there and the last place he remembers having his phone was in the sign in room for the game, just before they took a picture of them.

"I really need to find some help, where did Steph go?" Steve didn't have a clue what had happened to Steph or how she just snuck out so easily and quietly, but he thought maybe the phone he found would help all of this. "Right where am I going to find a charger for this? Will it even help? Must be something on it surely." Steve was having an argument with himself deciding what must be done before just acting "The kitchen draws maybe or the study downstairs?" Continuing his conversation with himself not sure of what next, he just knew he needed out of this room.

The two choices Steve has is to go back out the window he came in or the more logical choice of going through the door, moving towards the door trying his hardest to miss all the toys on the floor Steve notices a lot of weird things around the room which he never took notice of before "What's that?" Steve looks down and near the bedroom door lay a twisted discarded metal clothes hanger "Why does that look like that..."

Steves answer comes fast enough when he focuses his attention back on to the door and gives the handle a turn only to find that it's locked, giving it a good old rattle hoping it'll loosen up somewhat but no unfortunately all it does is end up falling back off the door. Steve quickly goes to try plan b the window, Steve moves quickly over to the window and with one arm tries to grasp the window trying his best and attempts to push it up but that is also locked.

"What?!? How is this locked" Steve is bemused "So, maybe Steph was trying to pick the lock, I'm assuming she succeeded but then why would she lock it again?"

Steve is standing by the window looking out at the blackness of the night sky almost day dreaming a little bit before realising that even if he got out the window then it would be very hard to climb with one arm so the door, Steve has to get out of the door. Leaving his post at the window Steve moves over to give it another go of getting out the door but this time picks up the metal hanger that had clearly already been used once.

Steve lifts it to the lock on the door and starts attempting to push it in the keyhole, twisting it and moving the handle at the same time even he knows full well that this is going to be near on impossible with one hand as he's twisting with his good hand and attempting to use his chin along with his neck to twist a loose handle that's he just placed back on.

So Steve now is moving on to his "Plan C" as he decided to say out that out loud to himself in confidence as if this one is going to be extremely ingenuous and he has fully thought this through, after looking at the door noticing that it clearly opens in he decides on his next move. After a few seconds of silence gearing himself up, hoping this is the correct move before just going for it "HEEELLLLPP." So Steves plan was just to shout for help and hope for the best, someone will recuse him, won't they?

"Fran you hear that!" David immediately hears the cry for help and freezes in a moments notice before signaling to Fran, with Fran's head lifting from her arms quickly rising higher and higher as the cry for help continues.

"Is that Steve?" Fran said in croaky voice with ears and head aloft like a meerkat.

"That's what I was thinking," David rises to his feet quickly leaving the toilet seat he was perched on and almost thanking god he doesn't need to listen to Frans crying anymore.

As David rose to his feet to listen furthermore and to potentially act on the cry, Fran isn't far behind lifting herself from the floor wiping tears from her damp eyes and throwing her hair out of her mouth and face, the cry seemed to stop for a minute but then it bellowed back with more noise.

Steve is relentless at the door crying out hoping for someone, anyone to help him and only stopping to take a breath although however he has no idea what the time is or how long he's been here only going off of the hope that his friends wouldn't leave him is driving his fight to get attention. His cries aren't all that he is doing he has now converted to bumping the door with his good shoulder at the same time as continuing his echoed voice "Heeeeeeelpppp please."

"Yeah that is definitely Steve and he sounds close," Fran said leading the charge out of the bathroom with some strength and confidence in her stride as she leap into the dark corridor waiting for the next burst of noise.

David too moved into the hallway within seconds of Fran, as she was sure that it has to be coming from the locked room as they had been in all the others, so he now lead the chase as he passed Fran in the hallway before heading straight for that room and put his ear to the door, only to get hit by the cascading bump from Steve on the other side.

"Ouch. Fuck, yeah it's this room," David says holding the side of his head after getting a small blunt whack, he also covered his ear with his hand and started rubbing it.

Fran runs over to the door "STEVE! Is that you?" Shouting back into the door frame hoping Steve would hear her.

On the other side of the door bumping his shoulder constantly hitting into the door and having the vibrations go through his whole body causing more pain to run through his arm however Steve's eyes light up with joy realising he isn't alone anymore and how amazing it feels. Steve can clearly hear his friends his dear friends so he backs off from the door ever so slightly and answers in a lower volume "Yes it's me, Steve! Thank god you guys are here! The doors locked I'm stuck in here."

David replies to him "Stand back I'm going to try and break the door down." He sounds so confident in his words however he would be the first to admit he has never had to do this before nor has he ever tried, so he doesn't actually know where to hit the door. "Is there a specific part of it or just the door," He mumbles to himself before taking a step back "How hard can this be" As he prepares himself to charge the door, gearing himself up he pushes his foot back like bull ready to charge toward it in mightily heroic fashion releasing himself and smashing into the door front.

A ' Crasssh' into to the door sees David go flying backwards almost back to where he stood with a tingling pain running through his shoulder and arm, he grabs his arm rubbing it trying to ease the pain or at least take his mind off of it. Fran is just standing there looking at David wondering what to do whether to help him or give it a go herself but she doesn't feel like she would be able to combat enough power to break it down herself.

"Coming again Steve, I felt it loosen. Stand back," David says breathing hard before taking a big breath and gearing up for round 2.

Fran backs off slightly after previously moving a little bit closer to David just wanting to help in anyway, however after a huff and puff David lets loose again running full pelt shoulder charging the door watching it bounce on its hinges having the latch and lock bend out the frame ever so slightly, it's almost there he can feel it.

"David! David it's almost done, just give it a big kick! It's come away I just don't have anything to prize it open with," Steve shouts out towards the others noticing the doors frailties.

Once again reeling in pain in the same shoulder David now at least knows he is almost there and one more should just about do it, he once again gears himself up to use all the adrenaline his body has left. David picks his slouched figure back up off of the banister rail relinquishing his arm off of his achy shoulder and brushes himself off ready to boot the door down.

'Thud!' A huge boot hits the door with force finishing off the door from its frame watching it fling wide up with Steve lucky enough not to be in the firing line but not only that he was now free. Although with the door flinging open the room gets covered in a huge gust of dust hitting Steve in the face along with the rest of the room raising a little cloud of old molecules however, Steve is no longer trapped in this creepy child's bedroom and he has been reunited with his friends, or at least some of them.

"Yes! Thank god," Steve managed to say while coughing his guts up with dust in his throat, waving his one good hand around the place trying to clear the air around him, and also indicating to his friends he was there and well.

Fran and David too turn away at first with the dust cloud hitting all of them, having it clear pretty quickly after a few seconds before having a gleeful Steve come coughing through the door, throwing one arm out towards them requesting a hug or some clarity that this is real. Fran throws her arms around Steve with a firm grasp to confirm that he is genuinely out and it's not just a figment of his imagination, he pulls back from the embrace with the other two immediately noticing the nonuse of Steves arm with Fran mentioning it first.

"Steve, what's wrong? Your arm you're not moving it?" Fran said as she then looked at Steve's arm noticing some blood stained on him after a few second also.

Steve gently looks at his arm once again attempting a struggled move or twitch of it at least but still nothing happened "Yeah I don't really know what happened, I reached into a fish tank and came into contact with a fish when all of a sudden I was in a lot of pain and passed out. I woke up and it's numb."

Fran took a step back to look at the state of his arm as the two of them were extremely shocked, David reached out and touched Steves arm picking it up before letting go of it with it proceeding to drop down with no control, David then decide to grip it harder almost squeezing it trying to get a rise out of him however he got no response from him what so ever, not even a little response. Time passed with David constantly grabbing and moving his arm non stop before eventually pushing his finger accidentally inside the wound on his arm.

"Ahhhh I Felt that!" Steve shouted out using his other arm to maneuver his wrist to see where on his hand the puncture actually occurred and it didn't look healthy.

"Jesus is that it!" Fran said turning away "I'm sorry," She said holding her mouth feeling queasy very quickly trying not to throw up.

"Yeah Steve that doesn't look great at all, we need to get you something for that!" David explained as he looked over his horrid wound, gradually feeling a little queasy himself.

"Well that is where I thought Steph was going," Steve said back before eventually mumbling getting more annoyed she had seemed to give up and leave "So where's everyone else? Steph said she was getting me something before I passed out."

Fran and David turned to face each other both pulling obscure faces before giving Steve the bad news "We haven't seen Steph in ages nor have we Jason, it's just us."

"What do you mean?" Steve lost for words "So, where is everyone?" He sounded just a tad bossy and sarcastic as he replied to them.

"Oh, they're down the pub Steve... Yeah just didn't want to invite you," David sarcastically said back before waiting a few seconds to give Steve a piece "Well they're obviously not here! They're missing, we're trying to figure this all-out."

A scowl almost comes across Steves face before he quickly motions to keep his mouth zipped locked attempting to re-lighten the mood instead as he realised maybe he was being a little sassy, although all of this was done without apologizing so this just lead to winding David up a little bit more, causing David to mumble and turn away for a second.

"Should've left him in the room."

Fran didn't initially realize what was going out and asked "What was that?" she asked David in a soft confused tone.

"I Said Steve, why was you reaching in the fish tank anyway?" With everyone now fully aware that is not what David said at all but it was best for everyone if they just moved on so he just answered him.

"My phone. MY phone was in the fish tank for some reason." Steve remembers completely that he had his phone, not just any phone and he hadn't told the guys yet so he pulls the phone out of his pocket.

"Your phone? Why would that be in there?" Fran questioned him looking rather bemused but she had every right to be this time, it was a very odd thing to have been in the room let alone the fish tank. "Does it turn on?"

"No it says the battery is dead so at least it is still working, we just need to find a charger, but I don't know if we would find one here," Steve replied to them with some optimism before realising it would be difficult to find one in this house.

All three of them straight away knew it wouldn't be easy to find a charger in this house, except maybe David as he did see a charger before except it was in the room he hadn't even told Fran about yet plus someone was in there earlier. David continued to keep it quiet for now so the odds of finding a wire anywhere else in the house may be slim as nothing plus to just conveniently find one laying around for them to just take and use would be impossible unless it was a genuine clue for a game.

"I think best bets are probably either the Study or the kitchen, maybe in the draws but I'll be honest I don't remember seeing anything in either place but we can look again if you want," David gives his opinion to the others.

"Yeah, you're right it's a thin lead of course but this phone might really be helpful," Fran interested in what the phone may hold on it or potentially they may be able to use it to phone someone.

"Yes, ok. Let's check the kitchen because for me personally that is where I keep a spare lead," Steve said while agreeing with them two of them.

Between the three of them they managed to agree on where to go and search, with the kitchen being the first destination but David still decided to kept the fact that he knows exactly where a lead is from the others because if he did tell them then they'd all want to search down there. David's main problem is he has no idea who the person downstairs was or if they're still there, so his best bet for now at least was ignore it so the three stayed together.

CHAPTER 21

Eyes opening into the darkness, the pitch black consuming the world around having nothing to see but the figments of huge trees standing tall, surrounding him like a full stadium without the cheering of fans instead being deadly silent as well as being terrifying. Jason has awoken outside somewhere lifting his sore head off the of the dirty woodland floor brushing the twigs and dead leaves out of his hair unaware of his situation.

As the freezing cold wind moved viciously through the trees hitting many leaves on the way making an unstoppable rustling noise for a few minutes at a time without stopping, having dark patterns flash across his eyes created by movement from the tall trees and branches. Jason's mind was running wild right now thinking of every possible worst case scenario that could happen to him right now. Jason's head kept twisting and turning not knowing which way to look for the noises he is hearing as they were happening from all around him.

"What was that!" Jason panicking calling out loud what his brain is thinking no matter how stupid "Please don't eat me, I've got so much to live for." Upon talking to the wind and darkness Jason gets no reply no voice coming back at him or no noise from animals anywhere near him, he is alone, so very alone.

Jason who as of right now is sat on his cold wet arse, hands and arms pushed onto the floor for balance knows he needs to get up so using all of his might he manages to move slowly onto his knees before moving up onto his feet holding on to the trees nearest to him for balance as he eventually makes it up right.

"Where am I..." As he got to his feet still using the tree as support Jason had a look around to see if he could recognise at all where he is, spinning on the spot looking in every possible direction possibly even in a few directions twice as in this darkness it is hard to comprehend what is what.

The darkness was set to consume the area for many an hour now so he needs to decide now which way to head hopefully actually try and work out which direction the house or anything is even in, this decision is virtually guess work right now. Jason has no idea where he is or what is lurking out there in any direction with the noise of rusting leaves and twigs breaking behind him, he decides to head forward from his final facing point, hopefully away from any more noise.

Walking along the woodland floor stepping on everything around with everything seeming to make a snap or a crunch adding to the fear that is pounding away in his chest making him feel like his heart could burst at any moment. The noise of the surrounding area is starting to get quieter with the wind slowly dying down to a normal level getting caught up in the trees a little bit more. Jason is extremely cold by now though he hasn't a clue how long he has been out of here but he is certainly not dressed properly enough to warm up and more importantly nothing he has on him will help him survive for too long.

"Oh god, if only I'd watched more of Bear Grylls survival programs." Jason was trying to keep his mood and spirits high making jokes to himself, taking his brain away from the fact that his situation is dire.

Walking in the dark woods getting more lost by the minute with nothing to guide him anywhere, let alone anything that could help him indicate where he may be even just a little sign would help massively. The woodlands continue to surround him with as the more he walks, the more he turns, spinning around the more confused he gets as now everything looks the same and yet nothing looks familiar if only something could stand out.

The wind echoes through the forest once more but more mellow and spookily than before almost as if the wind is carrying noises towards him just to toy with him, scaring him to the point where anything will do right now just something to hide behind and feel safe. The blackness of the night can play with peoples mind more than anything else especially being alone in the woods and in a weird sense he has a feeling that this isn't even real. Jason has picked up the pace still moving in the what he feels is the same direction, hopefully the correct one as-well but no one could tell him that however as he just randomly picked a direction walk in.

Jason keeps the pace moving continuing along his path, in the distance he can see what looks like a car however it just has a dark outline to show case it as something different to trees and bushes. Time has no concept to Jason right now as he doesn't know how long he's even been out here but it certainly seems like a long while or at least it could be, he wishes he had some clue. The dark outline in the distance which he thinks could be a car, could potentially be Jasons savior as the ghosts and ghouls of the woodlands might snap him up if they're real, so he wants shelter so quicker and quicker Jason moves towards this shining light of potential.

As he got closer to the outline he realised it was indeed a vehicle "A Car! But who's? Oh who do I care, I hope it's open then I can drive to safety! " Jason breathing heavy mumbling to himself as he continued his journey through the tall intimidating trees.

He had just reached a dark SUV type car, possibly a 4x4 he wasn't sure as he had no idea about cars but he didn't want to start learning about them as he froze to death in the woodlands.

Jason crept slowly around the car checking all the doors to see if any were open and to his surprise as-well as his sheer delight one of the back doors was actually open so he opened it slowly and moved himself into the car escaping the wind and noises straight away.

"Thank god!" Jason said as loud as he could but under his breath, almost shouting and whispering at the same time as he clambered into the back of the car curling up onto the back seat, closing the door behind him quietly yet efficiently. Jason ducks down between the front and back seats using a blanket that was sitting in there to cover and feel more secure. Jason was clearly a child at heart hiding under the covers from the monsters, nobody knew he was as terrified of the dark as he was if only they could see him now.

Jason although he was only hiding from some trees and darkness in a car, he felt so much safer for the first time in a while as this game was really starting to take its toll on him, slowly chipping away at his 'I'm not scared' demeanor. The back seat of the car was pristine clean with no mess at all with Jason quite surprised at a car in almost the middle of nowhere being spotless having the only mess in the car coming from Jasons muddy shoes as he got in the back, but no matter what the the state of the car Jason decided he was going to stay there for a while. Jason's placed his hope in this car especially as he doesn't really have to move straight away, just to stay warm some more as the car was still quite chilly but lucky enough he found a big blanket and threw it over himself almost hiding himself in plain sight.

Over in another separate location a set of weary eyes are awoken and strain to stay open as the sudden bright light hurts piercing against the cornea, it would be much easier to keep them closed and fall back into the darkness letting it consume them but alas this isn't the way. Steph has awoken in a chair with her arms bound to the arms of the chair and her legs the same, a strange situation to be in considering she doesn't really understand as to how she got there.

"Where am I?" Steph mumbling and grumbling to herself whilst trying to allow her eyes to adjust to the bright lights followed by an attempt to rub her eyes before a sharp pain made her realise her arms and wrist were tied down by strong tape.

Slowly and more surely the panic is beginning to strike Steph hard as her eyes were really starting to adjust allowing her to see her situation, this is certainly no longer a game for what is really going on has a much bleaker ending than winning money from a game. The room around her is still slightly blurry and hard to make out in her present state, but all it seems to show right now is that it is aesthetically clean, very sharp in every aspect and very bright.

In the background noise is apparent, not loud or out of the ordinary its precise noise was made from movement of a working person however, who or what they were doing is so much harder to comprehend or predict. The direction of the noise was coming from through plastic with the apparent door opening made entirely of plastic strips that does not act in anyway, shape or form of a noise barrier but it was simply easier than constantly touching or opening a door especially for hygiene reasons too.

Steph sat there in the chair attempting to move her arms and legs to break free but just ended up hurting herself a little bit with the tape rubbing profusely against her bare skin as this happened she could hear that the noises have changed, there is a lot less foot traffic now than previous it now sounds like someone appears to be at a small work station doing something.

The person at the station wasn't even making much noise it almost sounds as if it was just a few items that keep being interchanged landing back and forth onto a metal tray of some sort with Steph trying to listen out for anything specific like a voice or an action to indicate what might be happening in there. As her ears were working over time trying to work out what was going on, the noises continued to go on for a while with the same kind of pattern it's quiet for a little while, then an interchange of some sort and then the same again.

The noise stops all together after the last drop of whatever the person was using back onto the tray, then a voice 'Ah beautiful, nobody would ever know', who's voice it is was hard to tell as it didn't sound familiar but it does come with a slight accent certainly not like their accents. Out of nowhere footsteps seem to arise again with purpose and they appear to be heading straight for Steph, her first thought is to close her eyes again and pretend to have not awoken yet as she is terrified of who it is so that is exactly what she does. Steph closes her eyes and relaxes her limbs hoping not to be spotted having her ears open up listening to the footsteps get closer pounding the floor with boots, squeaking ever so slightly on the sparkling clean floor it was a terrifying sound for her to hear with no idea who it is.

The plastic sheeted doorway bursts open swaying and hitting itself with force, fear has set on to Steph as she is desperately trying not to make any kind of movement what so ever staying as still as possible to keep her anonymous for at least a few more minutes. The person has come through the opening moving closer but not directly towards Steph, they haven't come in here for her with the footsteps appearing to stop at a location inside the room and then rummaging around. The person started to grab what sounded like something made of cardboard but she couldn't tell 100% if it is cardboard, the person had certainly been there for a while but suddenly appears to have what they need as the footsteps head back away from Steph again very quickly.

As the noise penetrated back through the doorway once more leaving the plastic in its wake Steph started to feel safe enough to open her eyes again and look around for what they were getting from the room with her eyes less watery and blurry than before, it should now hopefully be easier.

Her eyes scanned around the room and in doing so she could see a trolley as-well as what looked like a hallway heading in an opposite direction from the plastic sheeting she heard crashing about a minute ago, the only other stuff she could see were two hefty freezers sitting simultaneously next to each other with a pile of cardboard boxes in front of them, all an array of different colours.

"Boxes, they were grabbing boxes. But for what?" Steph mutters under her breath feeling like she has cracked what the person wanted, before a voice could be heard coming forward from the new hallway she had noticed, followed by some footsteps.

"Hey, Yo I'm here. Are we ready?"

With the other voice of which came from beyond the plastic curtain gave back a reply of "Yes, very ready. We need to shift all of them out of the freezer ready for the next batch which i'll be taking tonight before we dump this place for good."

"Sweet I'll start stacking them." The voice had reached Steph long before the footsteps but not before long the voice was matched with a figure and they were here right in front of Steph talking into the other room before turning and seeing Steph awake. Steph hadn't any time to prepare for this as she couldn't tell how close this person was before it was to late, so her eyes were wide open staring at this person not knowing who the person was.

"Ahhh YO... This girl is awake in here"

Steph panics and continues to stare directly at this person she can clearly see it's a man but she had no idea who he was, she didn't recognize him by face or voice before then shortly closing her eyes and hoping that it wasn't true and it was all a dream..

The same man who her eyes had been fully fixated on spoke again "Aha I saw you! You can't pretend to be passed out now. But I will put you back to sleep to save you seeing too much" The man giggled as he walked away and disappeared into the other room, coming back with a rag and a small bottle of chemical with his left hand holding the rag putting it over the top of the bottle pouring some out onto it liquid onto it before moving closer to her.

Steph with her eyes now open at this point knowing she has been spotted "No no no please don't... I'll do anything just don't hurt me"

The strange man looks at her confused before replying "Who's hurting you? I'm making you go to sleep and get the rest you look like you need" He laughs as he forces the rag over her airways as she struggles trying to throw her head away hoping to not be succumb to whatever it was but to no avail. The man with all his limbs free and not attached to a chair will always win that's just obvious as Steph falls back to sleep with the picture of this man fixated into her mind as the last thing she saw.

The mysterious man saw that she had eventually stop fighting back and succumbing to the liquid in the cloth, so he put the bottle down close to where Steph had been sanctioned not seeing any use to put it back as he and his accomplice had a lot of work to do "Right so what boxes are we moving first?" He called out toward the other room.

The person situated in the other room replied shouting the information back as clearly as he possibly could "Right, we want Orange, black and Yellow going in the car first. Then the red and pink boxes to one side."

The man hears the instructions and agrees so he moves over to grab the trolley to move it into position in preparation for piling up the boxes, moving it into position he then heads over towards the large freezers starting to grab the boxes that he needed first. After pilling up the first colour boxes he wheels the trolley away taking it to the 4x4 parked outside and begins to load it up with only the light inside in the truck to work with, keeping everything as quiet and secret as possible with no idea who or what is watching him.

The 4x4 is loaded with the first batch from the trolley so he heads back inside to grab the second load, knowing this will take a fair few loads moving back inside before parking the trolley back in front of the freezers so he can continues to stack them up.

He asks "Did you say you were doing any more tonight boss?"

With the other person replying "Just the people left in the house so just a few more but don't worry I will be able to move them all by myself so as long as you get the majority out of the way then we're all good, so in case anything goes wrong in a few hours we've got enough to continue."

"Sweet, sounds good. I Imagine these are going to the same place?"

"Yup. Same Place. Oh I left something there for you as well as I had to take care of something earlier."

"Ok. Anything I should be worried about?"

"No,. But we'll deal with it properly later but for now, it should all be fine."

The suspicious man continues his job of moving the boxes, colour by colour shifting the boxes out and into the car, within 30 minutes the freezers were almost empty as-well as the car being virtually full up and ready go, so he heads back in to tell his boss "Right boss I'm off, any issues let me know and I'll run back."

"Good, remember quickly and quietly, did you grab the phone I left out for you in case you needed it." The boss replies without ever even leaving the position he is in, merely just shouting back toward the other person.

The man confused to what on earth he was talking about so he wanders in through the plastic strips to see what phone was being spoke about "Errm, no what phone?"

"Hmm I see, that means." The mystery person went quite before just signaling for the man to go and continue with what he was up to "Time is of the essence."

The mysterious person continued standing in the room looking at his boss as he was taking a look over to where he had left the phone wondering who was smart enough to get down into the basement and more importantly why would they take they phone.

After only a few seconds had passed the guy told his boss more information he hadn't said previously."Err ... Boss I thought you should you know that one of the metal doors was open before I came in, I closed it but just wanted to ask if you opened it?"

The other figure turned to look at the man with beady eyes almost looking into his brain to telepathically tell him the answer, staring deep into his idiotic soul. "No. Of course it wasn't me as I would have closed it to keep it what it's meant to be," Again staring at the man hoping for answer to his rhetorical statement but he gets just a blank stare so he intends to reply to himself " A SECRET! Moron, just go and close it on the way out." With a roll of the eyes the boss just turns back away from the man and continues doing what he was doing.

The mysterious man didn't reply back to his boss and just carried the last batch of boxes to the car as he decided there was enough just space to put everything in the boot so long as he re-stacked them properly, once opening the boot and stacking the boxes correctly in his motor colour by colour he did manage to fit them in properly. Once the trips back and forth were done as well the items being stored correctly in the boot the time had come for him to drive to his location, so he prepped himself to get into the car and drive away.

CHAPTER 22

Jason had heard nonstop footsteps by the car he was hiding in as well as rustling in the boot this was getting extremely terrifying for him as he cowered down even more than he was before just hoping and praying no person could see him. The noises appeared to stop dramatically after constant noise for a while as-well as the boot now seemingly closed, Jason has now realised that he should of made an escape in one of the opportunities when the footsteps went quiet but he hesitated too long and now the moment was gone as the footsteps came back but this time they came to the front of the car with the driver's door opening and someone getting in.

Jason did not move a muscle from the position he was in he merely laid there and just let it be instead of fighting it, the car turned on and he was now a trapped passenger in a moving car in which he had no idea who was driving or where they were going.

Jason was starting to breath real heavy but yet was covering his mouth with his hot breath flowing out of his nose instead, he was laying about being lazy yet calm but now he's gone and got carried away in a mysterious car feeling every bump and curve of the roads as the car twisted and turned following the road ahead. Jason didn't dare move himself as the thought of being seen was awful so he stayed motionless with his eyes broadly open underneath the blanket.

As he continued along the road with the radio playing quietly in the vehicle, he was in such desperation to look up and see where they were and who was in the car especially at times when the car stopped for what he assumed were lights or traffic but instead continued to ignore the temptation as hard as it was.

As the car travelled along gaining speed at times it was impossible for Jason to work out any coloration to where he was to where he is, although where he was now sounded like it had some traffic and other life at least with the noise of people on the streets. The journey seemed to take a while before coming to a halt shortly before hearing what sounded like a garage door squeaking as it lifted till it was open, with the car driving in and the door shutting soon after, but where were they.

Jason moved the cloth away from his head ever so slowly lifting up to visualize where he was as he heard the person get out of the car, lifting it just high enough to see out the window closest to him without moving the cloth off from much else of his body. The windows view was certainly a garage with the light coming on shortly after with the room being illuminated properly and brightly, Jason could see many tables set up with what appeared to be a few big freezers next to all of them.

The noise of the footsteps came back again very shortly followed by the man, Jason managed to get a very brief look at the man and it first glance he did not seem to recognize him not even a little, but as he came closer to the car Jason ducked back under his cloth before hearing the man go past the window heading toward the boot so he lifted his eyes back up again to get a glance as to what was going on.

The boot to the car did open and the previously put in boxes were now starting to get unloaded with each colour being put onto a different table as organization seemed rife here, box after box moved from the boot of the car being placed in the correct place before eventually everything seemed to be emptied out of the car. The boxes were done, they were unloaded and at this moment the man shut the boot moved forward to the driver's side opened the door and wound down the window closest to Jason a little before locking the car fully with no way out.

"You wouldn't think I'd notice when someone is in my car?" The man asked Jason, with his cover now fully blown "What are you doing in there may I ask and who are you?"

Jason lost for words struggling to put a sentence together as he once again slowly lifted the blanket off of him a bit more before eventually putting a few words together while still being scared out of his skin in this unknown environment " Err...I'm I'm Jason."

The man laughed profusely, "Oh you're Jason, should have guessed. Said you were an idiot," continuing to giggle to himself while poor Jason looked confused as to why the man said that.

However, he now had his back now up a little "What?! Who said I was an idiot?" attempting to defend his corner against this random man, not that it mattered right now.

The man simply replied "All of them," and backed away from his car moving over to the table where he had left a phone previously, picking it up and pressing the screen on it eventually putting it to his ear presumably to call someone.

Jason lay there in the car going back underneath the cloth hoping he'd wake up properly and this would all be just scary dream, oh how good it would all feel after this but that was a dream and not the reality he was facing. As the man listened to his phone Jason frantically looked about the car for a potential weapon or an exit but all doors were locked and the window seemingly not being opened anymore however, in the background the phone had now appeared to connect to someone with Jason managed to hear a few words and what harrowing words they were.

"Yes ok, I'll deal with him. Do you need anything from him... Mmmhm ok, alright? Quick and easy got it, no noise."

Jason didn't know what to expect but he was trembling as it couldn't possibly mean good news could it but the man knew how to play Jason as it was too easy to get him out and where he wanted him, he didn't even need to use force just play with his weak mind. The man moved closer to the car slowly and menacingly watching Jason's eyes tear up a little showing nothing but fear moving slowly about in the car as well as griping the door from the inside hoping he could hold the man off from opening it.

"Congratulations Jason," The man said with glee and joy as he reached the car window, watching Jason's eyes turn from fear to confusion "You were successfully the first person to make it out of the house."

"Wait. What?" Jason left stunned in the car loosening his grip on the door and getting into a more comfortable position "So, what do you mean? Like what do you want?"

"Well seeing as you were the first out, that means you're the winner!! You get the £50,000 to do whatever you want with." The man told Jason exactly what he wanted to hear, someone congratulating him and giving him the credit he feels he deserves "You have played this fantastic and are a well-deserved winner, if you head through that door over there you will find yourself back in the reception room where you will sign for your prize and your friends will catch up with you if they make it out."

Jason couldn't believe it he was getting the adulation he felt he needed as well as deserved, what a day for him, so he sat up properly now to move his eyes closer to the window to see the door in conversation, he was imagining all the things he could do with the money and for sure his friends couldn't laugh at him now as he was the winner outsmarting the rest. While looking at the door he heard the car unlock as well as watching the man back far away from the car smiling at him in joy giving him a slow clap as-well.

Jason clicked the door handle from the inside slowly pushing the door open and the man didn't move from his position, giving Jason confidence to continue. Out Jason stepped from the vehicle closing the door behind him as the door clicked closed Jason viewed the room but without really taking any more of it in as he was too overjoyed with winning but he did stop to ask a few more questions

"Wait, if I've won how do my friends get out?"

"Err, your friends are going to be given a little bit more time to escape but if not then they will be informed of your victory and would be transported to this location to meet you."

"Right, right. So, what is in all boxes and freezers?"

"The boxes hold different clues that we change and replace every now and again, they're kept here because they need to be sterilized."

"Ohh I see. You guys are legit, that place was scary man but my god you know how to make a good game! Can't wait to show the others my victory prize."

"Would you like your prize or not sir?" The man fed up with the lethargic small talk and just wanted Jason to move onto the other room.

"Would I?!" Jason didn't need any more convincing, he was sold so he stopped talking rubbish to the guy and started moving.

Jason moved away from the vehicle slowly walking towards the aforementioned door but slowly turning back every now and again to see if the man was in the same position however to his surprise he was smiling away in the same position which brought joy to Jason's fearful heart. Upon reaching the door Jason heard the man tell him 'It's just down the corridor' as he turned into the doorway seeing a corridor bend round to the left so Jason followed it, slowly but he still followed it round.

Walking down the corridor which lit up as he walked down it Jason was smiling away thinking about how lucky he was, as he felt he didn't actually do much to win and yet he still felt deserving of this prize considering the way his friends were talking to him.

Whilst thinking about this win Jason eventually began to slow his walk down and thought back to what he had even done to get to where he was "Wait a minute, how did I even get here to win, I just woke up somewhere?" As Jason thought about this and softly mumbled it to himself, he span around to see the man standing back by the door still smiling but almost in a different style now as-well as the fact he could move so quickly and quietly.

CHAPTER 23

Back in the house David and others needed to find a charger for Steves phone so they had moved back down the kitchen to start searching the place with Steve placing the phone down on a small kitchen table in case anyone were to find one, with the gang splitting up in the kitchen going back through the all of the drawers. The group were searching extremely thoroughly in each hiding spot in the kitchen finding some interesting items but none of them were the what they need.

It seemed that they were looking for ages and ages with no luck however while searching they then heard a noise come from the hallway.The random noise appeared to be coming from the front door as it opened with the sound causing Steve and David to spin around on the spot and they decided to crouch down in an attempt to be stealthy, well some what stealthy.

"The door?" Steve as he turned and crouched whispered to the others.

David nodded at Steve "Fran stay here," he whispered.

Steve even with his ailment right now moved with David and headed forward slowly towards the front door as they heard it close and shut slowly, with a voice echoing into the front room.

"Hey guys are you in there?"

David and Steve immediately stopped their movement before looking at each other slowly and now standing up straight, is that Andrews voice they can here coming from the other room. Once they stood up straight they decided to continue walking closer to the hallway entrance in the front room hearing footsteps head towards then, low and behold Andrew walked through the door looking really rough almost looking like he'd been in the woods this whole time.

"Andrew?!" David called out in shock at seeing him standing there in the flesh.

"Where on earth have you been?" Steve added moving over to hug Andrew in relief.

David moved over too with Fran now poking her head out from round the corner to see what was going on, seeing them all embracing with Andrew in the front room she was so excited to see him back and even if he did look like crap, Fran ran over and joined in the hug just jumping on all of them throwing her arms around everyone involved. After a good few minutes the embrace had run its course and everyone backed away a little bit before Andrew began to start explaining what had happened to him.

"Well i'll be honest, it's been rough man I'll tell you that for sure! I woke up basically in some room by myself not really knowing where I was all I knew is that none of you were there and I was completely alone. I didn't have anything on me, well I still don't! I've got no phone no information, not anything at all!" Andrew took a deep breath trying to compose himself before continuing. " I got told that someone will find me but I didn't know what was going on. I got spooked. So eventually I managed to get the door open and get out of this room, but as I got out of the room I found out I was in the middle of some woodland! It was dark and terrifying, After a while of wandering around in the dark I finally started making my way towards here. Oh and by the way I can tell you for sure that we're in the middle of fucking nowhere!!! I noticed what appeared to be Jason getting into a car and driving away. I assume he Is not with you guys then?" Andrew said attempting to explain as much as he could.

David straight away came back at Andrew "No, surprisingly Jason disappeared about an hour or two ago," anger and disappointment could be heard in his tone as he turned to Fran looking for support.

"Oh Wow. Why would he drive off and with who?" Steve said quite confused at that information.

"I Don't know! I am just as confused as you guys, I did try and call out to him but he didn't answer. So what do we do now?" Andrew said " Do you mind if we sit and you guys can fill me in very briefly?"

"Sure that would be lovely." Fran was delighted to see Andrew back so she encouraged them to sit for 5 minutes and have a chat.

As they sat down to discuss what had gone on for them Andrew just quickly insisted he was desperate for some water after running around the woods for all of his time so far, so he stood up quickly and wandered into the kitchen leaving the rest of them sitting on the couches mumbling to themselves about having Andrew back while he grabbed a glass of water, coming back a few minutes later ready to listen and learn.

"Sorry about that, right guys what has happened?" Andrew said with curiosity wanting to hear all the news.

The rest of the crew sat there and explained to him everything they had found out or learned during this process so far with Andrew just sitting there listening with intrigue, one by one they said their bit coexisting in each other's stories and Andrew couldn't believe the things they had found in this game.

"So, is that phone on the side in the kitchen. Was that the one you found in the fish tank Steve?" Andrew asked the question.

"Yeah that's it!" Steve whose arm was still almost nonexistent replied back.

"So who had the other phone, you Fran or David? I couldn't remember who said it sorry." Andrew poked for more answers making sure everyone was telling the truth.

"It was David, he said he had the other one," Fran replied to Andrew as he just nodded in response.

"So, we were looking for a lead in the kitchen for that phone when you suddenly turned up Andrew, David said to move on quickly "So, we good to get back to it now?"

The rest of them felt David's urgency to move on so they could get back to what they were doing and they agreed, so they all stood up to get back to the kitchen with now four people searching instead. Heading back into the kitchen splitting up and searching the few places left untouched and thankfully for them it wasn't long before David spotted a lead on of the top kitchen cupboards, while being a strange place to keep it David was overjoyed with the find.

"Guys Guys a lead!!" Chuffed, David told the others and threw his arms sky high.

The rest of them seemed to be just as joyous as David with all of them moving over to the phone on the table with Steve being the one to pick the phone up and passed it over to David who plugged the lead in next to the table and pushed the cable into the phone watching the screen light up to confirm power was on and charging had begun.

They had to wait for the phone to charge up with all of them standing there watching this phone screen hoping for it to eventually light up properly and turn on, hopefully it will harbor some kind of information. After waiting a good few minutes in silence as nobody said a thing just waiting in anticipation, the phone eventually lit up starting up slowly as they all wanted the vibrating to confirm that it is in fact on and working.

Everyone looked at each other in anticipation hoping to maybe call someone or find out where they are, however all was not as it seemed as the phone bleeped on it was clear from the start that this wasn't Steves phone but just a phone that looked a spitting image.

"What?! It's not mine, but it looked a spitting image of mine?! So, who's phone is it then?" Steve was bewildered picking the phone up to look at it, certain that it was but maybe he was wrong.

The phone came on properly now showcasing a picture of the house in the day time on it as its wallpaper, it didn't have a lock on it so you could open the phone right up and within seconds they realised that there was zero signal on it so any call to the outside world was certainly not going to happen.

"Oh wow, that's just great! No signal what a coincidence," Steve huffed and puffed as he looked at the phone and its limited qualities right now.

All of their disappointment could be felt flowing around the room surrounding them as they hoped for something more but as they opened up the phone and looking through it more, it soon became pretty clear that there was nothing on it at all. The phone also had pretty much nothing on it regarding calls or messages, however on the phone were pictures seemingly from this house a night or so ago.

"There are pictures on here are of us lot in this house, possibly from before our minds went blank." Steve said as he scrolled through the phone before showing the phone to the others and laying it back onto the table so everyone could see properly.

With the phone now on the table they as a group now all started scrolling through the photographs on the phone, it appeared that they had a party in this house as weird as it seemed, also everyone was present at the party but they just don't remember it. In the photos it seemed as though Andrew was wearing a different set of clothes to the ones he had on now, Steve picked up on this straight away considering he found Andrews other clothes in the bathroom but the others had no idea of that, but why would Andrew have changed.

"Wait, so where are those clothes Andrew?" Steve wondered as he pointed to the close in the photo.

"I have no idea; I just woke up in these," He replied confused himself as to why he was in a different set of clothes, with Steve giving him a weird look.

"Wait did you find Andrews other set of clothes somewhere or something?" David asked as he picked up on Steves strange look towards him.

"Yeah they were in a pile on the floor," Steve told David.

"Where did you find them?"

"In the shower upstairs, very strange place indeed."

"That's weird because they weren't when we checked in there," David curiously said as he looked at Steve.

"Maybe someone planted them there? Who searched the room with you David?" Andrew came back into the conversation so he could get some info and make his own judgment about what was going on and who may or may not seem suspicious.

"I did, me and David searched, I can assure you that there wasn't any in there when we checked. But," Fran stumbled right at the end of her sentence.

"But what?" Steve asked wanting to hear the rest of the sentence.

"Jason was up there before we searched the bathroom and he has gone missing since," Fran confessed to the others and put it as nicely as she could without actually accusing him.

As they were all having a conversation trying to get to the bottom of the mystery of the missing clothes, they all stopped for a second and looked around at one another before coming to the conclusion that it was very suspicious considering what they now know about Jason. They decided to continue to look through the photos to see if anything else in the photo album was of any help and what seemed to be a reoccurring theme was Jason.

On the phone many photos that they had come across seemed to capture Jason talking to a few people in the back ground that no one in the group knew, which wouldn't be strange at any other party but this was one party that no one even remembered having so how did Jason know so many people.

"Look, who is that Jason's with?"

Everyone looked harder and closer at the photos seeing the party pictures continued with Jason in the back chatting to what appeared to be some random lady that no one had seen before and in other photos he was seen to have been in the kitchen messing about with the knives before not appearing in any more pictures. The rest of the group were in other photos showcasing them in more pictures celebrating and partying, before one by one people were no longer in the pictures and it was just Fran by herself drinking in the living room.

"So, let's try and understand this, Jason disappears after playing with around in the kitchen with a few people and a knife for some reason. Then we all slowly move out of the pictures and I wake up in a room somewhere in the bloody woods?!" Andrew angry about the situation feeling like he has been completely hard done by and thinking about Jasons involvement.

"Well maybe there is some other explanation for this as none of us woke up in a great state, it's just nice to have you back with us Andrew," Fran second guessing herself and once again not going to fully accuse Jason just yet as she felt bad.

"Well where is he now? And we all know he fancies Steph and where is she now?" Steve getting right back onto Jason's case and taking a swipe at Steph assuming she may be in on it.

No one else said anything for a few minutes as they had a think about the potential situation they're in right now wondering if it is potentially life threatening or just a game gone badly wrong. The kitchen was filled with silence as nobody knew what to say with the pictures eventually grinding to a halt with nothing more to show but they felt like it showed enough.

The phone gave them some information about the state of the house and why they all woke up feeling a bit groggy but it didn't help pinpoint their location, with no signal or location on the pictures it was still a mystery and one that needed solving soon.

"Guys I just want to apologize about suggesting this, it was my idea because I thought an escape would be fun I'm sorry, I shouldn't have dragged you guys through this." Andrew apologetically said to the others hoping they wouldn't be too annoyed with him, but thankfully no one said anything bad back to him and merely just replied with a few smiles and faces to suggest they don't blame him.

One by one they moved away from the kitchen with them all going and taking a seat in the living room again to each take a moment to work out what they had just seen in the photos, because as much as there was not evidence of any wrong doing by Jason, but it certainly did put him in a strange position more so considering it was him who pulled the bloody knife out of the shed outside. The group knew they had to work out what they should do next as they had enough people now and information to work out a plan so surely if Jason could make a way out of here and sneak away then maybe they could too.

"Andrew just wondering, where did you see the car?" Fran asked as she had no idea about any car before then.

"Errr.. just somewhere in the woods, I know it sounds weird but I looked back and I couldn't see where it was anymore." As Andrew said that back, the rest of the group thought it sounded a bit weird as he knew where it was apparently but couldn't point it out.

"Hmm. So, you know where it is but won't show us, is that it?" Steve said, with everyone now questioning each other and tempers starting to flare up a bit.

"What do you mean you don't know where it is?" Fran wondered.

"Guys guys. It's fine I know what he is talking about," David backed up Andrew with the rest of the group confused and turned their attention to him, so far David had said nothing about where he'd been really or where he found his phone.

"How do you know?" Steve wondered and now staring at David instead of Andrew.

"I found a secret room and its exit was outside in the woodland, where there was a car and potentially it could be the same car but it did take me a little while to get back too as it's dark." David explained himself but a lot of it fell on death ears with people annoyed at him keeping this a secret for as long as he has.

"Why on earth are we just hearing about this secret room David?" Steve asks as it was strange he didn't mention anything to anyone.

"I just thought it sounded a bit insane that I had found a secret room in the basement, is it even a secret I don't know! I'm sorry ok I thought I could solve this alone and I started getting in my own head about everyone," David apologetically replied trying to make everyone know he wasn't a bad guy but it ended up sounded like a lame excuse.

"So you don't trust us?!" Steve got annoyed with David immediately.

"No, I do. Maybe I didn't trust myself, I don't know! I said I'm sorry," David again apologised as they started to get off track a little.

"God get away from your egos for a second! David did you find anything down there?" Andrew Said.

"Yes, I found a phone but it doesn't appear to work it just displays a time." David said "See look as he flashed the phone to Andrew displaying a time of 5.01, it appears to be a countdown but I don't know till what, but I reckon I know roughly where that car was positioned if you think we should look?"

"I don't think we should all go incase Steph comes back she'll need to know where we are?" Fran passed the questionable statement to the others curious of their reply.

"Good idea Fran, maybe you and Steve stay here because of his arm while me and Andrew find Jason and that car?" David made a good suggestion.

"Yeah sure, no worries here," Steve quickly agreeing after still feeling some pain in his upper arm but also, he knew he'd surely have the easier job of just waiting there for a while instead of trekking through the dark woods.

"You sure its best if we split up?" Andrew asked unsure of everyone's intentions right now as there has been a lot of mistrust going around already.

"Yes. Trust me it'll be fine as long as we know what we're all doing," David said taking charge for once.

Andrew was unsure about the whole splitting up thing and was trying to make sure everyone was comfortable with the situation before diving right into it "So, will they keep that phone on them or should we take it incase we get signal or maybe to ask Jason if we see him, about the pictures I mean."

Steve wondered that too "Oh, that's not a bad idea maybe he'll be able to explain that it was all a misunderstanding or we could get a call out to someone?"

"Yeah we should give him a chance to explain himself at least." Fran said trying to give Jason a say before he gets hung out to dry without even so much of a say so, even though she was heading that way herself and she kind of started the whole suggestion it was David.

"Yeah, fine we'll take it and see if he'll have anything to say on the matter." David says walking towards the kitchen table to pick up the phone once more, to take it with him as he along with Andrew would trek to try and find where the car was positioned hoping to see if there we any clues lying about.

"Oh actually first of all there is one other idea," David piped up bringing something else to the table.

"And what might that be Dave?" Andrew wondered, as he was very much curious about this idea.

"Well, that room that I got into I managed to do it by going under the stairs by using a photo I found which I left with some stuff in hallway albeit in a bit of a mess but If we can find that photo then we won't need to head outside to find the car," David telling more of his secrets to the rest, hoping to find an easier way to search for this car.

"That's a great idea, let's look for the photo. That would get us to the car quicker and easier right?" Andrew agreed asking David a new question.

"That's right," David answered.

CHAPTER 24

The crew had a plan and that plan was going to be lead by David who was taking the team into the corridor to search for the photograph which lead him into the secret basement the first time, which also is a much easier route to get the car. Moving into the corridor all anyone could see was a chair sitting upright, placed near a bin with a few books scattered about on the floor as-well as on the chair with Andrew being the first to question what had even happened.

"So David, what are we looking for exactly?" Andrew asked as he walked over to the mess that still existed staring at such random objects.

"Well, basically I had a little tower built using that chair, the bin and some books with the photo on top because that is what I needed to do to get the door open, so the picture should have been with the bin I would imagine," David says with everyone still looking quite confused "But nothing is how it was left, so did anyone touch it?"

Realising now what had actually happened before now informs Fran of why all of those items were in the hallway in the first place and how they got to be lying dormant on the floor, as everyone had a look among the items still there no one seemed to be able to find this picture David was talking about. As people searched hard for this picture suspicion started to rise onto David and they started to question this apparent picture, upon thinking back on seeing everything in the hallway Fran remembers it was here but mainly Jason who moved stuff.

"Where is this picture then?" Steve asks.

"Yeah, sorry David I can't see any picture here," Andrew says as he stands in the middle of all the items on the floor.

"It's so weird it was here guys I swear, it looked like a picture of the hallway and you needed to match up the reflection to the picture......" As David was mumbling his way to the truth trying to assure the others than he wasn't lying, Fran popped up with a solution of where the photo may have gone.

"Oh.. Guys, I just realised it was me and Jason who saw this mess on the floor.... and it was Jason's idea to tidy it up, he was first over to it and before I said anything he started picking stuff up! Saying he was going to move it," Fran explained with sorrow to the others with her head lowering and looking at the floor.

"Jason!" Steve expelled annoyed at how he kept on coming up in conversation and realising he was at the heart of most of their problems so far.

"So, do you think he would have removed the picture from the hallway to stop us getting into that basement room you're talking about David?" Andrew wondered curiously.

"Well, I don't want to start pointing fingers but it certainly doesn't seem great so far on Jason's part." David so frustrated he turned away facing the position of where the door under the stairs would be, however it blended in so perfectly that it was near on impossible to actually see where the door was hinged so they wouldn't be able to force it open without some indication of where it was.

"So, what choice to we have now?" Fran asked as they was back at square one.

"Well same plan as before I guess, the guys go into the woodland area to find where the car was or is and potentially another entrance to the basement room," Steves tells the others believing this to be there only option.

The group who are now still situated in the corridor seem to have made some kind of plan that they wish to follow, with Steve who will be accompanied by Fran staying behind and will wait here to see if Steph arrives back or not. The other two, David and Andrew moving out of the house into the woodlands in hope of finding the car as-well as the entrance to said basement. It must be said that not all of them are fully comfortable with this plan but they feel it is the best way to move forward right now in their search with everything else they've tried so far coming up in failure.

"Ok, so that settles it then. Come on Andrew you're coming with me," David states.

Andrew looks at David with very little confidence that he does in fact know where he is going but as of right now he has little choice or anything else to go on, so he has to keep some belief in him otherwise what else are they going to do. So he agrees to go with but not without looking at the other two wishing he was one of the people left behind.

"Ok, sure. Let's go!" Andrew says while gulping and breathing heavy to prepare himself to go into the darkness and cold of the night sky.

The two of them led by Andrew go to the front door attempting to open it, however like earlier the front door was still locked from the inside so they needed to find another way out of the house, with David's knowledge of how to get out of the house limited he asked Steve and Fran which way out they could take.

"So, one more thing guys." David turns to the others in the front room "How do we get out because the front door can't be opened from the inside, and i've only exited the house one way." David went and checked the front door just to double check just incase for some strange reason and didn't want them to look stupid, but just as he knew it was locked.

"It's so strange, does it genuinely not open outwards?" Andrew asked David when watching him try it also "So, weird so how did everyone get in and out then?"

"Well, there is a window upstairs to climb out of or Jason smashed a window in the kitchen?" Fran exclaimed.

"Oh that was you guys!" David remembered being jumpy from that earlier "Yeah sure we'll climb out the kitchen window. Yeah Andrew?" David said motioning towards the kitchen and looking at Andrew.

"Nothing is ever easy is it." Andrew huffed and reluctantly started moving towards the kitchen with David speeding past him to become the leader again.

Upon reaching the kitchen they hadn't actually noticed the broken window before but as they moved further into the kitchen it became clear and apparent which window it was and with David reaching the window first, he asked Andrew to hold the curtain away while he placed his foot through followed by the rest of him but there was still broken glass in the frame so being careful was advised.

David clambered his way through the window just about making it through the window unscathed landing on the soft mud outside slipping about a little bit but not really understanding what he was standing on, he looked around in an attempt to understand which direction they were facing however none of this looking familiar to David which was not a good start.

Andrew was next to get through the window trying to hold the curtain out of the way himself and not cut himself on the glass, with David not helping at all from the other sides as he was too busy looking around. Eventually Andrew made it through and seemed annoyed at David for not even attempting to lend a hand giving him a dirty look, not that David could see it him properly.

"Come on then. Which way then if you know best," Andrew sarcastically said towards David seemingly now annoyed and questioning whether he actually knew where he was going or whether he was just acting like he did.

David span around 360 degrees looking in every possible direction hoping to see something to jog his memory but from where he was and what he could see nothing was the same he had no idea from this point of the house. "Errm, let's head around to the front door I should be able to tell from there as I think it is around the other side of the house." David said as confidently as he could hoping Andrew believes him before starting his walk, still looking around keeping his eyes open.

David led the charge round the house to get toward the front door moving from the side of the house, almost feeling his way round due to the fact it was so dark and was so incredible hard to see, but eventually he made it to the front of the house. David could see the outline of front door in front of him only turning back to see if Andrew was still following, in which he was. The night sky was in full flow with there only a few stars around to light it , it was becoming one horrid foggy night with their vision getting more blurred by the minute so time was of the essence but once the front door was almost in reach Andrew had an idea to help the others.

"Hey, should we leave the front door open in case they need to leave easily for any reason?" Andrew asked David thinking it was a good idea.

"Err, could do? Actually, no. They won't need to escape, we'll come back for them," David said back before once again just walking on.

"Ok sure," Andrew just once again agreed almost keeping quiet letting David have this operation running the way he wants it to, although he was confused as to why he didn't seem like he wanted to help the others so really quietly Andrew clicked the door latch out and just tapped the door open ever so slightly so David didn't realise.

David moves a few metres away from the front door attempting to retrace his steps hoping to remember which direction he walked in when coming back from the basement, pointing in certain directions looking for certain tree layouts. Finally, David believes he had the right angle and direction to walk in, believing in himself he tells Andrew before starting his walk.

"There, see them trees. I'm pretty sure it was over in that direction," David tells Andrew before starting to walk in the dark dragging his feet through the frosty wet grass.

Andrew wasn't sure what he was even talking about as he attempted to look in the dark at these trees that were pointed out to him before realising that he was suddenly on his own because David was already on his way. Andrew gasped at the sight of him so far away already he couldn't believe David just left, leaving Andrew having to move quickly to even stand a chance of catching up to him.

After a brief power walk Andrew caught up to him, walking side by side in the grass with company from the mysteries of night sky, it was certainly cold almost forcing them to walk faster into the unknown just in an attempt to warm up. Davids steps were large and precise stepping on whatever lay beneath him traveling towards the precious car position, as best as they thought anyway because in this darkness it was hard to judge whether or not they were going exactly the right way.

They shivered as they walked grabbing their own arms rubbing them like mad as they walked trying to warm up slightly as the wind picked up and took over pushing cold air at them, they wandered ever closer to the woodlands with David seeming to be slowing down a bit as he seem to start to lose his baring, turning his head frantically trying to re-evaluate his positioning even looking back at the house every now and again to see if it seems like they're still walking in the right direction.

"What's wrong David?" Andrew asked.

"Nothing. Everything's fine, it's this way," David stayed sure of himself and continued walking although in a slightly different angle hoping Andrew wouldn't notice.

"Ok, just asking as this seems slightly different way," Andrew said as he picked up on the change straight away "Maybe it's just me, I don't know."

David didn't answer and carried on walking the way that he suggested to go, moving into the unknown with the confidence of a bull, some might say arrogance but either way it was a poorly thought out move leading to nothing but danger and confusion. Andrew followed suit watching him move into the woodland now with the cover of the trees blocking out what little light the moon was giving them, but the woods certainly was not the place they wanted to start moving around aimlessly in without a proper idea of where the finish line was.

"I don't like this David, we're now lost for sure!! Just admit you don't know where we are it's not a big deal, we'll figure it out," Andrew said giving David confidence that he doesn't blame him but that they should work together.

"No, it's fine. It has to be this way surely," David telling back with confidence once more "See the house is there so, the thing should be ..." As David turned around, he could no longer see the house properly and it certainly wasn't the angle of the house that they had started with.

"The house is no longer there David!!" Andrew moaned at David for not ever wanting any help, they were a team and he needed to start acting like it.

"Ok Fine! I'm not 100% sure where we are,"After some huffing and puffing David finally admitted it, before taking a few minutes pretending to re-work out where they were.

"God. I knew it," Andrew said while shivering away but also not being any help as of yet, which wasn't fully his fault "I Need a whizz too so can you wait here while I go."

David fed up and disappointed agreed to it before slouching himself against a tree, he was genuinely gutted that he'd managed to get so out of coordination so easily and while waiting for Andrew to come back he watching the night sky pass. The stars of the night passed slowly but not before they seemed to stop and position themselves in such a beautiful way he thought to himself, any other time apart from now and this woodland along with this skyline it would be stunning to look at. The enjoyment of the sky is non existent as of right now as he is stuck in the woods trying to find a car that is no longer there waiting for his once missing friend to come back from having a whizz.

"Sorry about that David, couldn't stop!" Joked Andrew looking at David in a gleeful manor only to have David not reciprocate that happiness.

Something was up with David as he was very quiet seemingly lost inside his own mind trying to figure out where it all went wrong, life feels like it has gone nowhere and this is almost epitome of it, so close yet so far, all the information to point to somewhere yet still unable to make it.

Andrew moved closer to David to tell him something. "David. David," Andrew trying to talk to him.

"What! I know we're lost, I don't know where it is ok! I thought I did but now I can't find it sorry, don't need to keep reminding me!" David snapped and jumped down his throat without giving him the chance to even finish his sentence just assuming what he was going to say.

After a few seconds of silence allowing David to calm down Andrew then popped back up again to finish the sentence he was trying to say "Ok, calm now? Because I was going to say David is that, I think that is the car over there," with Andrew pointing over into the distance to a dark shaped outline.

Both of them strained their eyes over to the outline hoping out of nowhere some light would beam on it to confirm what it actually was, however that was just a pipe dream as no light would just suddenly appear right now. A hint of a smile came onto Davids' face he looked over at Andrew and motioned his head in a way to suggest 'come on let's go' heading over the what they assumed might be the car getting closer and closer to the isolated dark figure. They continued moving across the dark floor snapping every twig that they stepped on as they felt panicked yet excited, surrounded by these tall trees which shaded them fully from any potential light.

Andrew and David moved through the dark woodlands using what little moonlight they had to continue as the car was almost in reach now after feeling like they left the kitchen window ages ago dragging their feet across the ground with only a rough idea of where they should have been going, but soon they felt they were about to complete what they set out to do.

"Well at least it is actually a car," Andrew smirked as they got over to the car confirming it was actually what they thought which was a relief for once.

They had reached the car and it seemed to be roughly the same colour size and shape that David remembered, as well as being similar to the one Andrew thought he had seen Jason get into, although it was dark when he looked over. As they stood looking over the car something was wrong, something was different and apart from the car itself David didn't recognize anything else as well as the fact that he could no longer see the fences hiding it or any rough idea of where the basement doors were.

"Andrew, I don't feel like this is where I saw the car before! This feels different," David panicked moving back away from the car slightly turning his head frantically looking for someone familiar.

"Is it not?!" Andrew now also seemed to be panicked after going off of Davids intuition.

As they two of them moved closer feeling safer together, the question of whose car this was started to make them very curious with them now almost no longer able to see the house only just very faintly but it had become clear they were in the wrong place. Twigs snapping along with crunching of leaves started to suddenly come into ear shot as it appeared someone was coming, as they now turned in a 360 degrees spin trying to work out where or who was coming.

The wind blew into their faces as they saw a figure appearing slowly from behind the car causing the two guys to move further back although this would hinder their vision of this person, but they didn't want to take a risk so they only moved slowly at first.

"Stay back!" Andrew called out trying his best to act toughened and not afraid of what may be. "David what should we do?" He mumbled as he questioned to David.

David stayed quiet before answering with a simple and short answer "Maybe we should run."

They both span on the spot ready to run back into the woodlands assuming that would be safe, maybe going back into the dark would be even safer than having it out with whoever that is. Once the two of them had spun around they soon came to realise that someone was behind them also, this person could be seen brandishing what appeared to a crowbar or something like that as it was hard to distinguish exactly what it was.

All they knew was that they were trapped in a place they don't know confronted by some maybe not nice people.

CHAPTER 25

In the house left behind are Fran and Steve with his poor arm
still numb with pain still present in the upper region of his arm
and heading towards his shoulder, with him complaining
about the immense pain he was in. The two of them were
taking refuge over on the couch to have a sit down, relaxing,
taking a minute to just chill seeing as everything has been
crazy so far.

"How's the arm?"

"Numb and extremely painful if that makes any sense at all, I
mean it isn't numb like it was earlier and yet I still can't really
understand what happened."

"I wonder what fish that was because it sure as hell seems to
have done you dirty," Fran expelled to Steve.

"I have no idea, haven't a clue about fish! But whatever it is,
it's a nasty thing," Steve replied while breathing heavy,
seemingly sounding like he was struggling a little but still
attempting to stay strong.

Steve was visibly still in a lot of pain with his arm actually
looking quite red, especially around the wound however Fran
was so intrigued by his injury and the state of it she moved

closed to Steve shuffling down the couch until she was next to him, softly grabbing his arm and pulling it closer to her so she could inspect it.

"The cut you've got seems to be infected we're gonna have to clean that somehow, and think about covering it." Fran gasped when she saw it, as on closer inspection she noticed straight away that it doesn't look good at all with Steve in pain and coughing a fair bit. Fran decides to offers to get him some pain killers especially as she thought she had seen in the kitchen earlier as well as some water.

"Stay here Steve, I'll grab some stuff from the kitchen to help you," Fran lifts her butt off of the couch as heads into the kitchen.

Fran had moved into the kitchen with her starting to grab the items she needed by starting with grabbing a bottle of vodka she had seen to sterilize the wound also grabbing a tea towel seen on the side to dress it after. Fran grabbed the cupboard handles flinging them open knowing she had been in them already and trying to remember which one had the pain killers in, eventually stumbling on the right one seeing the painkillers on the top shelf. The painkillers were still in date lucky enough so once she had compiled all of the necessary items, she moved back into the living room carrying the items over to Steve.

"Right, this is going to hurt to Steve so grit your teeth." Fran said that as she opened the bottle of vodka moving over the top of Steves arm, looking him in the face to get his consent before starting.

"Do it," Steve says while gritting his teeth preparing for the sting and pain of the sterilization.

The bottle gets tilted allowing some alcohol to drip onto the wounded area splashing off his skin as well as running off his fingers and onto the couch, causing a screech of pain out of Steve as the alcohol flows into his wound however it's not long before Fran throws the bottle down grabbing the tea towel and wrapping his arm in it.

"Ahhhh!" Steve cries out as he tries to hold himself still.

"Not long now!" Fran tries to reassure him as she finishes up with her bandaging. She had finished rubbing the alcohol into the wound cleaning it making sure she covered it good and proper making sure it would disinfect it properly. The alcohol stung Steve like crazy as it went over the wound however, the struggle was over soon enough with the tea towel being tied up properly almost closing the wound.

"That feel any better Steve?" Fran said after she finished helping Steve.

"I mean it stings like hell but it is probably for the best yeah, thank you," Steve was thankful towards Fran and her caring ways.

"Ooops! Don't forget these." Fran said as she almost forgot she had got some painkillers in her pocket, pulling them out and handing them over to Steve for him to engulf them in hope it'll help him a little bit at least.

"Oh thanks!" Steve said grabbing the box of tablets off of Fran, reading the box before opening it and popping two pills out of the packet throwing them into his mouth in a swift movement. As Steve held the tablets in his mouth he starting looking around for a glass out water or something but he couldn't see anything, so he swished the tablets under his tongue before asking "Did you get the water?"

"Ah Sorry, forgot about that." Fran genuinely forgot and apologized, she quickly stood up from the couch moving over to the kitchen to get a glass of water.

Fran leapt into the kitchen yanking open a cupboard before pulling out a glass with it being surprisingly clean and she took it over to the sink, spinning the handle on the sink attempting to turn the water on only for it to fail and not come on. The water not coming on was weird, with Fran turning the other handle only for that not to come on as well, which led to Fran moving to the fridge to check for some water or drink inside there, however the fridge was empty not even a trace of water or anything inside so Fran decides to just go back into the living room to inform Steve.

"Steve, there isn't any water or anything. I'm sorry, will you be alright?" She asking him apologetically and somewhat panicked, spit them out if you can't swallow them.

"What? Fran why are you saying it like that?" Steve asked watching Frans' face go crazy with thoughts looking like she was going insane inside.

"Oh nothing I think I'm going crazy, this game is getting to me. I just thought Andrew had some water earlier, but maybe it broke after that I don't know!" Fran said questioning herself as she was sure she could remember Andrew saying he had a drink earlier.

"Is it a big deal or something? It's fine, I'll do without the water." Steve confused turning away thinking the same thing that maybe Fran has gone a bit crazy, but didn't say anything more before just staying quiet and smiling.

Fran came over properly now instead of just staying near the door of the kitchen incase Steve was annoyed, once in reach of the couch she now sat down making herself comfortable, casually wondering what her and Steve should do while they wait for the others to return but all she came up with was worrying.

"Steve do you think the others will be ok?" Fran asked Steve beginning to tear up just a little bit worried about everything going on.

"We will have to trust them I guess, what could go wrong? They're together so they should be ok, Steve replied "Honestly right now I don't know as this game has gone way too far and I think we could all just do with going home now."

Time passed as they sat there waiting for any news to come their way but it soon became apparent that none of this was going to fix itself. The two of them felt like they needed to do something to help so they started to get curious as to what they could be doing something now instead of sitting here like some couch potatoes waiting for it all to fall in their lap, but they hadn't a clue what they should or even could do.

"Steve we can't just wait here! We need to do something, they seem to have been gone for ages and we haven't heard anything back. Should we go and find them?" Fran says with a small amount of confidence.

"Like what? What could we possibly do?" Steve moaned wondering where Fran was going with this.

"Well I'm going to go and find them because I can't just sit here so get up and come if you want," Fran told Steve in a stern voice as she got to worried just sitting there waiting for some news.

Fran stood up in a meaningful way, with a purpose of getting ready to leave the room and ready to move outside to find the others, Steve just stared at her wondering what he should do. Steve hadn't a clue whether he should stay here by himself or leave the partial safety of the house. Steve wasn't sure if he should veer outside into the dark woodlands with Fran, he was trying to weigh up the best option for him to stay safe and them to stay together at the same time.

"Fran! Let's think about this for a second, the two guys left a while back and haven't come back yet and straight away you want to run into the woods?" Steve said trying to convince Fran to use her common sense a little bit more.

"I mean, you've just explained why we should," A frustrated Fran replied to Steve almost throwing her arms up with the pointless nature of him right now.

"Ok, maybe I worded it wrong. Two guys are out there together they should be safe, and then there is you and me, I still have pain in my arm so please explain what are we going to do that they couldn't," Steve said while expressing a little bit of anger at the nature of Frans' huff and puffing.

"Ok fine I get it, but we cannot do nothing Steve... There isn't anything else left for us in this house we've known that for ages. So, do you think we should just sit here and do nothing or should we actually try and do something," Fran gave as good as she got hoping to convince Steve to get into gear.

The two of them were stuck in a predicament because they both made good arguments, because yes this house was dire and if it was made for a game then it was an embarrassment as nothing had particularly epitomized an escape room, merely a childish attempt to make one but giving up before you'd done anything. Frans' argument was also very good because they should find the others as there is strength in numbers but Steves' point was solid as it dangerous, dark and no one knows where the others are or what has happened.

"Right we need to make a decision, if we go out there we take something with us for protection. Agree?" Steve says to Fran hoping they could agree on something and make some kind of plan.

"Like what? What do we take?" Fran wonders as she takes a glance around the room seeing if her eyes catch anything they could use.

"I Don't know but if you wanna go out there then we need to be prepared because if for some reason something has happened to them, then we need to be prepared incase anything were to happen to us, understand?" Steve explains to Fran talking a little bit of sense and almost setting a ground rule.

"Ok, fine we'll grab something. Errrm," Fran stuttered as she continued to look around the room for something to grab and use in case they needed too. Fran couldn't see anything in the front room that seemed right or even feasible to take so, she moved into the kitchen opening one of the drawers and grabbing a rolling pin she saw earlier before turning back to Steve " This? We could use this."

Steve looked back at Fran and huffed, he didn't like the fact that was all she could find but it'd have to do "Yeah, sure. That looks alright, I guess."

Fran was now more excited yet more panicked than before pretending to swing the rolling pin around like she could actually be prepared to use it, seemingly ready for what could happen outside forgetting this was a real-life situation. Fran could feel it slowly and yet more frequently the adrenaline flowing through her veins, with all of it building up to the point of exploding but at the same time she was absolutely petrified of going out there in there dark.

Steve managed to get himself up off of the couch having a quick stretch to ready himself and test the arm at the same time, it was no better than an hour ago but what could he do, so he moved over to Fran taking a closer look at the rolling pin and gently rolling his eyes.

"Ok, ok we ready then?" Fran asked Steve, ready for their expedition.

Steve reluctantly agrees pointing to the door with his good arm showing Fran out the door first, offering his hand for the rolling pin only for Fran to shake her head in reluctance and clearly insisting she holds it. The whistling of the wind outside is calling the two of them offering its elements too them, Fran took a deep breath and a quick glance at Steve before she went to open the front door and to her absolute shock it actually opened. It was brutal outside the cold wind coming in and surrounding them as it crashed the door wide open in the process into the wall marking the wall with the handle.

"Jesus it's cold out here," Fran shivering straight away looking back at Steve and waving for him to come closer, to follow suit but he did seem somewhat reluctant as he would much prefer to stay inside but he wanted to stay with Fran too.

Fran moved over the threshold to fully get outside taking it all in whilst looking at all the dark figments waving about in the background making it seem even more intimidating than she originally thought or even remembered it to be. Steve still laboured and lingered behind not making too much of an effort to catch up to Fran, dragging his feet through the living room wanting to just have a seat and wait for everything to blow over.

As Fran saw Steve dragging his feet taking his sweet time she eventually got tired of waiting for him, a huff and a puff came from Fran before she turned away from Steve and took a step into the actually darkness. She straight away bumped into someone in the process and it terrified her into just mindlessly swinging her rolling pin smashing them over the head and with a thud they hit the deck hard and fast.

"Ahhh oh my god!" A panicking Fran screamed dropping the rolling pin after clumping them with it, almost jumping 10 feet in the air all in one motion.

Fran stood silent at the front door not even looking at what she had done she just had tears rolling down her face through her hands as the desperately tried to hold them back.

Now Steves feet are in motion " What happened, Fran?!" Steve raced over to the door going through it seeing Andrew laying on the floor with Fran cowering still covering her face with her hands.

The silent scream now emanating from Frans mouth is painful to watch as she peaks through her fingers and sees it was actually Andrew on the floor has made her feel so much worse. As he lay on the floor Fran believes to herself that he might be out cold, moving about fidgeting in her stance trying to forget what has just happened. Steve was standing over Andrew looking down on him, unlike Fran he could see clearly at this present moment and noticing that Andrew isn't in-fact out cold which is great, but the bad news is that he is clearly now in tremendous pain.

"Oh my god Andrew, are you alright? What happened?!" Steve bent down to talk to Andrew in hope to keep him awake and responding.

Andrew scrambled on the floor holding his head in sheer agony lying next to the rolling pin that had just clattered against his poor head knocking him down, his head dripping with blood ever so slightly causing more concern. Fran was moving around so much still in hysterics panicking attempting to explain what happened but she couldn't get any words out right now as she was breathing so heavy she didn't have time to speak.

"I I I.. He, he startled me. I didn't know he was there, I turned and he was there. I jumped and hit him by accident on purpose, I don't know!" Fran kept muffling her words and she tried not to cry her eyes out completely after hitting Andrew in the head.

Fran moved from the position she was in removing her hands from her face uncovering her flushed face, with just a small number of tears hitting her cheek bones as she wiped them away and began moving towards Andrews to see if he was ok or if there was anything she could do to help.

"Andrew I am so sorry I didn't mean to ... I got scared and I am so sorry," Fran continued to sob away, with Steve noticing that she did seem completely scarred from the accident.

Andrew stayed down still holding his head and rubbing the small amount of blood across his forehead instead of off as he couldn't see what he was doing but he slowly maneuvered himself onto his arse still very unstable at the moment, using his free hand to hold himself up while Fran ran over grabbing his arm helping him up with Andrew eventually getting to his feet thanks to help from Fran although she was the reason he was on the floor.

"Oh, Andrew I am so so sorry, are you ok? God please say you are." Fran apologised again while picking Andrew off of the floor, she felt terrible and just wanted to hear Andrew say something to give off the notion that he was at least somewhat ok.

Andrew moaned and groaned slowly managing to get back to his feet, now standing upright but a little bit dazed he was helped by the other two back into the house and over to the couch almost dragging him over there before plonking him onto the couch. Andrew basically landed from a standing height onto the couch with little attempt to stop himself, Fran noticed the blood over him as it had dripped down him leading her to promptly grab the tea towel she had just used for Steve. Once she had picked it up she doused it in alcohol once more to sterilize it she gave to it Andrew to put on his head to wipe away the blood hopefully.

"Thanks." Said Andrew taking the towel off of Fran, straight away putting it to his head causing an immediate sting and a moan before attempting to wipe away where he believed blood to be but he obviously could not see where it actually was.

Watching him struggle Fran knew that it was only right to offer to do it for him "Here, let me do it Andrew," Grabbing the towel back off of him and started to slowly was the blood out of his hair as best she could, "I am really sorry."

"It's fine honestly, I shouldn't have scared you. I mean I didn't mean to anyway," Andrew mumbled back to Fran taking some of the blame to make her feel slightly better.

As Fran squashed the towel onto his head where the cut was, holding it on the wound for a few minutes as Andrew started to feel a little less dazed with him slowly coming back too, the others were able to see this straight away and were delighted. However after allowed him to have a moment to recover Steve stood back watched Andrew get cleaned up by Fran, he began to get curious.

"Andrew, just a question... Why where you at the door?" Steve asked Andrew with probing intentions.

"I was coming back to tell you that me and David got jumped in the woods and I lost him, we got close to what we thought was the car place thing, what we were looking for but when we did two people appeared and chased us with some kind of blunt objects. We ended up losing each other. I don't know where he is! what should we do?!" Andrew said as quick and as clear as he could.

"Shit." Steve belted out "What the F is going on!!"He really started to lose his temper having no idea what is happening and his confusion is getting him stressed to the point where he is going to lash out at someone unintentionally.

Steve paces up and down the living room clenching his fists kicking bottles as he walked past them, the agony of this disastrous time here is really fueling him right now. Andrew stayed still on the couch watching Steve stress himself almost making a statement of intent to try and fix this, before eventually realising he won't do anything as it takes a strong person to act on something and actually stand up to make a change. Fran who was still by Andrews side also was watching Steve wondering what he is thinking because he was very slow to actually want to go outside and help before this, so this behavior of now wanting to do something is odd.

"Right. We can't" Steve says without any more context.

Left confused by his comment, Steve gets a reply from Fran "What? We can't what Steve?"

"We can't do this; we need to leave."

"What!?" We can't just leave."

"Fran, Steph is missing, I'm hurt, Andrews hurt, David's missing and Jason well he's missing but a lot more suspiciously! What are we supposed to do?" Steve says raising his voice flaring his tonsils, willing to give up right now and cut his loses no matter how big they were.

"Steve, I know it looks bad but we need to stay positive," Andrew said trying to calm him somewhat in hope that they could actually put a plan in place.

"No we don't need to stay positive this isn't a fairy tale! We need to leave this house now and go and find help!! We can't stay here."

"Steve please think about this, we can't just abandon our friends" Fran pleaded with him to just rethink, their friends needed them and he just wanted to walk away.

"I'm not staying. I'm going to find help!! This is ridiculous, staying here will not help our friends." Steve says as he started preparing himself to leave the house as the door still holding itself open letting a lot of cold air in.

"Where you even going to go?" Andrew asked him with some intent, wondering if he knew where he'd go then why hadn't he gone before now.

"I don't know, but I'm going to walk down that path there and find the street no matter how far it is then I'll find someone. Get a phone and call for help," Steve explained his plan to the others hoping to convince them that it was actually a decent plan.

"We don't even know where we are Steve, you could be walking for ages," Fran said back once again trying to get him to rethink.

"Well it'll be better than here," he says.

"Really is this what you're going to do Steve?" Andrew stands up asking Steve face to face, " You're just going to run away down that road and leave us?"

Steve pushes past Andrew causing him to stumble back re-adjusting his footing to stable himself, while seeing Steve cascade towards the door with it still open turning back only to see Frans sad face looking at him, wishing he would stay hoping he would change his mind however it seemed as though Steve had snapped and was fully intent on just leaving.

"Steve please." Fran now sobbing "We need you, I don't want to lose anyone else."

Andrew saw how upset Fran was and moved over to console her, hugging her tight as she fell into his shoulder. "Steve c'mon man, don't do this." As Andrew finished his sentence Steve moved out of the door onto the grass heading towards the only small road out of there, moving quickly down it with no looking back.

Steve moved down the dark path leading away from the house following its concrete route wondering where it would take him, he hadn't even had a thought about stopping as his mind had been made and his journey had begun however where it would lead to, well nobody knew that. Andrew wanted to make sure Fran was ok but also wanted to get to Steve, he had to come up with an idea to keep her safe and get to Steve as even he knew that now with David gone too they had to get Steve back with them for any chance of getting back home safe.

"Fran, we need to get Steve back but you need to stay here and stay safe," Andrew informed her wanting her to trust him but how would she stay alone here and feel safe.

"What? You can't go out alone as well Andrew you barely made it back last time."

"Fran, please trust me. I will be ok... What I need you to do is going into the study and lock the door behind you barricade the door only coming out when you hear my voice again. No one else's, you understand?!" Andrew dished some safety orders out to Fran as-well as having piece of mind that she was ok.

"Andrew?! Don't go."

"Fran, You will feel safe in there and no one will be able to get in to get you and I promise, you will be safe... nothing will happen to you, I will be back." Andrew had gained quite a liking for Fran in-fact he had always cared for Fran a lot and now almost sacrificing his wellbeing just hoping she will be alright. "Please, do you understand?"

Fran didn't fancy chasing Steve down the path especially as she felt he wouldn't come back anyway, especially after Andrew came back and told them about David.The other option of staying was also something she didn't like the sound of but really what choice did she have as of right now, with both really poor options leading her to eventually agree to one of them "Fine, I'll go in the study but I'm blocking the door too!"

"Good thank you and remember no one else voices, only mine because I'm the only person here with you now, so trust me?"

"Yes I do but Andrew?"

"Yeah?"

"Please come back soon and be safe."

"I will and I am so so sorry about your mother. She seems like a lovely lady, I know how much I adored my mother, so please go and be safe for her so we can get you back to her," Andrew said as a last time goodbye for now.

Standing there still with his head brandishing a bit of blood on it, he looked and smiled at Fran whilst she teared up before giving a smile back at Andrew for his kindness before reluctantly moving out of the room.,Fran moved down the hallway past the chair and bin heading toward the study. Once more Fran turned back and smiled at Andrew as he smiled back before running back to him and placing one final hug on him giving him a kiss on the cheek for caring for her so much, wanting to help, after that she ran back over to study being watched as she closed the door locking it as many times as she could followed by the sound of the red couch screeching as it was getting dragged and pushed in front of the door.

This was Andrews time and his plan was simple, go and get Steve using his help to then find David and hopefully find the car or basement whatever was first, it all seemed simple enough. After Andrew had heard Fran secure herself in the Study knowing she was safe, he burst through the front door closing it behind him and began in his pursuit of Steve down the long path pacing powerfully with big stride after stride coming with a deep breath, this was almost like a sport for him right now but it seemed to paying off.

Andrew realised just how fast he had just power walked up the path when he could faintly see Steve very far in the distance and with the discovery so soon he began a light jog wanting to catch up with Steve as quickly as possible. Outside was still very cold with the wind still whistling loudly and the natural life moving about in the background this was no place to be waiting around very long unless you were comfortable in these kinds of surroundings. His eyes were fixated, like a lion on its prey as he moved quickly covering ground like it was nothing as the figure of Steve began to get bigger and bigger the closer he got, not much running was needed any more as he was so close.

"STEVE!" Andrew bellowed out, getting closer hoping he might eventually hear him "STEVE!"

Steve's walking pattern seemed to change ever so slightly indicating he did in fact here Andrew but wasn't sure how to react to it only slowing down enough that he could catch him up with him instead of interacting with him, a tap of the shoulder from Andrew wanting to him stop for a second to catch his breath and to have a word with Steve apparently obliging and stopping.

"What do you want Andrew?"

"Well apart from the obvious things in life I want you to stop being irrational, be the leader we all know you are and help me find the basement thing David was talking about," Andrew said nicely giving Steve some encouragement he felt he needed, playing to his ego.

"You think I'm a leader..."

"We all do, you're the bravest and probably strongest."

As Steve gets complimented, he doesn't realize Andrew can see him smirking and getting excited over his comments even if he tries to hide it away and not show it "Well how are we going to find it?"

"I think I know where David went wrong, because between me and you ... he didn't seem to know where he was going he isn't savvy like you," The compliments kept on coming Steves' way and inside he was loving it.

Even though he tried to stay calm, Steve started believed the things he was being told and fell for his own ego "I guess I am a good leader. Fine let's do it but not because you said so but because this path doesn't lead anywhere, I can already tell."

Andrew looked at him funny "Sure it doesn't. So, you're in?"

"Yes, let's do it. So which way?"

"Right it's this way follow me alright?"

Steve agrees to follow Andrew nodding to give his approval with Andrew turning away and rolling his eyes at Steve high on his horse and began to move off of the path, onto the grass again heading back into the woodlands. They walked along the woodland floor which started to feel like Deja vu for Andrew but this time he is not following he is leading, with Andrew leading the hunt Steve and him were making good progress, getting closer to what Andrew believes is the right location all they had to do was keep going as well as battle through the trees.

"Almost there Steve," Andrew says waving his hand in the direction he believes it is in.

Steve keeping up the pace behind Andrew, watching him drag his feet through piles of leaves and mud with no worries or break in his stride "Sure, no worries."

They continued their pursuit through the darkness with Andrews compass brain working well breaking twigs and branches as they go while showing the tall long standing trees they were not afraid of them and they did indeed make good progress. As they battled the elements they eventually started seeing the car they were looking for although at first it was just an outline before it soon became a full figure and they could see it clearly.

"That's it, that's the car I saw Jason get into before," Andrew softly whispered to Steve loud enough for him to hear but not loud enough to spook anyone.

"Do you think he's come back?" Steve wondered as he understood what Andrew had told him.

"I don't know but maybe that's who jumped me and David before so we have to be alert and keep our eyes open Steve, otherwise we will end up in trouble!" Andrew explained to Steve as he was still in the lead.

Steve nodded and agreed with him as they got closer together still moving ever so slowly towards the car getting within touching distance of it before looking inside it to see if anybody or anything was in there, although dark inside it seemed to look pretty empty. Steve looked behind the car seeing fences like David had described previously and on the floor lay two patches of the grass that ever so slightly seemed different from the rest, almost looking fake.

"Hey Andrew, does that look suspicious to you," Steve said while pointing at the floor.

Noticing what he was talking about Andrew too questioned it " Yeah, hmm it does actually."

The two of them moved over to the odd-looking patch on the floor, with them both bending down to see if they could work out why it seemed different so the guys felt their hands over the patch of land with it feeling tough and oddly shaped, it was obvious that something was differently but what. They remembered David had said something about the doors opening upwards so this might be the only logical explanation, if these were them doors then they needed to find the handle to open them.

Both of them felt around the fake grass trying to find a handle of some kind with Andrew eventually finding a handle and pulling it until it clicked unlocking itself and started lifting up this heavy metal door allowing it to open and showcasing its inside with a ramp heading down into some tunnel by the looks of it.

"Oh my this is it!" Steve said "I knew we could do it, David must be in there with Jason."

"I guess so," Andrew replied "Do you want to go in first, it'll do you good showing you came first for them and they'll appreciate that."

"Thank you, I appreciate that. You're being a good friend right now," Steve smiled pleased with the nice gesture and moving in to the basement they'd finally found.

CHAPTER 26

Steve was first into the secret basement as he took a few steps on to the ramp and quietly began to move down it with Andrew too stepping into the basement behind him, moving down the ramp seeing the dry concrete walls and ceiling with nothing of colour around. Everything in this basement so far was just as plain as the walls were but they must admit this basement was very well put together with an incredible structure to it, the two of them continued to slowly move down the hallway with no idea what to expect but the thought of potentially Jason being down here or David crossed their minds and inspired them to continue going.

"Hey! I hear voices," Steve said looking back at Andrew motioning for him to follow closely.

Andrew nodded back signaling for them to be quiet as they moved further down the hallway getting closer to the voices they could hear, the voices were not any that they recognized and it seemed as though there were at least two people hanging around. Steve lead Andrew into the other room creeping around the corner, straight away noticing Steph and David tied up on chairs as well as being gagged. This shocking scene was so hard to witness seeing his friends bound and gagged feeling as though something in Steves heart snapped, breaking him down inside to outside he virtually stopped in his tracks both physically and emotionally, he shut down.

"Guys!" Steve mumbled as he was fighting to hold back his tears "I'll get you out of this." As Steve was telling his friends that he is going to help them and get them out of this situation, their muffled screams came back at him making so much noise to get his attention.

"What?! What's wrong... It's going to be ok we're here now!" Steve now says in a louder voice smiling at them although still with tears in his eyes but he began moving over to them, trying to talk over their muffled voices.

As Steve walked over to the others to help them the other voices that he heard made their way through the doorway coming into the room to interrupt this nice heroic moment catching Steve in the act of savior. There were two of them, one male and one female, they were both dressed in dark clothing inconspicuous to vision outside for sure and they were standing there staring at Steve and Andrew whilst brandishing blunt pole like weapons.

"Don't move a muscle," The mysterious girl said standing there with confidence.

Steve who was facing away from the two strangers at the present moment jumped turning around to face these two brutes as he heard the lady shout at him, having one of them move over to Andrew immediately and seeing the ladies face turn very angry and looking into his soul "Andrew look out."

"Don't talk to him, how's that arm? Surprised you're up and moving about," Laughed the mysterious man as he and the girl had a good old giggle about the whole situation.

"How do you know about my arm?" Steve asked the mysterious dude who was over by Andrew.

As the mysterious pair looked at each other and answered it seemed as though it was plain and obvious "Well... Cameras obviously, we've seen everything that's been going on. Did you really think you were alone in this house?"

"What do you want!!?" Steve angrily replied getting more stressed by the second.

Steve stood in the middle of everyone turning his head nonstop to look at everyone wondering how to get out of this, when he looked over at Andrew he looked calm as he stood there silently he also hadn't moved since those two walked into the room. What a situation to be in right now, Steve could have been down that path way and maybe to safety now who knows however, thanks to being convinced by Andrew he isn't as he decided to come back to help and here he is.

"TELL ME! What do you want?!" Steve was getting more and more angry by the minute to the point where he felt like he would explode.

"Look, just calm down will you. What do you think you are going to do with one and a bit arms." The girl laughed as she mocked Steve completely, as she was not intimidated by him what so ever.

"Don't tell me what to do," Steve fought back with words whilst eyeing up the hallway from which he came, wondering whether to make a break for it or to attempt to stay and fight.

"Go and get him a chair, he is not leaving," The girl gave the orders to the other guy with him listening willingly.

"Sure" The guy agreed and turned away from Andrew before heading back into the other room once again through the plastic sheeting to find another chair.

It was at this moment when the two were split up as-well as being partially distracted, now was the time Steve decided to act and within a moment he bolted past Andrew who was still static, running back up the ramp screaming back at the others "Guys I'll come back with help I promise, Andrew C'mon!!" running back down the hallway and as fast as he could, Steve clambered back through the floor opening.

All this did was provoke a smirk from the girl who was left standing by Andrew "Thank god, thought this was going to be too easy. It's no fun without a chase and we're still making good time." As she decided to make chase moving past Andrew back up the ramp grabbing a gun seemingly out of nowhere and she too also climbed through the hatch in the floor. Once outside the ramp she gave out a huge "WOOO Let's do this, I will find you!" she was doing all of this with a smile on her face.

As David and Steph sat bound to their chairs with no other choice, they were sitting near the two big freezers with Steph not having moved in a few hours, both of them looked over at Andrew motioning for him to come over and help to untie them. Andrew saw a moment so he moved over to both of them and took their gags off of them coinciding with the man coming back through with another chair, fear ran through them seeing the guy return with a chair and seeing Andrew helping until them. The man continued moving toward them with the chair held aloft, before slamming the chair in front of Andrew and motioning for him to sit.

Steph pipped up "Please don't do this, Andrew help us!" screaming for Andrew to continue untying them.

Andrew looked worryingly at the man as he motioned for him to sit on this chair before then looking back at the other two who look terrified begging for Andrew to help them, he was stuck in the middle just like Steve was a second ago eventually deciding to sit on the chair and looked at the others and apologized.

"I'm sorry," A simple yet apologetic voice from Andrew as he parked his butt on the chair.

They both dipped their head in solitude and David come back with "It's fine, it's not your fault."

As Andrew parked his butt on the chair looking around the room as it started filling up with silence, they all sat there as the man stood watching the 3 of them sitting on the chair completely still, no one wanted to move about at all with David eventually pipped up.

"So, what do you even want because this clearly isn't a game! So what do you want, money?" David asked the man as he stood in silence.

"Answer us, please... We just want to go, what have we ever done! We're good people we don't deserve this," Steph said before calling out the man "You're a monster!"

"Well," Andrew said out of the blue.

Both Steph and David looked over at him trying to turn their bound bodies as much as possible before Steph once again talking but this time aiming it at Andrew.

"What? Well?? What do you mean well," She said while sounding very stressed.

"Well, I just wouldn't say your good people who don't deserve this," Andrew replied "We have all done some bad things in our time."

"Don't side with that huge tit!" David said nodding his head in the direction of the man, questioning why Andrew would even say that.

Andrew started laughing and pointing at the man "A huge tit, David that is a good one!" he giggled away while David and Steph laughed at little, but more in a confused way wondering if this was part of the game "You haven't been called a huge tit before have you Doug."

The man replied to Andrew, not only confirming his name as Doug but his association with Andrew "No, I'll be honest that's a new one."

Silence filled the room straight away with the others being left absolutely shocked looking at Doug and then back at Andrew over and over again, stuck in that motion like time had been paused on the whole universe, with their minds blown watching the two laugh together with it feeling like a personal attack to them and their intelligence.

"What?! How do you know each other!?!" David blurts out hoping this was all part of the game.

"Is this some kind of elaborate joke or part of the game?" Steph asked Andrew as well as Doug hoping for an answer.

"Oh, no this isn't a joke or a game. This is a reckoning," Andrew replied and after a few silent moments he speaks again "Ok, you deserve to know the truth... So, in your final few moments I will tell you."

Panic runs across the face of the two of them after hearing that sentence really sets things in stone, it's a horrid thought to think this could be your last moment and have nothing to do about it especially as they have no idea why. Tears slowly build up in Stephs' eyes ever so slightly dropping down here face speechless completely just waiting to hear Andrew say what he has too.

"You see. I'll be the first to admit the game this year wasn't as good. I didn't make it as well as I have done in previous years, it was a bit bodged so I apologize for that because you deserved better there, but the overall plan worked. Separate you and get you all in here," Andrew started saying before being interrupted by Steph.

"So all the things that happened around the house?" Steph shocked getting a few words out.

"Yes, it was Doug who scared you guys upstairs forcing you out the window, more so to see who would stay in the room but bravo you all jumped out. He also snatched Steph from my childhood bedroom bringing her down here. David you were incredibly smart finding your way into here which I didn't think was possible for someone to find but fair play. However you took a phone that I left out for Doug, what did you think you'd do with that?!"

David looked at his pocket then replied "So, if it wasn't for us what was it for?"

"Well for Doug and Kate. Oh Kate by the way is the beautiful lady hunting Steve and the phone was simply so I could contact them and so they knew how long we've got left."

"Time left till what?" David said very slowly and in a confused tone, wondering what he was on about.

"Well we always give ourselves a time limit because we don't like it to drag on for too long." Andrew explained in a very sinister way.

"So why fucking drag us through all that shit, why not just bring us in here in the beginning when you drugged us!" David shouted out making sure Andrew could feel the anger coming at him.

"You are correct, I did indeed drug you! We use a nice little drug that makes you forget the last 24/48 hours sometimes fails in a few moments but overall works well. If I brought you in here from the start where is the fun in that, you see we like a challenge we like to give people a fighting chance, for example why do you think we let Steve run before getting him it's all about the survival and finding out what you lot are like under pressure.

You can only tell what someone is like when placed in a situation like this like a caged animal using only its survival instincts and as soon as you guys were in this situation you did turn to animals, being rude and nasty to each other so quickly! The only person who was nice and stayed nice was Fran, thus why she will be fine in all of this," Andrew continued.

Complete silence filled the room with nobody being able to comprehend what was going on right now, all the information Andrew had just told them seems so crazy like it couldn't actually be real.

CHAPTER 27

Andrew sat on his chair like he was sitting on a throne, king of the world in this present moment but no one else in the room actually knew what the end goal was right now and they still had many questions to ask and information to find out.

"Where is Fran!!" David once again shouts at Andrew.

"First of all, please stop shouting it's rude David. Do you see me shouting?" Andrew huffs as he looks back at Doug rolling his eyes in discontent at Davids' rude behaviour. "Secondly, she's safe and totally fine, plus she won't know any of this ever happened. You see all of you have been lying or generally rude or worse over this time that I've known you, what I do is I find a group of people and sometimes, like in your case I make friends with them, before finding a way in the circle then evaluate whether or not to use them or leave them."

"What do you mean use them?" Steph asked.

"I don't touch or mess with nice people, genuine people because I have morals. It's only people that don't deserve chances like racist, criminals, even cooperate arseholes! We are all on this planet together so why not be nicer to each other, you see nobody is nice any more everyone is only ever out for themselves, people are born with no decision on life but to live, it's society that drives them into horrible people."

"You twat you've got us bound to a chair because we were mean to you once?!" David says in shock.

"It's not just because you were rude once David, you're missing the point but anyway look. My mother used to live here and still would but unfortunately, she died of lung failure admittedly 30 cigs a day wasn't great, I mean I did tell her to stop but hey. Anyway she could have been saved but didn't manage to get a new liver quick enough, because she was low priority, thrown away by society and ignored by most." Andrew said while welling up ever so slightly before pulling himself together before continuing "She had an amazing clothing range that she ran from upstairs, everything was handmade, pushing it into the small lift hatch and lowering it down to here where I would pack it and send it away to our shop. I loved it, I loved her we worked together for at least 10 years and she was my perfect mother, she was the perfect mother."

"You've missed the point where we give a shit you prick, so get to it," David violently abused Andrew, spitting at him in disgust.

Doug came running straight over to David using one hand to grab him by the cheeks very hard and point his finger in David's face as a straight warning before turning to Andrew telepathically questioning if he should do anything to him as he continued to squeezes Davids face, with Steph groaning and mumbling for him to stop.

After wiping the spit off of his face Andrew and walking into the other room to get an antibacterial wipe he then motioned that it was fine "Don't stress Doug I deserved that. If you let me finish I'm getting there David, god so rude. My mother taught me to hand stitch things to such perfection that you wouldn't even know, but I lost her too soon we even tried a private hospital for a liver but we didn't have anywhere near enough money and I vowed from then on that people would be able to get the things they need, no matter where they came from."

The reality was slowly settling in for the two of them with both of them on separate occasions seeing boxes and freezers in this room, even now as they sit there they can see some empty boxes lying about. This wasn't a game anymore and it hadn't really been the whole time, well not for them anyway but for Andrew and his team it was, they were loving the thrill of the chase. However, with time still ticking on and Steve running around the forest being chased around by Kate, Andrew decided maybe the time was now to start finishing off his game before anything else happens.

"David or Steph. Hmm, let's start with beautiful Steph." Andrew said while moving his pointed finger over the two of them before choosing, with Doug still standing over by the bound friends ready to take one.

Doug let go of David's cheeks pushing his head back at the same time as Davids' head bounces off of the back of the chair with some force, with Doug's attention then moved over to Steph and now standing in front of her chair looking her up and down smiling knowing what's in store for her. He then grabbed her head by some scruff of hair and laughing at her right in her face as they locked eyes with their emotions in them totally different.

"Andrew please please, don't do this," Steph begging and pleading with him.

"Give me one good reason why I shouldn't and I mean a good reason," Andrew listened almost seemingly ready for mercy.

"Because we're friends and I'm not a bad person I swear," Steph cried and begged "I'll do anything you want, anything."

"Urgh Steph no thanks but this is really embarrassing, especially from such a so-called hard girl. Ok Fine, I'll save one of you. Out of you and David who do I save?" Andrew asked them.

"Me, always me" Steph answers so quickly smiling after as she could feel the glare of Davids eyes burning into the side of her head " Thank you!!"

"See, such a selfish human. Never ever thought of anyone but yourself. If you said David then it may have been different and I may have thought about it but you're like most others in this crappy rat race we call life." Andrew rolls his eyes in predictability from Steph "Get her on the chair Doug."

"Nooooo Please!!" Steph begs harder than before.

Doug doesn't care for Steph's begging tilting her chair and dragging it along the floor screeching as he makes his way through to the other room, as the plastic sheeting lifts up and comes back to slap Steph in her face. David sat there in his chair speechless not knowing what on earth to do or even how quickly Steph had chosen herself with everything going on David needs to desperately escape. Doug reaches the surgical chair in the other room that David used as a hiding spot earlier in the day, Doug had now stopped dragging Steph's chair letting it drop back and sit up straight bouncing on its legs threatening to fall over, he turned walking away to open a draw rummaging through to find a needle and a small bottle of liquid.

"Doug please you seem like a good guy," Steph now tried her luck begging with him instead.

Doug laughed as he pushed the needle in the bottle drawing out some of the liquid inside "Do I?" pulling out a confused face turning to Steph while continuing to hold a needle full of liquid very menacingly.

"I'll do anything, just let me go," Steph attempting to slightly seduce Doug, hoping this will work.

"Oh, will you now...anything?"

"Yes, anything you want big boy," Steph continues her desperate approach.

"I don't want any of that thank you, I've been told everything about you plus it's not really the best time," As Doug moved closer pretending to be seduced before insulting Steph.

Doug put the bottle of liquid back then coming back to Steph who wriggled and moved about frantically hoping to be able to get out of the chair and bounds to no avail, before Doug grabbed her head tilting it to one side pushing the needle in her and allowing the liquid to flow out of the needle into Steph with it causing an almost instant effect. Steph's head flopped down after a few seconds allowing Doug to undo all of the ties attached to her before lifting her out of the chair and throwing her onto the surgeons bed. It was all so precise and accurate with Doug pulling a sheet, covering Steph's body after removing all of her clothes putting them into a pile to one side in fact even neatly folding them.

Doug came back into the other room where Andrew sat with David in silence on his phone, scrolling through it as if nothing else was going on right now showing David all kinds on dumb stuff that he has come across with him being less than interested right now.

"Boss, she's on the table ready to go.".

"What are you going to do to her! Why won't you answer me!?" David demands from Andrew.

"Well if you've never noticed, during this whole time I've known you and the others I've been collecting data. I know all of your allergies, all of your illnesses and who's for what blood type" Andrew was meticulous in all the research he had done in the past, a master in what he does this was all now just second nature to him.

"You are sick! How many people have you done this too?!"

"I'll be honest, the answer will shock you David."

"Leave us alone please."

"I respect you David, always have it's a shame to do this to you. However just for my satisfaction and my respect for you, I will at least explain what will happen. I have a naked Steph laying on the table and I'm potentially going to remove all of her vital organs one by one putting them in specific colour coded boxes ready to sell to a private institution who will be able to offer them out at a reasonable rate to people who genuinely need them." Andrew tells "But we've all seen how Steph has lived her life up until now so her organs may be shot or no good, so we might just kill her and frame someone."

David was shocked, gob smacked with tears immediately filling up his eyes "You fucking monster, is that really what your mother would have wanted!"

Andrew stood up from his chair he was perched on walked over to David and punched him hard "Don't you ever mention my mother!" before walking away to get prepared for his victim before laughing and turning back.

Tears dropped from David's eyes but more from bottled up anger than sadness wishing he could actually do something rather than just be sat here like an animal led to slaughter, shaking violently attempting to break his chair or somehow break free but he was well and truly bound to his chair. As Andrew moved past Doug into the other room, he whispered something in his ear getting a cooperative nod bad from Doug who immediately turned to David and walked over the him clenching his fists cracking his knuckles with David cowering as much as he could while only being able to move his head.

Andrew walks over to Steph looking at her naked body lying there and taking it all in, only moving away to grab a small box and put on an apron and gloves. Inside his box lay all the tools he needs to devour Steph's insides, before he began Andrew started feeling over Steph's body for business and weird pleasure using a pen to mark over certain areas to make incisions on her to get everything he needs. Once fully marked up using his pen Andrew knew he had to double check using a few machines he had in the room whether or not Steph's organs were actually any good, Andrew took a swig of his drinks as he powered up a few of the machines.

David was bleeding from all over his face after being on the receiving end of quite a few brutal punches from Doug, Andrew knew David had some wits about him so any potential break out plan was not even being allowed to be considered. As David spat out blood some originating there but some dripping down without him being able to stop it, he looked a beaten man he was struggling big time even spitting out some of a tooth that had broken off, with the chances of him getting out of this is now extremely low and you could see it in his eyes. Once he had given David a painful beating, he moved over to clean the blood off of his hands, washing them in a sink keeping the figure of David in his peripherals as he was slumping down on his chair.

Doug finished by the sink going to join David on the chairs, sitting on the chair next to him and started talking casually. "Andrew is fantastic with a needle, no one will even know what he has done once he's finished. You won't feel anything don't worry, it'll be painless." Doug was just as sadistic as Andrew laughing as he explains things to Andrew.

Nothing more was there to be said to David so Doug sat there in silence pulling out a newspaper from his jackets inside pocket, flipped it open and started reading it with some of it out loud too just expressing his disgust he found inside it. He seemed to sit there for a ages reading this paper, watching David still wilting next to him, as he waited for the call from his boss in the other room with time slowly just ticking on. As he sat there David could feel himself almost leaving his body every now and again, Doug had really given him a beating and it felt like a psychological beating as well but while he tried to hang in there, he just began to get drowsier before eventually passing out

"Doug in here please." Andrew's voice came through from the other room requesting Doug's assistance with whatever Andrew was doing being finished.

Without an ounce of thought Doug got up out of his chair throwing his paper down on it as he did, smiling and looking at David completely passed out "Look after that will ya." Walking away Doug laughed pushing apart the plastic sheeting into the other room going over to Andrew, looking at Steph's body which was now clothed again and the boxes still piled up next to it.

"Right she's done, I couldn't do everything I liked as she has been terrible to her body but hey! I'll stick these in the freezer and I want you to take her body back to the house chuck her somewhere upstairs and slight her throat with the chef's knife, yeah?" Andrew gave the orders "Use the little lift if you want, with little blood in her system you should be able to squash her up a little bit," smirked Andrew.

"Sure boss, no worries." Doug respected the order and grabbed Steph's body putting her into a fireman's carry walking her over to the little lift enclosed in the corner, having Andrew open it as only he knew where exactly it was and how to open it. Her body got thrown into the lift and Doug moved away taking a pair of latex gloves off of the side and leaving the basement room going through the outside doors as they may have been room for Steph but there certainly wasn't room for him as well.

CHAPTER 28

Outside in the dark cold woodlands a chase was afoot with Steve was being chased down by Kate. Kate was running him down with a gun through the elements, as much as this was a game for her because of the darkness the odds were a bit better for Steve than what most peoples would be, maybe even possibly 50/50 and this was one chase she knew she could not fail at. Steve's feet were racing across the floor crushing leaves as he goes making as much noise as possibly right now, breathing heavy swinging one arm as he goes the other not so much. As the surrounding forest witnessed this foot chase through itself, Kate appeared to gaining ground on Steve slowly but surely as well firing a few warning shots his way because her objective wasn't to kill Steve, if possible.

Shot after shot ever more blazing close to Steve in and around his path way, his breathing only got heavier and his route only got more erratic trying to zigzag amongst the trees hiding away from the bullets, before running through a big settlement of bushes tripping as he did causing himself to tumble down a small wet muddy hill. Kate could hear the cries and screams of Steve in distance as he tumbled landing on his arm too causing more pain, before it all went silent for Kate, has Steve landed on something odd shaped causing a bit of discomfort.

Steve had not hurt himself well not badly at least, but he had gone quiet mainly because he'd found a small bit of cover to duck behind, he lay on ground being inconspicuous with him desperately grabbing his own mouth to keep his pain and breathing under wraps.

Kate continued her run moving through the trees breaking twigs as she went by eventually catching up to the bushes that fouled Steve, she wasn't as brisk when passing through them taking her time to push the bushes apart squeezing her way through the bushes safely. As the night sky kept the forest dark with no moon light really penetrating into it, the darkness would extremely hard for everyone so they had to rely a lot on noise to be able to hide from or even find each other.

"Come out come out where ever you are," Kate calls out in the loneliness of the dark.

Kate slowly has the bushes fold back behind her as she comes out the other side of them and as she comes out to the other side moving ever so softly now, the noise from the forest has almost come to a standstill, not even the wind was rustling about at this present moment. Kate stands still taking in all the surrounding information watching for any movements or potential dangers as she span her head about body around. She decides to take a few steps further along the path now moving away from the bushes from once the noise had last been heard being made from Steve, as she steps forward turning around every few steps taking a moment to browse but her site of Steve appears to have vanished.

"Where are you, you piece of shit," Kate mumbles to herself as she begins to not like the situation she was in.

Steve for the moment is safe hiding in his spot in the bushes, he was able to see Kate from where he is right now watching her wander a bit further away from him causing him to have a few moments relief to actually catch his breath a bit. Steve, hoping Kate would never look this way tried to move ever so slightly further away with Kate moving ever so slightly out of his view causing him to push on the ground to shuffle himself forward snapping a few twigs and in this silent woodland it was a big arrow pointing to his rough location. Kate's head turned rapid and sharply like a predator seeing its prey, she felt like that noise was rattling through her ear drums showing her basically where it came from.

The dirt turned beneath her following her boots as they swiveled 180 degrees with her head not moving away from the direction in which the noise came from, eyes fixated onto a small section of bush that Steve was hiding in. Steves eyes lit up at the sight of Kate now staring directly in his direction slowly cautiously walking towards him aiming the gun at the bushes, while still keeping an eye on everything in case it was a decoy. Panic was settling in for Steve as he started trying to shuffle back to where he was hoping to find a new point to move to, slowly motioning backwards in an army man crawl away from his hiding place in desperation hoping his last few moments were not inhibited by some twigs.

Two shots fire in the air 'Bang Bang' ... Followed by silence, no more steps had been taken just yet. " Come out, it'll be easier for everyone. I know you're back there," Kate said out loud while aiming the gun back at the bushes looking for even the slightest bit of movement.

Steve had managed to back away from the bush eventually getting to a different tree and getting to his feet ducking behind that tree, poking his head round the side of the tree watching as Kate made her stand shooting her gun in the sky as she spoke to the surroundings. Kate finished her stance in the woods continuing her pursuit back in the direction she was heading as she hadn't noticed any movement yet from the bush, getting closer to the bushes she assumed the noise had originally come from, she armed her gun again while continuing to point it at the bush. Her footsteps got lighter on approach with one hand softly reaching out into the bush to pull away half of it away throwing her other hand through with the gun pointing straight in.

"Aha!" Kate said as she moved through the bush.

Empty, the bush was empty as Kate moved further into it realising Steve was not in this bush but what was clear is that someone had been, there were fresh marks in the mud with Kate inspecting the bush looking for a clue of which direction the suspect had moved in. The beady eyes of Steve watched from a distance while Kate was she doing what she needed too by the bush as she searched for any clues but it was in this moment Steve wasn't sure whether to make a break for it now or whether there would be a better opportunity that would arise, but he had to make a choice.

Kates' chase seemed to go cold quick once no body was found in the bush and the mud marks that lay beneath didn't offer much in the way of direction, she stood up tall once again surveying the surrounding area, looking for any small type of noise or movement but for once Steve was doing really well to stay calm and be silent. Kate decided to start moving away from that bush although continuing to now move in that same direction which was slowly towards the tree collection Steve was now hiding near, he was running out of time to make a decision.

Where Steve was hiding was behind a tree in the middle of a few small bunches of trees, he had some cover and unless she knows exactly where to look or he makes a move or a mistake he could potentially be safe but realistically what is his game plan right now, just stay in the woods forever surely not however does he save his friends or just run.

As Kate moved nearer to Steve somewhat appearing to target the trees he was in, she got closer and closer with her gun pointing directly towards them, Steves heart started to race in anticipation of the end. Steve panicking and looking around for anything he could use to defend himself in case he needed to, looking on the ground he saw a big rock that he picked up holding it in two hands and just prayed he didn't need to use it. Kate crept ever and ever closer virtually staring at Steve without realising, her gun pushing past the tree Steve was at as it seemed to be parallel with him right now as he saw it up close ready to turn and point it at him.

Steve was about to get found out with it being game over but to his rescue a noise of a few twigs breaking in a different direction became into play, a big deer walking past causing noise like nothing else right now. Kate turned fast her gun pointing in the other direction pointing it at the deer almost pulling the trigger at first site but stopped just in time as she noticed it was the deer but as she was now distracted by the noise, Steve poked his head out the trees seeing Kate right there facing the other way. The gun that was pointing at the deer slowly dropped down to waist height and a small sigh was let out by Kate with that sigh indicating to Steve that even she too was quite fearful of the dark at this point and with that this was now Steves' chance to make a run for it, better late than never.

Although Steve by this point had chosen a different approach and without thought unleashed this huge rock into the back of this ladies head, smashing it onto her and dropping it in the same sequence. Kate immediately dropped the gun completely collapsing in a heap within seconds, without a murmur only the noise of her hitting the deck made a thud that echoed around the woods as well as the rock following suit and hitting the deck bouncing and rolling away. Steve hit her with as much force as he possibly could as he let his fear and anger take over with no self-control present.

"Shit! Should I have done that, Steve gasped as her watched Kate bounce off of the dirty floor panicking about something else now, but it was just survival wasn't it?

His immediate thought was one of despair and potential regret having to remind himself that he was possibly going to die if not, so survival of the fittest in a sense but even that wasn't enough to manage to wipe that from his memory however with his situation desperate and the fact he'd been out here freezing his arse off he was glad that situation was dealt with somehow. Now after a few seconds of rubbing his head in discontent he moved down towards Kates motionless body rummaging around in her pockets picking up a phone as well as grabbing the gun while he was at it although he had never used one before.

The phone opened up straight away with no need for a passcode or anything as it was clear she didn't believe anyone would ever get it off her as well as probably needing it at a quick moment's notice and thank god for Steve it had signal so things could be on the up, he no longer touched the body and basically ran away back in the direction he came from but only a little until he felt safe a bit safer in case she did wake up from death. Steve pushed buttons on the phone checking whereabouts he was which appeared to be 10/15 miles outside of their main city in a location that he had no idea about, his second action was to get some help immediately so he rang the police.

"Hello Police here."

"Hi hello, we are under attack! I need assistance!"

"Could you elaborate at all sir, where are you?"

"Errm just outside the city, I'll be honest I'm not too sure but whatever location this phone is linked too! I just whacked a person with a rock who was holding a gun, who was trying to kill me and there are 2 others that have my friends please hurry." Steve said so many things at once trying to rush the conversation so he could get the police her asap.

"Did you say gun sir?"

"Yes a GUN!"

"Ok Sir, sit tight do not engage. We're sending a unit now, just keep the phone on for a few more minutes so we can find you."

Steve agreed and just put the phone back into Kates pocket hoping police will arrive very soon before now taking a closer look at the gun he'd just told the police about, but honestly not knowing a thing about guns he had no idea how to check if it even had any bullets left in it but nobody else would know that either, so he attempted to carry it with confidence and guile heading back towards the basement where David was being held along with Steph.

CHAPTER 28

Back with Doug he had finally reached the house walking in the dark across the muddy floor, getting to the house opening the door leaving it ajar and going straight into the front room moving across its dirty floor to get to the kitchen. Once in the kitchen he puts on his latex gloves with a snap of latex hitting back on his wrist and moves over to the knife block to find the Chef's knife sitting on the side near it. Doug picks up the knife spinning it around to have a good look at it seeing dried blood on both sides of it and a little splatter on the handles, taking it out of the kitchen to head up stairs and to get a squashed Steph out of the lift.

Doug walked back through the front room kicking a few bottles out of the way almost in a football sense to pretend celebrate before heading up the stairs to the first floor heading into the room with all the knitting stuff in where the lift was situated. In this room at the back was the small lift that had Steph in, pressing the button in the room to open it so he could finish what was asked of him.

Once the lift had opened its doors and like a rag doll he had dragged Steph out of the small enclosure hitting her body parts on everything, he lifted her back into a fireman's carry walking her into another room of his choice, so he settled on the front bedroom which was already a complete mess thanks to everyone else so it helped him out massively especially as it already had Steph's DNA more than likely already it in. Doug walked into the room properly noticing the mess and launching Steph onto the bed before quickly getting on it, Doug did not mess about with her moving behind her body lifting it up and slitting her throat making sure he wasn't disrupting the blood splatter at all, whatever blood was left in her anyway.

The blood splattered across the room dripping onto the bed also, the knife was now covered in fresh blood as well as the previously dry blood, Doug now let go of her head letting it drop onto the bed and got up. He walked out the room closing the door behind him making sure to get her blood on a few things before getting outside the room and while outside the room, as well as simply throwing the knife in the bathroom next to door to make it seem like someone was trying to wash it off. Doug's job here was done for the minute heading back out of the house and going to make his way back over to the basement to tell Andrew it was done.

Andrew who was still in the basement now had David in the other room sitting by the surgical bed, sorting out the syringe drawing from the same vile of liquid that Doug had done so previously with Steph, as he got ready to start with David.

"Freeze!" Steve said as burst his way through the plastic curtain holding a gun up in the air aimed at Andrew, after slowly creeping into the basement without anybody noticing "Wait Andrew what's going on?! Where is Steph?"

"I'll be honest Steve I don't have time for this, you missed the big speech earlier so I'll give you a super quick one. But I will say congrats for getting past Kate."

"What?" Steve said now confused at why Andrew was where he was and why the other guy wasn't there.

"Steph's now dead, David will be in a minute and I'm taking their organs and or blood. Problem?"

"This is all you?!"

A Small shrug from Andrew to imitate a 'Why thank you'.

"Well you sick fuck! We were your friends, how could you do this?!"

"Oh honestly Steve you missed all of the explanation earlier, I can't actually be bothered to go through it again."

"Tell me!"

"No. Now where actually is Kate? She Failed I imagine but what's happened to her."

"Yeah she failed!"

"Is she dead?"

"Does it matter?! Vicious bitch," Steve said while tearing up in sheer anger wanting to do something so badly, he now feels like he would have let his friends down badly for leaving so will not do the same now.

"Well. You too are now a murder if she is," laughed Andrew at Steve, making him feel like they were the same.

"Well the cops will know the truth when they get here," Smirked Steve back feeling like he had done real good.

"So, let me get this straight" Andrew started saying as he saw a smirk come across Steve as he felt like he had got Andrew in a trap, "You called the cops to come here after you murdered someone? Ahaha smart move idiot."

"Errr... well they will arrest you and once they do... Err I, I'll be fine," a mumbled and muffled answer came back from Steve as what Andrew said now does actually make sense some what but he thought surely he could explain it.

"God you're bad at this, so what you're gonna kill me now? Then what?"

"Then I'll save David and Fran, then we'll get out of here leaving you here for the police," Quite the plan from Steve standing there ready to win.

"Got this all figured out haven't you, so C'mon then make your move." Andrew knew psychologically how to get to at him.

"Don't tell me what to do!"

"I'm not but you're annoying me, wasting my time and clearly now thanks to you! I have less time, so if you are going to something then please now do it," Andrew said in a meaningful tone moving a step closer to Steve initiating the first interaction of this prepped battle.

"STAY THERE!" Steve screamed at him, with David still passed out sitting by the surgical bed.

"Steve do you even know if that's loaded?" Again another step was taken by Andrew towards Steve as he was digging away at his solid Stance.

"Yes, I do." Steve bluffed hoping Andrew wouldn't realise that he has absolutely no idea.

Steve still had the gun and was still pointing it at Andrew although now it wasn't with the same conviction as it once had, with his position of strength now slowly wavering as Andrew took more and more steps towards him as well as digging at his mental state. During this period there was little movement from David trying to get free and help as he was only slowly just coming back to after fainting before starting slowly to make some kind of noise to try and distract Andrew but he seemed to be the cold hard killer that he looking like. Andrews posture hadn't wavered once during this encounter if anything he was thriving off of it, bringing more passion and power through his veins with that only growing stronger as he watched Steve wilt from the inside.

"You see Steve not everyone can be so calm and collected in the face of danger, you are not that type of person and never have been clearly. I see fear in your eyes, I do not see confidence or determination. A real killer would have done the deed already, but you have halted, frozen like a deer in the headlights," Andrew said taking a few more slow steps towards Steve as he could see him start to doubt his abilities. "I am fearless" Andrew continued to say as his movement continued too.

Upon that Andrew leaped forward with his now enclosed range of Steve pushing the gun to one side attempting to take it off of him, but as this happened Steve woke up and accidentally fired the trigger with the gun going off firing towards David going straight into his chest. As they continued to tussle for power over the gun another 2 shots fired off hitting things in the room, Andrew shoving Steve against the wall behind forcing him to drop the gun slowly over powering him because of his limp ability to use one arm properly.

As Andrew wrestled Steve to the floor managing to get on top of him, swiftly punching him in the ribs a few times to wind him almost like Gengis Khan they were precise and endangering, David was in the background screaming away well it was more a mumbled scream being in pain from a bullet to the chest with no way to put any pressure on the wound as it poured out with blood. Andrew turned around noticing the wound to David and knew that his window for a good surgery was now fading as he couldn't afford him to lose too much blood, causing him to get frustrated and losing a little bit of his accuracy become more erratic before getting off of Steve while he was rolling around in pure agony, going to find something to cover David with before seeing the gun close by quickly moving over to where the gun was and picking it up straight away pointing it over to Steve.

"You idiot, you've wasted so much of my time!" Andrew furiously shouted.

"Wait wait," Steve putting his hands up after seeing a gun pointed to him now.

"Why should I?! You've caused panic in here and called the cops?!"

"Yeah but I could help you escape," promised Steve.

"You think I need you to help me escape? You clearly couldn't even get a phone out of the fish tank," Andrew faked laugh as he said this, still absolutely furious losing a little bit of his calmness.

"Well... well," Steve stuttered trying to find another reason to let him live or to convince him to let both of them go.

"Shut up you twat. I never liked you, you're an arrogant piece of shit, plus I don't need anything from you as you've had venom in you and that doesn't do well with organs," Andrew said before cocking the gun once more.

"Andrew please..." Steve got half way through his sentence before releasing a bullet into Steves head, rendering him dead.

Andrew went back over to David quickly picking back up the syringe that he had dropped in the earlier confrontation quickly squeezing it into David's neck, he dropped it straight after and moved to grab his sowing equipment to patch David up before ripping him apart, blood splatter everywhere is not going to help. Andrew had finished patching him up just enough to stop the blood, time was now no longer on his side with more than enough time already wasted, so he had to chuck him on the table really quick and get on with it.

Andrew stripped David cutting off his clothes which he doesn't normally do as cannot put them back on the patient but needs must, David got marked up with the pen quick time and prepped for surgery with Andrew working as quick as possible but he quickly had a few seconds to himself to compose himself as this needed to be precise.

Doug rocked up not long after with him deciding to take his time with a smoke on the way back, strolling in the basement dabbing it out on the door frame to come in as casual as you like without realizing what had just occurred. Doug witnessed Steve on the floor as soon as he had come through the plastic sheeting, his eyes filled up with stress and apologetically asked what happened.

"Shit, boss what happened?"

"Well Kate failed didn't she so I put a bullet in his head, in a quick explanation."

"Shit, is she alive?"

"Who knows, who cares. Where have you been eh?"

"Sorry I stopped for a ciggy!"

"Typical we don't have long left stop wasting TIME! Now take that gun and wipe it clean, then put it back with Steve."

Doug didn't mutter another word he just stayed in silence feeling awful for taking his time so he just immediately done what Andrew had asked, picking up the gun washing it clean and putting it back Steves hand making sure to get his prints all of it properly. Andrew attempted to salvage as much as he could from David but with him losing so much blood beforehand it didn't go very well, so he stitched him back up to a high standard covering wounds as best as he could followed by virtually just throwing David on the floor straight off of the table in anger.

"Right before we sort out David go and find Kate! See if she is actually dead and if she...Fucking bury her or burn her, I couldn't care less. Just do it now," Andrew moaned staying in his now foul mood.

"Sure, I'll be as quick as," Doug was a loyal man and had an iron stomach seeing dead people even, even seeing his friends dead in the past had done nothing to him.

Doug snatched a shovel from the previous room and began to move fast outside going to look for Kate, moving into the dark woods attempting to work out with path she may have taken as for right now everyway looked the same and the way Steve originally left the basement in sheer panic then they could have gone anyway but, eventually settling on a direction to start walking and tracking Doug heard a noise is the background.

"Cops!" Doug said before dropping his shovel running back to the basement bursting in the hallway running through the plastic where Andrew had finished packing the boxes.

"What's the panic?"

"Cops!! Cops are basically here and sound like they are coming fast."

"Oh sugar! Right quick let's chuck all these boxes in the car. Go go go," Andrew grabbed a few boxes straight away running out to the car before putting them in the back as quickly and neatly as he could.

Doug followed suit taking as many as he could carry safety and running outside to put them in the back of the motor, it was nowhere near as organized as before. The boot had not been coloured coordinated, the boxes had just been put in whatever way they came out the rooms. Box after box got pilled in as they just dragged the previous few boxes from Steph from out the freezer as now it all had been compromised and no evidence could be left, the sirens in the back ground became louder to the two of them but finally they managed to fill up the car with all that was required and decided to just leave David there and go.

"Doug get in and go now! Go to our location!" Andrew said as quickly as possible knowing he had a plan.

"Done... but what are you going to do?!"

"I'm not leaving Fran alone, she can't be involved in all this plus that's a good easy way out for me, my alibi."

"What?! Just kill her and let's go?!" Doug was confused as to why he now cared so much about Fran.

"No! Now go Doug, I'll meet up in an hour," Andrew grabbed this huge man by the scruff of the neck pushing him towards the car door "Doug, we've got this I promise. Go!"

Doug eventually agreed mainly because the sirens were getting closer and jumped into the motor, straight away opening up the exhaust pipe with the tire spinning like mad and moves off flicking mud backwards. Lucky enough there was a second way out of these surroundings, separate from the main road in so Doug would be able to get out unseen if he left now, as Doug span off like mad Andrew stayed behind and closed the doors to the basement behind him to get rid of the glare from inside so it was invisible to the outside world, before attempting to run back to the house to find Fran. The logic behind him going back for Fran was weird due to the fact that they had never spared any one before let alone go back for them, however this game hadn't gone as well as some previous ones.

As Andrew got to the house the front door was still ajar from Doug, getting turning around as he got there seeing 3 police cars come flying into the area lighting it up like mad, with blue flashing lights everywhere causing slight panic. Upon getting inside the house he slammed the door behind him hoping he wasn't seen entering, once the front door was closed and had a look out of the window to see how long he had while catching his breath, he ran over to the study door and started banging his fist on it.

"FRAN FRAN!"

Fran was still inside cowering away as she had been for ages since Andrew asked her too. "Andrew?!"

"Fran, you gotta open up!"

"Ok, Ok. What's been happening?"

"Come on hurry!"

"I'm trying!"

As Fran panicked to move away the couch and other items, she piled in front of the door to keep her safe Andrew began to spin his web of lies "Sorry, it's just that a lot has happened here and we're not safe we need to go now."

Fran eventually moved everything away from the door and yanking it open revealing a tired looking Andrew who moved over and hugged her smiling in delight as he did, Fran hugged back reciprocating the feeling. The hug once finished felt good for both of them, Fran was so happy that Andrew had done what he said and came back for her, in that moment a slight amount of calm filled the air.

"Fran, do you trust me?" Andrew asked her.

"Yes, you said you'd come back and you have."

"Right good." As Andrew said that and embraced Fran again, he put a syringe into her neck what he had taken from the basement just before running over here, releasing the fluid into her having her pass out into his arms. In that instance he picked up Fran in his arms properly and started carrying her over to the front door before banging on it like crazy hoping to attract the attention from the cops.

'Bang Bang Bang' " HELLP" Andrew screamed in the crack of the door.

The police were rapid in their response coming up to the door with. "Stand back from the door," Without a second thought the police smashed the door off its hinges, it opened rapidly flying open quicker than it did earlier with the wind.

As soon as the police told him to stand back Andrew made sure the police could see him holding Fran in a friendly way, so once the door had opened and the police came flying in the police never saw him as a threat only a victim. As one officer stopped with Andrew the rest stormed in searching the house as well as before asking Andrew what happened and calling for medical attention.

A Police woman questioned "Sir, is she ok? What has happened here?"

"Some maniac was running around with Knife and some other guy had a gun so me and Fran, that's this girl here, we were hiding out in the Study." Andrew replied putting on a soft scared tone, to get the police on his side.

"So who called us?" Questioned one of the officers.

"I'm sorry ma'am I don't know but I am so glad you are here! There has been a lot of commotion in this house and yet we were only here for a game! I do think the guy with the was below us somehow, maybe a basement or something. Please can we get her to a hospital! She just randomly passed out."

"Sure, can we have your name sir as we will need to bring you in for questioning," The Police Officer requested.

"Yes sure, it's Andrew Miller."

"Thank you," The Police Officer helped Andrew outside and made sure to call for an ambulance.

As The police searched the house Andrew could hear a lot of chit chat going on with specialist units being called to come and inspect certain things in there, as well as having a unit start sweeping the woodlands outside. Andrew could have potentially made a huge mistake coming back for Fran however he cannot back down now, otherwise it'll look even more suspicious so he kept up this charade of being a nice friendly person.

As the ambulance rocked up a few minutes later, he and Fran were bundled into the back of it with Fran given oxygen and put on the bed in the back, Andrew had the ambulance door close in his face as he sat in the back with Fran and looked out the back window at the house slowly disappearing in the distance with him now working out how he'd finish his plan off now that he had to improvise a little thanks to Steve.

As the ambulance left the house zooming off in the background it left the police behind who were in the process of thoroughly sweeping the house, coming with them coming across Steph's body as well as the knife and various other things they classed as evidence, although as of right now the could not find a basement entrance in the house let alone a basement of which Andrew spoke of. The second squad continued searching the surrounding area outside and it would surely not be long before they found the other entrance and possibly find David and Kate. The house was in a state from the way everyone had treated it with Andrew being the only one who hadn't spent much time in the house and hadn't touched much so his presence would not be felt in the house by the police.

It wasn't long after the police swept the house that they called for professionals having the forensics team turn up later to sweep it themselves, they came through the house checking it all for prints as well as the knife and Steph's body conversing with the police and spending hours searching the house collecting evidence. The team also found a rock in the kitchen lying on the floor which appeared to mirror a trajectory of being thrown through window, on those two items the forensics team worked out that there were prints on all of these items that looked similar but without checking they wouldn't know yet. The Female who was in charge of this investigation spoke to the head of the forensics team to find out what they had now knew.

"So let's make sure this area is all cordoned off properly, I don't want anyone else in or out of this building," The Police sergeant exclaimed.

"Yes boss, it's all cordoned off," The second in command replied.

"Right, what have we got," The police sergeant.

"Right sir, we have 2 people we know of right now the ones who left in the ambulance and information of a basement but no signs of it right now," The second in command informed.

"And forensics wise?"

"We have a body of course, a knife which seems like it was used in that attack and in the kitchen we found a rock that appears to have smashed the window sir where someone may of broke in... These are our main clues right now, as well as an open laptop found in the other room so that may have some clues on it once we crack it," The forensics woman explained to the sergeant.

"Right good work, we need to find this basement! What about the team searching the woods?"

"No find yet sir," The second in command told him.

CHAPTER 29

The flashing lights lit up the city as the ambulance went flying through town towards the hospital as Andrew sat in the back holding onto Frans hand as she lay there passed out on the bed, having the paramedic checking her over looking at her vital signs. As the paramedic checked over Fran, he had a few questions that were requirements to ask as he needed to know the basics of the situation.

"Sir, can you tell me what happened?"

"I'm not sure, we were hiding out in the study of the house and as we managed to escape from it just before the cops turned up she appeared to faint, at first I thought it was something more serious as I didn't know why just randomly fainted," Andrew started moaning with his eyes tearing up a little "But thankfully it seemed like she had just passed out, maybe through fear or terror I don't know."

"Oh ok sir, it seems as though she isn't too bad and doesn't appear to be hurt or anything in anyway. So it's quite possibly that she just passed out due to excessive panic or fear but we will check her over properly once at the hospital," The paramedic said feeling for Andrew right "You done the right thing having her brought in straight away."

"Thank you, Thank god," Andrew wiped away his teary eyes as he said it Are we close sir?"

"Yeah, we're about 2 mins out then we can double check."

The rest of the city flashed by the window at Andrew as he stared out the back before having the ambulance pull up sharply at the hospital, having Fran thrust out of it very quickly and up the ramp inside the hospital watched by a standing Andrew. Andrew stood dormant by the ambulance listening to the calls of the staff at the hospital yelling at him that all will be fine, as he then moved towards the hospital following the bed lethargically lagging behind eventually getting to a door and being told he can go no further for the minute and to please wait to the side as the police were coming for his statement.

Andrew smiled and walked away moving over to the chair he was requested to sit on, there didn't seem to be too much discontent from Andrew with him agreeing to wait and give a statement. As he sat there waiting which seemed to be quite a while, he got a call from Doug and before he took it, he checked the people around him to see if any cops were around.

"Doug what's up?"

"Right the stuff is all safe and sound in the freezers back at the shop."

"Fantastic and Jason?"

"Jason Is going to be put in position now, we're just loading him back into the motor."

"Doug you're a legend, Shit I gotta go, Feds. Let me know when you're away and clear."

Andrew hung up the phone before he was caught using it and stuffed it back into his pocket on silent while now slumping in his seat appearing to mope, feeling sorry for Fran. The police walked in the waiting room where Andrew was situated as told, the police came over with one sitting on the empty chair next to him and one standing in front of him as imposingly as he could. They seemed to appear apologetic towards him as he sat here alone waiting for his apparent dear friend, waiting for the results of the checks the doctors were doing.

"Hello sir, I'm Officer Harris and this is Officer Rick. Are you ok?" The police woman asked.

"Yes, as ok as I can be! Wish it was me in there instead of her." He laid on the sadness straight away in his speech.

"That's sweet of you, is she going to be ok?"

"Honestly I don't know, nobody has told me anything."

"Well I hope she will be, I'm sorry to do this but can you tell me everything you know about tonight."

"Sure, I mean I'll be honest with you. I don't remember a lot, just that someone was running around with a knife and he seemed to be having it out with some guy with a gun!"

"And where were you in all this?"

"I only remember from being in the forest although I don't know how I got there! Then running away from the crazy person with the knife into the house and slamming locking the front door behind me, basically then just hiding with Fran inside the study hoping not be found!"

"Did the guy with the knife follow you?"

"I think so, I remember hearing a window smash and footsteps upstairs"

"I said to the officer before about noises coming from below indicating a basement or something but I don't know how to get down there!!"

"Ok Thank you."

"I do remember that it appeared to be another few people arguing, one of them called Jason I think,"

"Did just you and Fran, come to this house and why may I ask?"

"No it was me Fran and a guy called David, we were here to play a simple escape room or so we were told!... Oh sorry and a girl called Steph."

"So there were 4 of you?"

"Correct."

"Ok, Thank you sir. We will be in touch, what was your name again."

"...Andrew ... Miller"

"Ok Mr. Miller Thanks for that, get some rest."

"Appreciated."

The police closed their notebooks taking all the information they felt necessary from Andrew at this present time and informing him that he was good for now but they would be back once they knew more, Andrew watched the police leave the room before standing up himself. In his mind he knew Fran wouldn't remember a thing because most people don't when given the drug that he gave her, so upon standing up he had a big stretch of the body whilst having a little giggle to himself, proceeding to leave the hospital without checking on Fran knowing in the long run she would be better off. Walking through the clean building that was the hospital sanitizing his hands as he went and discarding of his jacket in the bin outside the hospital, he assumed this virtually to be over.

It was early morning at this point having his phone go off from the alarm he set ages ago, although this one hadn't gone as smoothly as some of the others, he still feels like he had done well and feeling like he has got away with it, just in time for his alarm to go off as well. He walked away from the hospital walking to the cab parking and grabbing a cab heading back into the town Centre not far from the shop where Doug had been accumulating the boxes from which he was told. A black cab picked offered to take him, driving to his destination he had requested and virtually ignoring all the questions spoken by the cabbie, on arrival Andrew paid him his fee also waving him goodbye then walking down the empty dark street before heading down an alley towards the shop where Doug had been.

Once there Andrew made a call "I've got stuff, it's got to go now it won't last long."

The voice on the other side of the phone gave a plain and simple response "Ok, I'll be 5."

Andrew unlocked the shop and went inside with it filled with a couple of people there who help out however, Doug was not there as he was busy dealing with his Jason situation right now. This well-oiled machine of a company that Andrew owned did not only just deal in organs, it's just that was how it all started and it has spread like wildfire since then however, organs are not easy to come by in a big supply for his work is vital for the business. Within the next 30 minutes the man on the other end of the call hand came to the shop and cleaned out all of the boxes that had been lodged in the freezer, no longer being anything to do with Andrew they were out of his hands for good being paid handsomely for his services, job done.

The work had all been completed for the night and the swift transaction topped it off with the good being extracted, moved and then sold within a matter of hours, so he said goodbye to the others working in his shop after informing them to leave so he could lock up before leaving. Andrew left the shop walking back down the narrow alleyway in which he came from, before moving on down the street heading towards his apartment feeling the early morning vibe in the air and it was at this point that tiredness really hit him.

Andrew got into his apartment closing the door behind him followed by walking into his kitchen and moving over to the cabinet where he grabbed a whiskey glass out of it as well as a lovely expensive bottle before pouring a glass and drinking it all. A big sigh of relief was breathed out straight after feeling like he'd done a good deed and it was finally over, something seemed to be over but it certainly was not a good deed what he had just done with his accomplices.

Andrew poured another drink, although this time he took his time with it and really savored it, moving over to his table to take a seat to just chill out for a bit while waiting for a text from Doug to all but confirm things had been taken care of. Eventually that text came but it took another 20/30 mins along with another glass of whiskey but the text came, with Doug letting him know that all was in place. Thankfully for Andrew the day was done, everything was in place and he was at home, he could rest.

Within a few days the police had eventually found the entrance to the basement in the woodlands, on the way to finding the basement entrance in the woods the police found a poor lady in the woods who appeared to have been bludgeoned over the head with something, and on her corpse they found a phone with a dead battery. Once the police had broken open the doors and forced their way inside finding bodies of two guys whose names at first were unknown, no wallet or ID were found on them so they were a mystery at this present moment, so all they done was for now was have it all cordoned off. The police had however managed to get into the laptop seeing pictures of groups of people on there, of them pictures they'd found most of them had appeared missing over the last 18 months but before now nobody had any leads, so this just added more confusion onto the polices portfolio.

On the bodies that were found in the basement held few items on their person, one of the two had a phone on them and had a few papers in his pockets taking those items in for evidence and examination, while the other had a gun in his possession. The room that they were positioned in was a strange as it was surgically set up being immediately obvious to the police but it was barren with nothing in any of the freezers nor the cupboards, nothing of actual use or evidence. The only thing in the room which could potentially be useful to them was a few screens which computed cameras across the house, the police were in the process of checking the computer but of course it eventually came up empty with no saved data or anything to help find out the names of these people. The police searched and stripped the room for anything useful with not much to be desired strangely, with them only able to guess potential outcomes of this room available now.

Once back in the lab the police managed to crack the two phones that they had come across, giving valuable information although yet to understand it fully but it was a start and at least some information to go off of with them scratching their heads so far. The phone found on the woman out in the woods was pretty bare in terms on pictures or calls but one called made on it was a call to the cops about someone with a gun, which potentially could have been the man found in the basement. The other that was found on the person with the gun had many pictures of what appeared to be a party with all known suspects in it except one and that appeared to be one person they hadn't found yet, he always appeared to be the one in the photos brandishing a weapon which has now been confiscated for evidence and potentially used on the poor girl upstairs in the house. This person was also seen conversing with the woman found in the woods during this party in the photos, so maybe there's a question of these two working together and it went wrong.

After finding out these bits on information the police contacted Andrew using a number he gave them with him agreeing to come in for second questioning, once in the custody of the police Andrew answered a whole range of questions related to all the photos found on the phone along with questions regarding the people they found diseased. Andrew was complicit and answered all the questions he was asked, telling them all they wanted to know, as well as confirming what they thought that Jason was the main man they needed to be talking to. The police questioned whether Andrew knew any idea of Jason potential whereabouts, if he had over heard anything about where he may or may not be going but Andrew had informed them that he didn't stay in Jasons vicinity for long enough with the police thanking him for his help in this investigation.

Fran on the other hand got in touch with the police to tell them that Jason had been trying to get into contact with her after she was aware they were interested in talking to him, Jason was saying about coming over for a catch up as he hadn't seen anyone in a while and was feeling a bit weird wondering where everyone was. The police took note of Frans information taking immediate action to move on Jasons' apartment with a squad, the plan was to take him in for questioning and search the property as he was suspect number one and nobody had seen him since that night, almost vanishing.

Using the information Fran had given the police about Jason and his whereabouts a police squadron were in action within hours of receiving this information heading straight to Jasons' with a warrant, knocking in his door and getting him with lightning-fast precision. As the door to Jasons' apartment flying off of its hinges Jason was left in a frozen moment, gob smacked and confused causing him to resist due to his unwavering request that whatever had happened, he was innocent in it all. The police dragged Jason to the station to start an inquest.

"Right we are here at 1.40pm, I am detective Charles and I am starting this interview with Mr. Jason Pegg." The detective clicked the button to initiate the recording of the interview "Right Sir, can you please tell me where you were on the night of the 21st of November?"

"Err What is this about?!"

"We were hoping you could tell us."

"I was at an Escape room house until I was virtually kidnapped and taken to somewhere else, I didn't know."

"Can you elaborate because we no record of you being kidnapping, especially not from what we've heard from everyone else?"

"Well I'm telling you now! Where are my friends?!"

"Who was you at this escape room with?"

"Fran, Steph, David, Steve."

"And what about a guy called Andrew Miller?"

"Well I know an Andrew but his name isn't Miller, but he was supposed to be with us but we never saw him."

"Right so do you have any idea who kidnapped you or why?"

"Well... it was kind of me who got in the car, but they didn't know I was in there and then they drove off."

"So, you broke into a car? And you are now claiming kidnap, that is not how kidnapping works sir."

"No! They separated me from my friends!"

"Well to be honest sir it sounds like you done that yourself!"

"When was the last time you saw your friends?"

"When I was at the house..."

"Ok, and did you notice anything strange there?"

"No not really."

"We had reports of people vanishing?"

"Oh yes we got spilt up a few times."

"Split up.. So, a few people went missing before you and then you seemingly just left the premises in a vehicle afterwards?"

"Well that doesn't sound great but the person who found me in the at the other location said I had won the game."

"Which person, what game?"

"I don't know, just some guy and the escape room, I told you."

"Then what happened?"

"I sat and had a few drinks got a bit drunk in the location he had me in, then I woke up at home."

"So you had a few beers with your kidnappers, did you? Do you know where the place was?"

"No because I was taken against my will."

"Yet you sat and got drunk with this person?"

".... Err"

"Interview paused at 1.58pm."

Another detective comes into the interview room to inform him that he has some information, with Detective Charles pausing the interview to go outside to find out the information, as the information is shared with Charles, he feels like he has enough for to get Jason.

"Interview starting again at 2.05pm," Confirmed the officer.

"Who's Kate?"

"Kate?! No idea," Jason looked very confused at this point.

"Well we found a phone in your apartment sending a message to a woman we found in the woods, Dead. And you were seen pictured with her at the 'party' at this house."

"I don't know a Kate and don't remember a party, so you have the wrong person sorry," Jason said with some confidence in what he was saying, but it just came across arrogant to the officers.

"I'm terminating this interview at 2.15pm... Jason you are free to go for the moment but do not go anywhere as we will be in touch real soon."

Jason didn't say another word leaving the room in the hump as well as being confused to what is going on, wanting to get a few answers himself and deciding to straight away ring Andrew to see if he knew anything however, no answer. Jason knew roughly where he believed Andrew to live and decided to head straight there from the station with some intent as right now he is being accused of something potentially major, with nobody answering him he had to go searching for answers.

CHAPTER 30

Andrew was in the process along with Doug right now of setting up another 'escape room' with more unwitting people but thanks to Steve he had to wait until the police had moved on from that house or they would have to find another house to work with which would take even more time. As he and Doug was chilling at home trying to sort this out and getting good ideas for new versions of these escape room after this poor attempt at one, they were interrupted with 3 vicious bangs to the front door, Andrew had Doug go and open the door while he continued.

"You?!"

"Hmm Ok...." Doug didn't know what to say knowing this would be an issue.

"What are you doing in Andrew's apartment?! Also, when can I expect my prize money, I won didn't I?" Jason somewhat still believing he is owed money from the game he believes he won, being none the wiser.

Doug rubs his eyes with his fingers unsure what to say next almost bursting out with laughter with Jason still believing there is a prize for it, thankfully to his rescue came Andrew from around the corner.

"Doug who is... Oh Jason, long time how's things?" A smug giggly Andrew replied without trying to make it too obvious.

"Don't how's things me! Why are the police on my case and where is every one?"

"Oh have they? What for?"

"Questioning me accusing me of... well saying I had something to do with our friends going missing, who's missing?" Jason didn't know a thing; he had no idea who why missing or why.

"Well David, Steph and Steve... And they're not missing, they're dead."

"What?!"

"Yeah, so if I was you, I'd starting running."

"Why?"

"Because that is called murder Jason and the cops know it's you so..." Andrew says with a bemused look on his face at how stupid Jason was.

"But It wasn't I was with him!" Jason points to Doug angrily before looking back at Andrew who is smirking back "Oh my... it was you."

"Well maybe you're smarter than we give credit for Jason, yes it was me yet the police know it to be you". Andrew laughs away "So better run Jason, as there isn't a way in hell or heaven that you could link me to this, so goodbye and errm good luck I guess? Come on Doug we have things to."

As Andrew walked away back into the apartment finished with this interaction, Doug slammed the door in Jason face while he continued shouting from the other side warning Andrew that he will get him and how he won't get away with this. Jason walked back down the few steps it took to get to the front door of Andrews apartment getting to the bottom step and just slumped to the ground with his head in his hands starting to cry having a complete break down for a moment, acceptable in this situation. As tears flood Jasons' eyes rolling down his face like a flowing river he knew he had to do something, he couldn't just sit back and be accused of something that he is positive he had nothing to do with it.

The only way Jason could clear his name was to find some kind of evidence that puts Andrew in the frame instead of him, the actual criminal here but how would he do that, how would he find something that links Andrew and clears him in time without getting sentenced for this. The main thing Jason right now would be knowing where to start as right now he doesn't know whether to head back to the escape room house to try and find something or head to the place he got taken too however, they both posed a problem as he has no idea where either one of them are. Jason heads home fast knowing he has very limited time as the police were hardly friendly with him, upon getting in his house he straight away gets up a map of the city on his laptop and zooming out to get some of the surrounding area on it to hopefully find something because thinking back he felt like the journey he had couldn't have been more than a 15/20-minute drive.

Jason frantically searched the map hoping for a result he managed to find 3 big-ish estate houses situated in the distance so he circled all 3 on the map, there potentially may still be police at the location so he'd have to sneak past them which would be extremely difficult, however if there were then at least it should point to being the right house. Having the map open he wondered if he could guess where the other location, he went too was but that was proving a hell of a lot more difficult as he had no idea at all about, recognizing the interior of it yes but the outside he has no idea. Jason decides to act and act now, like a panic animal he is now just relying on instincts and they say go, check all these estate houses he's marked on the map, so he goes to his car and gets in it readying to go start checking which one it possibly is.

As Jason attempts to work out where the house is, he knows he could do with a hand with this as well as someone to actually believe in him, so he decides to make a trip somewhere beforehand. Jason drives along heading 10 minutes away from his house before parking up and getting out, he heads towards the front door of this house and rings the bell. He stands there for a few minutes praying this person would help him and he stands there twiddling his thumbs, before someone answers the door and stands there staring at him in silence.

"Fran, thank god," Jason goes straight over to hug Fran

"Where have you been?" Fran gives a small hug back "The police have been looking for you?"

"I know I spoke to them."

"I told them you were looking to get in touch."

"The think I murdered our friends."

"What?! They're all dead!"

"Wait what, you didn't know?"

"No, I don't really remember much, I just got told they may be missing."

"No, everyone is gone except me you and Andrew."

Fran breaks down in tears grabbing Jason again giving him a much tighter hug this time, she had no idea of this atrocity. "Andrew is the only one I've seen and he hasn't mentioned any of this. Why wouldn't he tell me?"

"Can I come in for a second?"

"Sure come in Jason, I'll make a tea." Fran says inviting Jason in for a drink, thankfully willing to sit down and speak with him.

"No time for tea Fran, sorry." Jason heads inside past Fran and goes into her front room, sitting on the chair Jason begins to spill what he knows. "So, I don't know how to say this but Andrew is the person that killed them... I know it sounds strange but I know it's true and the police think it's me! I need to clear my name Fran and quickly!"

"Wait Andrew?!"

"Yes."

"But he has seemed so kind. How do I know it's not you?" Fran nervously testing the waters.

"Fran if it was me do you think I'd even come here."

Fran did not know what to believe she was caught here in the middle, with little to no memory of anything that has happened and now being given this awful information with no idea what do to about it. Fran stood up from her seated position near Jason and walked over the window with tears still afloat in her eyes, she was reflecting over everything " So why wouldn't Andrew have killed me then?"

"I don't know. Fran what do you remember?" Jason asked in a hurry.

"Genuinely not a lot. I remember waking up in a hospital, with only the faintest memory of us in the house. Like the bit where we had woken up and started, that is about it after that it all becomes a bit blank," Fran replies honestly.

"So, did anyone tell you how you got out of the house?"

"Apparently Andrew rescued me and took me to the hospital."

"And no one told you anything about anyone else?"

"Nope."

"Don't you think that's strange?"

"Well maybe but also maybe Andrew was protecting me," Fran said still somewhat sticking up for Andrew.

Jason knows he doesn't have time to wasting as he has no idea when the police will come back for him and it may be too late, he has to move soon and fast, he needed to find a way to convince Fran he is innocent so she will come with him and help him but how would he do that "Fran please, I'm innocent I would never do anything to harm anyone. I got taken away from the house by a man named Doug apparently before any of that even happened, I didn't even know anything had happened to anyone before the police told me," Jason breaks down with his eyes tearing up once more.

"Hmm, so what do you want with me anyway?"

"I need your help to clear my name, I need to find the house again and find something that proves Andrew did it and not me."

"Like what? What would we even be looking for?"

"I don't know, I really don't... I don't even know how they died," Jasons' gut drops as he says those words knowing this is virtually an impossible task "I'm sorry, I'm just wasting your time... I'll leave but please know whatever happens, just know that I didn't hurt anyone." Jason stood up to leave knowing his time is short and can't even convince Fran he's innocent, he started walking away from Fran who was still facing out the window, staring out into the distance. As Jason got close to the door opening it, he heard Fran shout from back inside the other room.

"Wait!" Jason just stands there waiting as Fran comes in from the other room "Look, whether or not I believe you, I don't know! I really don't but honestly, I've never been overly fond of Andrew and what's the point in life without your friends.... I'll help, just don't kill me," She smirked to him as a friendly joke but somewhere inside he meant it, with Jason smiling back.

Jason's eyes water up again but this time for a nice reason, he can't believe Fran would give him a chance like this but she really is just a nice person inside "But why Fran?"

"Something in my gut tells me too, so what's the plan again?"

"Well I found 3 big estates in the surrounding area and I believe one of them is the house we were in. So the plan is to go there and find something there to prove the house was Andrews' and that I was not involved!"

"Cool, well what are we waiting for," Fran grabs her coat which is situated behind the front door as well as grabbing her keys motioning for Jason to come on.

Jason and Fran head outside with her locking the door behind them following Jason into the car with Jason showing Fran the map he where he has circled the estates are located and starts the car up. All of the estates are within a 10-mile radius of each other so hopefully it shouldn't take them very long to figure which one the house is, that is if any of them actually are the house, if not then game over maybe. They drive along the roads out of the city following country roads that seem to twist and turn all over the place with this car ride being a quiet one with not much conversation between the two of them, as they are on a mission to get Andrew but what they are looking for is less clear as neither one of them actually know what happened that night.

After a good amount of time on the road the first house appears to be just round the corner according to the map with Fran giving the directions although this map is a bit older and some of the roads on this map are no longer roads or they virtually unusable due to the flourishing woodlands, as they approach the first house using its long drive way in between a stunning row of flowered trees it is immediately clear that this is not the house. The car is turned around straight away screeching back down the long driveaway out of the estate as Fran crosses it off of the map using felt tip and starts her directions towards the second house in question.

"So did the police give any indication of what happened?" Fran asked Jason curious about him conversation with the police.

"Not really no, so I'm not sure what to expect or what to look for but when I got away from the house I got taken in a car to a separate location, so if I could find where that is or even the car that would be a huge start. Not by my will by the way, I virtually got kidnapped by that person."

The road toward the next house seemed to go on forever especially in this silent car as it ticked along with just a slight noise from the engine coming into play, eventually Fran told Jason to turn left, in which he did but this turn seemed to lead onto another old road taken over by the woods. This didn't even seem like a road anymore; it didn't seem like anyone even knew this road existed and yet the further he travelled on it the more it started to seem like a road again with tracks to confirm someone had used this. Jason budged the car slowly down this road not knowing what to expect as it slowly crushed over the top of small branches from the trees.

"Jason what's that?"

"Let's park this over there, out of the way a little," Jason parked the car more in the bushes hiding the fact they were there "That actually looks like the house in the distance," he said as he pointed through the trees.

"Yeah that looks somewhat familiar actually," Fran agreed even though they never saw the house from the outside very often especially not in the light.

Jason parked the car unlocking his door and got out with Fran following suit, they walked further inwards towards the house almost through the woodlands silently hoping to creep up on it, only to see in the distance that there were still two cops guarding the actual house and two other cops closer standing by some fences, it didn't make sense.

"Why are those cops standing there?" Fran questioned as she watched them stand there like guards.

"I have no idea? That's nowhere near the house?" Jason too was confused as he took more of an interest in them than the ones at the house.

Suddenly out of nowhere while watching the officers two doors opened up behind them, a light appeared and out stepped Doug carrying some items stopping for a moment to look at the cops as they looked at him, before of the officers offered a hand with the boxes and put them into what appeared to be their cop car which was parked nearby. Doug was happy for the help as it was looked like it was heavy carrying those boxes, before what appeared to be money heading into the officers' pockets, as one of them got into the car and Doug followed getting in the back pretending to look like a criminal, ironic really.

"Bribing the cops?!" Jason was furious "They're bribing the fucking cops!"

Standing in the bushes watching the criminal activity going on, the car with its traditional blue lights staying off started heading towards them down the path causing Fran and Jason to duck behind some bushes dramatically, watching as the car began get away down the dirt path with Jason attempting to remember some of the number plate at least, while the other cop just stood by the doors closing them to keep suspicion down.

As they watched the car drive away Jason knew what they had to do, coming up with a new part to his plan which was being made up as he went "Follow. We need to follow them!" Jason shot up and out of the bush "Fran let's go," He shouted back before Fran even got a chance to say anything Jason had run off back to the car taking the wheel instead of Fran.

Once Fran had eventually caught up to Jason and got in the car, he pulled off straight away knowing they would be a few minutes behind so they had to move fast to even find them, as Jason got to the end of the road he turned back towards the city in hope this is the way they went. Jasons panicked driving and pure guess work started to pay off because after a few minutes on the road and seeming as though they had missed their chance traffic came to their rescue, at the front of that traffic appeared to be a cop car so fingers crossed it was them.

As the continued along the same roads as this cop car in the distance having a few cars slowly moving out of the way and turning off of the road, it began to be possible to see the number plate as Jason looked hard at it and noticing a few similarities in the letters and digits he deemed in a confident tone that this was it.

"That's the car Fran, I'm sure of it!!"

"Yeah but now what?"

"Well we just have to see where they go, hopefully they go to the place I was talking about!! But even if they don't surely whatever they took was important to keeping their names out of it all, so we need to get that box of stuff," Jason explained actually making a lot of sense and almost coming into his element with this detective work, he might just clear his name after all.

"Ok, that makes a bit of sense... So, you say that guy works with Andrew?"

"Yes! That's Doug, the guy who drove the car and took me."

"If that is true then why would he be bribing officers I wonder," Frans confidence in Jason's innocence seemed to grow a little.

They seemed to be following this car for ages as traffic in this city at this time slowed everything, as time slowly ticked away on Jasons' innocence in the polices eyes they finally travelled back through the city into a part of town that seemed sleazy and grimy neither one of them recognized any of it but perfect place for criminals. Once the turned down a long stretch of the road a few seconds after the cop car they noticed that it had stopped and was parked up on the side of the road as Doug was in the process of moving the stuff out of the back of it and away down an alley.

"Look!" Jason pointed to the stopped car on side pulling over his car straight away, way further back down the road and boy was he delighted to have found this car, he could feel his reckoning coming.

"Where do you think we are?"

"No idea Fran. Absolutely no idea, but it certainly is a poor part of town."

The two of decided to get out of the car not long after they saw the cop car drive away and Doug wasn't in the car when it did, could this be the location they were after.

"Should we call the cops?" Fran asked.

"Well if we did then I feel like the car that just left would come back then we'd be done, we have to work out where he went and what's there."

"Ok," Fran agreed while nodding in agreement.

They were both very nervous as neither one of them were physically strong or even confrontational, they were the two most happy go lucky people in the group so this sort of thing was not in their nature but for Jason he hadn't another choice. Moving further down the street to where the car had been parked lay an alleyway and down the end of the alley was a plain door with no stand out features it blended in perfectly with everything without looking like anything, potentially a prime location for hiding something.

He and Fran ducked behind a wall as they spied down the alleyway waiting for some kind of activity, with it coming in the shape of the door opened with Doug coming out of it locking it behind him and heading down the path towards the two of them.

Fran crawled away with Jason in tow as they heading for a different piece of cover to not get spotted, ducking behind one of the cars parked in the street watching Doug moving away thankfully in the opposite direction in which they were hiding allowing their hearts to have a few seconds to calm down a little bit and beat a little bit slower, Doug continued walking down the street peacefully. While Doug moved away Jason indicated for Fran to come along as he crouched his way around the car before crouch running into the alley as he eyed up the door, Fran had followed suit moving behind Jason down the path into close proximity of the door as Jason tried the handle to double check if it was locked, which unfortunately it was.

"Damn.. How are we going to get in?" Jason said out loud while throwing his arms about.

"Err I don't know. Try and pick the lock?"

Jason turned around to Fran slowly and sarcastically "Oh Sorry I forget I have that in my repertoire," As he was getting desperate, he got himself a bit emotional looking away from Fran so as to not say or do anything too rude.

"No need to be a horrible Jase!"

"I'm sorry Fran, it's just I'm panicking."

"Yeah no need to take it out on me."

"You're completely right and I am sorry, thank you for being here."

As Jason stood with his head against the door resting it for a second, he had to think of a way to get in the door and potentially the only way in was to bust the door in or suddenly learn how to lock pick which wasn't exactly just going to happen. They had no idea if Doug would be coming back anytime soon so whatever they were going to do they needed to do it quickly, Fran had suggested things such a call a locksmith and pretend they had been locked out which was a good idea, but right now that would plain and simply take way too long.

"I'm just going to break in, I think there is a crowbar in my car wait here," Jason told Fran as he just left leaving Fran at the door and running down the street.

Jason ran back to his car as quick as he possibly could unlocking his car throwing the keys on the seat as he wrecked his car boot searching for his crowbar, eventually coming to the realization that the crowbar must lay in his old car not this one causing him to head back to Fran empty handed.

"No?" Fran asked

"Nah, New car! Stand back."

"Why?" Fran asked before seeing Jason take a few steps back and moving his foot back like a bull would.

"I'm going to charge it," he exclaimed. Jason ran as fast as possible hitting into this door bouncing it around on its hinges but it didn't seem to budge at all, this was a big solid door clearly made for some kind of protection.

"What if we wait until Doug comes back and try and get in then?"

"What are you crazy?" Jason questioned

"Well think about it, if he comes back with the door busted in then he'll know something happened, at least if we wait for him then we have the element of surprise," Fran actually made her suggestion make some kind of sense.

"But what if he doesn't come for ages?!" Jason stressed in his voice.

"Well if he doesn't come back for ages.... Then we will break in I guess?!" Fran just saying what Jason wants to hear.

"Ok, we'll wait. Let's head back to the car then," A disappointed Jason heads straight back for the car leaving Fran in his wake, knowing full well he could never just kick or barge that door down.

"Wait up!!" Fran shouts, running to catch up to Jason who had just left her.

Once they get back to the car, they both go to one side each and get in with Jason straight away slumping in his seat blowing out showing his disgruntled side armed with disappointment. Fran sat quietly in the seat next to him as they sat in silence for what seemed like a good hour, with tension filling the air as the afternoon drifted away there was no sight of Doug just yet, but eventually sparked up a conversation with Jason.

"Jason, you ok?" Fran said softly.

"I'm fine.... No I'm not, I'm a good person Fran! I've never wanted to hurt anyone or do anything wrong and yet here I am getting interrogated by the police over something I had nothing to do with! And now I'm trying to break into a building, what's happened to me Fran?!"

"Oh Jason." Fran feels awfully sad for Jason almost stunned into silence "Jason... you are a good person and I know you didn't do that stuff they're saying, I wish I could prove that. You're my friend and I really care for you."

"Thank you. Like all I've ever wanted to do was have fun with my friends and enjoy life, you guys are the world to me and yet I've never felt much respect from most of them. It's only you Fran that is kind and nice to me, I've tried my hardest for a few years to impress Steph and she still acts like I'm a child."

"I've always liked you Jason, sometimes people take longer to realise how great people are!" Fran smiles proudly at Jason with sincerity in her voice making him feel somewhat warm inside before coming to the realization he may never get a chance to prove anyone wrong.

"Well, I'll never get the chance because I'm never going to clear my name," Jason cries into his hands picturing his life trapped behind bars "I'm not tough enough for Jail, i'm barely tough enough for real life."

"Jason let's stay positive, It's not over yet!"

"Not for you it isn't your fine!" Upset and angry indirectly focusing it on Fran mainly because she is the only person here right now.

"No, look!" She points out the front windscreen with Doug back in view.

As Jason looks out the front window trying to see what was going on, he was finding it almost impossible due to the fact his eyes were filled with water, rubbing and rubbing them hoping to clear them. As Fran watched Jason frantically struggle to get his eyes to readjust after crying for a while wondering why it was taking so long, she thought it just best to tell him.

"It's Doug he's back! He's heading back into the alley! Let's go," Fran jumps out the car.

Jason too jumps out with his eyes finally feeling clearer from tears being able to actually see again, the two of them moved swiftly but sneakily down the road keeping low getting to the eyesight of the alley way and eventually getting there without getting noticed. Peeping around the corner of the wall down the alley they do indeed see Doug open the door with a key from his pocket followed by him going in, leaving the door to slowly close by itself, this was Jasons moment. Jason ran down the alley just about putting his hand in the door to stop it closing properly trying not to make any noise at the same time but Fran stayed at the end of alley for the moment seeing Jason stop the door from closing.

"Right, let's go in but be super quiet we don't know what's in here so stay behind me," Jason whispered to Fran down the alley as she just about heard him.

"I don't like this so much now," Fran was having second thoughts and started to get scared, not wanting to go running in that door with mystery surrounding what may be behind it.

"Can't back out now Fran?" Jason questioned her in this moment.

"Can I wait at the car?"

"Pfft Fine," Jason huffed but knew she didn't need to come in.

"Call me if there is any problems." Fran couldn't do it, she was too scared there was no way she could go in there and snoop around, making her way back to the car in rapid fashion with Jasons' key still sitting on the seat in the car.

Jason rolled his eyes letting Fran move back but he couldn't, he had to find out what was in here and whether it could help save him from what was around the corner for his life. Allowing the door close ever so gently Jason hoped it would make no noise as it clicked fully closed, once inside Jason moved further in to the building which was huge compared to what it seemed outside. A sound came from another room and it sounded like a garage door was opening followed by the noise of a car starting, Jason crept around the building to find where this was and catch Doug in the car maybe.

The building seemed to be pretty void of other humans but as he continued his journey around the building, he found the garage and it was exactly what it sounded like, a car was indeed leaving with Doug in the drivers seat of the car maybe this was the luck Jason needed. Doug drove out of the garage as the doors slowly shut once his car was out of the way seemingly a similar car to what Jason remembered and once in the garage watching Doug drive away under the ever-shutting garage doors, it was all being pieced together for Jason.

This was the place he was in before the garage confirmed that completely as he remembered certain things from the room along with the tables and the freezers, so all he had to do was to start finding somethings to clear his name.

"Yes! Now I just need to find something to link Andrew," Jason mumbled to himself as he gave himself a little fist pump to express his delight.

Jason in his delighted state texted Fran to inform her this was the place he had found before smiling away but his work was not done because he needed to find something to help him, as he searched the garage, he opened everything in the building starting with the freezers. Jason looked in the freezers but a few of them were completely empty, wondering what happened to some of the boxes that he had seen Doug place in there before. Walking around this building searching for items to help him, opening as many boxes and stuff as he possibly could but he was seriously struggling to find anything of significant use to get Andrew with and virtually running out of ideas. There was another door further back down the corridor he noticed one the way in, Jason headed back to this door and went to open it and to his surprise it opened with no worries and what lay inside could be what Jason needed.

The room that he went into was an office, inside this office seemed like it would harbour every little piece of information of how the plan to do the escape room and who was going to be involved in it, as well as information on previous groups and what had happened to them it was virtually a gold mine of information. All of the information he need was indeed here with sheer delight coming on his face, smiling as he found so many things that were incriminating but the only thing that appeared to be missing so far was Andrew's name on anything with only code names seemingly used in all of this or Doug's name, but never Andrews. It seemed very strange that he couldn't find anything with Andrew's name on it, but things were made clear very quickly and very brutally the more he searched through all these papers.

As Jason looked through all these papers his phone started ringing, it was Andrew.

"Hello."

"Hello Jason, How's things?" Andrew laughed "Free yet?"

"I've got you!"

"And by that what do you mean?"

"I've got information to prove you done it all, I broke into that safe house Doug took me too before so you are screwed," Jason said with real confidence.

"Oh.. And what would that be?"

"You're a murderer, a liar and just a general piece of crap."

"Not very nice is it, certainly not a piece of crap. I'm actually quite a smart person, if only you actually knew me."

"Oh shut up," Jason laughed a little bit with a tiny bit of relief.

"Oh wait just a question, does that information you apparently have say my name on it?" Andrew said slowly with emphasis on the word information.

"Err."

"That's what I thought... Jason you thought you had me, I knew you wouldn't just lie down because you're persistent little rat and I knew that, I'd even go as far as saying I respect that. Also, the police had been slowly sniffing around me more and some of my dealings, they knew of Doug's dubious past as well so what I thought I'd do is clean my slate and have you take all that suspicion down with you," Andrew explained.

"Wait...What?"

"I wanted to you to go there, I wanted Doug to lead you there and I got a little help in doing so. Jason you are going to take all of my crimes down with you! Oh Doug too, you are cleaning my slate because there is nothing to link me. You see this was never the plan at all but sometimes when things go wrong in life you have to just wing it and hope for the best," Andrew sadistically laughed down the phone " Good luck!!" And with an instant he hung up.

Jason eyes light up as he threw paper after paper off of the table and they all had the same name at the top with nothing remotely linking Andrew, within a few minutes' things had gone from bad to terribly wrong for Jason with things not looking up even more so now. His eyes and soul sunk into his body before disappearing leaving behind a lifeless body, with Doug coming back through the main door and bursting in on Jason in the office just to add to his pain.

"Wait Wait Wait!" Jason shouted at Doug.

"For?" Doug asked while brandishing clenched fists.

"You've been set up. We, we have been set up."

"What?"

"Andrew has set you up!!"

"What, don't be stupid you're just trying to get me to let you go."

"No seriously!"

"I have no reason to believe you!" Doug shouted almost admiring the sheer desperation of Jason.

As Doug was getting more and more furious he was interrupted by a noise, it was the bleeping of Jason's phone with a text from an unknown number 'Jason, I am sorry xx' as Jason took his phone out and read this message his heart sunk, it really felt like it was all about to get worse. Within a few minutes of Jason trying to get Doug to listen a noise of a huge crash and a bang flooded the building as armed police swarmed into the building, catching and surrounding the two of them inside the office room with nowhere to go, with guns pointed at both Doug and Jason.

Jason froze once more feeling like this was game over but Doug wasn't going down without a fight, trying to move back behind the desk and brandishing his gun at the same time causing the swat team to shoot him instantly with Jason feeling like he'd just witnessed it all in slow motion before getting body checked by an officer as he got taken to the ground and arrested on the spot.

3 Months later.

On a hot summers afternoon in the nicer part of town, a bright illuminated house party was in full flow with the music blaring and the drink flowing, this house party was full of vibrant young people enjoying themselves to the max. The sun was still in the sky but slowly settling down for the evening, the setting was beautiful something picturesque as time passed and people began chatting with people unknown from different social circles a somewhat peculiar conversation was starting to be struck.

"You are so fun! Where have you been all our life," A woman named Lauren said.

"Yeah I agree! Aha, we should do it? What do you reckon peeps?" Rosie asked her friends.

"Sure, why not, can you tell us again?" A Guy Fred asked "What was your name again?"

"Sure. It's a really cool, interactive scary escape room you would absolutely love it." A smiling figure was stood aside in the setting sun as it came over him while he was sipping his whiskey chatting to his new victims. Sorry, Friends. "Oh, my names Andrew, nice to meet you."